D0774138

WHITE BOYS DON'T CRY

JOHN FULLERTON was born into a military family. He grew up in Cape Town, attending boarding school, serving in the army and trying several jobs, including farming and finance, before a journalistic career spanning more than thirty years, twenty of them with Reuters. In all, he reported from about forty countries and covered a dozen wars. Fullerton lives in London. *White Boys Don't Cry* is his fourth novel.

JOHN FULLERTON

WHITE BOYS DON'T CRY

PAN BOOKS

First published 2006 by Macmillan

This edition published 2007 by Pan Books
an imprint of Pan Macmillan Ltd
Pan Macmillan, 20 New Wharf Road, London N1 9RR
Basingstoke and Oxford
Associated companies throughout the world
www.panmacmillan.com

ISBN 978-0-330-45270-0

Copyright © John Fullerton 2006

The right of John Fullerton to be identified as the
author of this work has been asserted by him in accordance
with the Copyright, Designs and Patents Act 1988.

Every effort has been made to contact copyright holders of material
reproduced in this book. If any have been inadvertently overlooked, the publishers
will be pleased to make restitution at the earliest opportunity.

1 3 5 7 9 8 6 4 2

A CIP catalogue record for this book is available from
the British Library.

Typeset by SetSystems Ltd, Saffron Walden, Essex
Printed and bound in Great Britain by
Mackays of Chatham plc, Chatham, Kent

Visit www.panmacmillan.com to read more about all our books
and to buy them. You will also find features, author interviews and
news of any author events, and you can sign up for e-newsletters
so that you're always first to hear about our new releases.

FOR

L. G. F.

Humans thrive in conditions that morality condemns. The peace and prosperity of one generation stand on the injustices of earlier generations; the delicate sensibilities of liberal societies are the fruits of war and empire.

JOHN GRAY,
Straw Dogs: Thoughts on Humans and Other Animals

The dream stalked my waking hours and waited in ambush until my eyes closed.

It was a game I could not refuse, and the dream always won. That moment, the instant of squeezing the trigger, repeated itself again and again in my sleep. Not immediately, and not every night, but several times a week, and it continued in this irregular fashion for years. Scotch and marijuana helped, but not always. Sooner or later it would recur, this nocturnal predator of my fears padding into my mind, taking up stealthy residence as I slipped uneasily below the surface of consciousness.

All I could ever hope for was deferment, and the price was a nasty hangover.

The sequence never varied.

I'd wake in a sweat, trembling. No, not with fright. Worse than that. Funk. Holy bloody terror. Not because of the process of killing per se, but because my victim, the woman Sipole, would turn her head towards me at the last moment, just as my forefinger took up the trigger slack.

It was a reproachful look.

The eyes seemed to say: 'How could you?'

Or perhaps: 'Do you really want this?'

And as I looked down at her, uncomprehending, I saw it wasn't Sipole any longer.

A change had taken place. The recognition, the eye

contact, always occurred just as the Tokarev leaped in my fist.

She still had the make-up on, the mascara was still smudged, and her perfume still lingered in the cold morning air.

The ruined shoes still lay in the sand.

Oh, I had my duty.

But in my nightmare it wasn't the face of the Security Branch officer any more.

It was the woman I loved. Frances. By then it was too late. I couldn't take it all back, much as I wanted to. The bullet could not be recalled. I'd killed my love; not just my love for her, but my love for life itself, for all forms and ways of living. We'd put ideas above everything. We'd made philosophy our God. We'd sacrificed the present for the future. That was our mistake. We'd sought a higher purpose, a salvation, to do good in the name of one faith or another, we'd dreamed a history that did not exist, and ended up in doing nothing but harm.

Sometimes Sipole became Frances, who became my wife, Annette, the bullet smashing into her pretty blonde curls, cracking the skull, the blood thick and black as crude oil, spreading into the sand of the Black Mountains, the Swartberge.

There is no purpose except to live life, I know that now.

The realization came too late for Sipole and many others like her.

For years I had trouble eating and sleeping. I spent too much money for far too long on something called cognitive therapy, but it didn't work nearly as well as my daily *daggazolletjie* and injection of single malt.

2

In the mornings-after I'd tell myself it was just a silly nightmare and that time heals everything eventually, even a killer's conscience, if I could only wait long enough.

DAY ONE

ONE

I swear I didn't know about the murder.

After lunch I order an espresso and wait for Josh in the restaurant overlooking Kloof Street. He said, 'I'll join you by three,' and when my watch shows four o'clock I can't sit there any longer, and pay my bill and go out into the crowds and order a beer at a table on the pavement outside Minetti's; I prefer the heat outside to the air-conditioned chill of the interior. A taxi driver sounds his horn and rolls slowly by, staring, then accelerates down towards the sea where the old docks used to be, beyond the reclaimed foreshore with its black glass towers, phallic symbols of triumphal Afrikaner capitalism, en route to the gated waterfront area of overpriced bars, boutiques and marinas. I drink my cold lager and watch people of all shapes, sizes and colours flow past. There is no sign of Josh.

Of course, I tell myself, he's a busy man, an important one in an era of rapid change, someone who can bend events to his will and interests; and he might have been held up by these same events, but surely he would have called me, or have had his secretary do so; he has my mobile number and I know he takes care over such courtesies. Missing an engagement, even one as unimportant to him as this, is so unlike him.

7

I can't help feeling anxious; I get up when I see the taxi again, and I am sure it is the same, not because of the colour or shape, but because I recognize the driver's cap and mirror sunglasses and the brown face behind: narrow, triangular and inscrutable like a cat's. All it lacks is the whiskers. This time he pulls into the kerb and the back door swings open and a pair of long female legs, shapely tapering legs, emerges, knees together, followed by the rest of the woman; and I know at once who it is before I see her face: Frances.

I feel a pang whenever I see her. It lasts only a moment, but it never fails to remind me that I have loved her, and that my love has remained unrequited. I love her no longer, but there is nothing so humiliating to the male ego as having to settle for friendship with a woman who loves another, perhaps has loved several, all of whom I know, or think I know.

Perhaps I've not so much loved the woman herself as what she has represented – a door to an unfettered life. Whatever. That's all in the past. I tell myself it no longer matters. She smiles and waves; she has a wonderful smile, and as she strides towards me she is head and shoulders above the legions of pedestrians. Her height, her effortless stride, her beauty, make her seem like another being entirely, separate, rarefied, apart from the rest of us. She does not have to say why she is here: it is obvious. Frances has come to meet not me but Josh.

'He isn't here,' I say.

'I can see that.'

The smile vanishes.

She glances about her, chin up, eyes gone cold.

Frances arches her back, her right hand on her hip, the

elbow pulled back. Her weight is on her right foot, her left pointed like a ballerina. It is one of her catwalk poses. It smacks of boredom, haughty indifference. It's a mask. She adopts it to wrap herself in a sense of distance from other people, a form of self-insulation. In this instance, from me. I know she isn't even aware of it. It's instinctive. It used to protect her from the camera; now she wields it to fend off the world at large; but all it does for me is underline her vulnerability.

I say, 'He was supposed to meet me for lunch.'

It's a lame remark. It is unusual for Frances and me to be alone; we usually meet *cum multis aliis*, in a crowd. How I used to long to have her undivided attention; now it seems we don't know what to say to each other, and she seems restless, reluctant to sit down, looking at the two vacant chairs and empty beer glass with something in her face that amounts almost to a suspicion that I have organized Josh's absence in order to have her all to myself. I am struck dumb, like the tongue-tied nineteen-year-old on our first encounter. She clenches her teeth, making her jaw muscles pulse; she is annoyed to be left stranded with a newspaperman, a whitey on the inter-mediate slopes of middle age with beery breath and with whom she plainly has nothing in common except a past that includes Joshua Schuter, someone who has never known, not even for an hour, what it is to be tongue-tied.

She gazes at me with a slight frown.

'What time did he say he would be here, Seb?'

'By three,' I tell her. 'He told me he had an hour to spare.'

'No message?'

I shake my head. 'Nothing.'

Now she looks as worried as I feel.

Neither of us cares for the conventions of greeting. We don't blow kisses, touch cheeks or shake hands. She looks at her watch, checks her mobile and plays with the strap of her minuscule handbag; she fidgets, in other words, the way people used to do with cigarettes and umbrellas in that diffident grey metropolis three thousand miles to the north now wrapped in tawdry winter rain that I used to call home. In a way it is still; London is the magnetic north of my personal compass, the needle always swinging its way there mentally, wherever I happen to be; like a drunk tottering mindlessly home in the wee hours of a Sunday, I've never succeeded in altering my bearings despite my best efforts. Perpetually changing course is a lifetime's vocation and it still is what some people, trying to be agreeable, describe as my successful career in journalism; a contradiction in terms if ever there was.

Frances is still slim, still supple. She works out, I know, and swims a lot, summer and winter. Her neck shows none of the telltale signs, the creases like rings in wood, of her true age; on the contrary, her brown skin glows with health as if the sun I detest breathes new life into her with the onset of the summer. Unlike white South African women of a certain age, Frances has not been turned into a mass of leathery wrinkles by the dry, salt-laden wind and broiling heat; rather the opposite, in fact: the country's climatic extremes, from the south-east trade winds' chilly blast to the hot hairdryer blow of north-westers, seem to suit her in every way.

I say, 'Shall we sit?'

She perches on the edge of the chair as if she's granted me a concession and shakes her head when I ask if she'd care for something to drink. She turns, as if seeing me for the first time, and appears to inspect me.

'You look worried, Seb.'

She does, too, but I'm not going to make it worse by saying so.

I say, 'He's usually so punctual.'

'He'll be here. Of course he will.'

She seems so sure of him; it is as if she wants to put me at my ease with her confidence in his devotion. Or perhaps she is trying to reassure herself. I wonder what it is they will talk about when finally he does materialize and I leave them alone. Josh has allotted me an hour of his valuable time, but I won't impose myself on them both. Whatever it is he wants to say to me can wait, though it is true that I am keen to have his 'take' – on an unattributable basis – on the new order taking shape.

Have they planned to spend the afternoon together, in bed? Will it be his place or hers?

Frances has never married; there are no children I know of. For his part, Josh broke up with his blonde, thin-lipped and disapproving Presbyterian wife some four years ago, and I won't presume to ask either of them whether Frances was a factor in the Schuters' separation and subsequent divorce.

Frances opens her mouth, changes her mind and looks away at the traffic that seems to increase visibly as the rush hour approaches. This hesitation is out of character; I know now she has decided to tell me something import-ant, at least to her, and she's trying to summon up the right words, the appropriate tone for whatever it is she has to say. Frances does not like scenes, and she hates to upset people unnecessarily, a trait I associate with those who are not so much kind or considerate as determined to get their own way with minimum fuss or opposition.

Manners are less a matter of temperament than intelligent self-interest.

When she does speak, it isn't so much of a surprise as a blow to my self-esteem.

'Josh and I are getting married,' Frances says.

I go home after an unproductive day – unproductive professionally, that is, in the midst of soaring hope and profound trepidation, for the first weeks of 1994 are a time of frenzied activity on the part of politicians and the schools of media pilotfish that cling in symbiosis to the notorious and accomplished alike. For my part I can at least console myself with the thought that I have, the previous day, contributed to the world's sum of knowledge of these great changes by having filed a broad thumb-sucker, a 'whither South Africa' of which I am, as usual, inordinately proud. It is election year. The threat of violence sweeping away all faith in a new, non-racial future grows closer with every passing hour as the Zulus of Buthelezi's Inkatha movement and the activists of the African National Congress wage war in Natal and the mining towns of the Reef – aided and abetted, of course, by white extremists while the police stand by and watch.

Even if, as everyone believes, hopes or fears, the ANC scores a notable victory at the country's first multiracial polls, what then? Will it be the old adage: give them parliament but we keep the money? Is South Africa going to fall into Josh's hands, to be plundered anew by international corporations, merchant banks and members of the City Club of which Josh is now chairman? This morning's local papers pose the same question. Where does Mandela stand now? Only a few days ago the ANC published its election manifesto, entitled 'A Better Life for All', but it is far from clear how its Utopian message is to be paid for. How will South Africa provide jobs and training for 2.5 million people in ten years, a million new homes in five years, a decade of free and compulsory education for all children?

Now I need to forget, at least to dull, both the worry of Joshua's failure to turn up and the ache of his engagement to Frances. Old jealousies die hard. She is marrying one of the country's foremost white liberals, and certainly one of its richest men. It will be an alliance of the times, a symbol of the new rainbow nation. I can imagine the media coverage, the intense scrutiny their wedding will receive in the Sunday papers. It is grist to my mill, too, of course. I can hardly complain. I know them both, and have done so for so many years. It gives me a front-row seat on their romance. Their tying the knot will give me space my heavyweight think-pieces can never command save on the slowest of news days. Celebrity is everything in a press dominated by self-made tycoons, profane men with the crocodile smiles of the second-hand car lot, backwoodsmen from Canada and Australia bent on respectability and a barony.

The few words exchanged with Frances outside Minetti's are in themselves a useful item for the rag's weekly gossip column. It shows I am still on the ball, still in there with human interest stories. I'm used to it. I have lived with the frustrations of my trade for a good many years under a variety of flags and have grown impervious to the fickle ways of what was once called Fleet Street, its circulation battles and the ravings of its monstrous child-editors. I survive by not taking it too seriously, and I tell myself a celeb wedding will do me nothing but good.

Best of all, I look forward to flinging open the French windows that lead from the rear of the living area of my little terraced town house on the slopes of Signal Hill to a secluded patio lined with geraniums, a deckchair, a view of the dying sun turning the amphitheatre of sheer rock into fool's gold, to rolling a reefer of Durban Poison, so resinous that its smooth and slightly aniseed taste will produce hallucinations in the novice – and all this to the sound of Bach. Not even Frances or her wedding plans can compete, and the question of Josh's whereabouts is almost forgotten.

Marijuana produces a sequence of effects, the penultimate being thirst and the last an urge to sleep, not unlike the qat of Yemen, only much stronger. It is dark when I go inside, drawing the doors shut and locking them. I'm barefoot and wear nothing more than a pair of white boxer shorts, for it is still warm and I am not expecting visitors. My deadlines have long since passed; the editors in that concrete wasteland called Canary Wharf can pick up agencies for any late-breaking news.

I light a candle and carry it about with me, setting it down next to the sink while I pour myself a glass of tap water and drink it straight off, refilling it and drinking again; artificial light, even dimmed, will only hurt my eyes. I need to shade reality in the aftermath of my joint. The Bach CD – three violin concertos – has finished, and Schubert's gentle Duo Sonata for piano and violin in A major fills the stoned space in my head when the doorbell rings; it isn't tentative, a quick buzz, but an insistent peal of sound, demanding and aggressive.

My first thought is that it is Josh come to apologize; perhaps it is his driver with a scrawled note saying sorry, and will I join him for a drink at his club. Perhaps it is a fellow member of the Foreign Press Association, much the worse for wear, who has decided to impose himself, or finds himself outside my door on his way home after several too many. It could be the loud-mouthed, heavy drinking ex-Marine, Brinkman of *Newsweek*, or the loquacious and preternaturally skinny Linda Gorstein of the *LA Times*, still recovering from a messy divorce and prepared to hit anyone foolish enough to linger within range over the head with her dreary tales of pitiless domestic warfare. But then, of course, I recall that most if not all have left for the north, to report a new bout of black-on-black violence.

The district where I live is by no means safe; it's a definite no-go area for tourists, and is marked as such in most foreign guidebooks; I chose Bo Kaap for the simple reason that I feel at home. It has a Mediterranean feel, and its largely Muslim population of Malays and so-called Coloureds (as members of the Cape's mixed-race community used to be called), along with that demi-monde that straddles and defies the irrationality of apartheid's racial classification, has been left alone for reasons I don't fully understand.

We're all African now, aren't we?

I'm careful to use the intercom positioned on the wall near the stout front door.

'Yes?'

'Mr Palfrey?'

'Who is it?'

'Police.'

I tell myself to stay calm. My first sensible thought is to hide my *zol*, my second to pull on a T-shirt and khakis, then fish my flip-flops out from under the sofa in the living room.

Take it a step at a time.

I have more reason than most to fear the knock at the door.

Don't think about it.

Take a deep breath.

'One moment.'

It is more like a minute before I return and start the laborious process of unbolting and unlocking; even so, when I open the door it is with the chain still fastened, and I have barely two inches through which to view the two men who stand waiting, a tall black man with a shiny, well-fed face, dapper in suit and tie, and a uniformed policeman out on the pavement, whether white or not I can't tell in the sodium-yellow pool cast by the street lamp.

'Can I see some ID?'

Confidence is everything, Palfrey.

Remember: you're a British newspaper correspondent. The rest of it is behind you. It's over.

The plain-clothes officer holds up his warrant card. He holds it close to the crack in the door so I can read it.

I take another deep breath.

'What do you want, Lieutenant?'

'Commandant Viljoen wants to see you, Mr Palfrey.'

'Can't it wait till tomorrow?'

Silly question.

'No, sir.'

He speaks good English, almost without any trace of an accent, and he's confident in dealing with a white man and a foreign correspondent; both qualities still unusual in 1994. Racism takes the underdog one of two ways: it produces either aggression on sight of a member of the Chosen Race, or slavish subservience. Neither applies in this instance. Something in his manner tells me Lieutenant James Mabaza is that rare animal, a black graduate; perhaps he's in line for one of the top jobs the authorities have promised to make available for fast-track promotion throughout the civil service and armed forces, in this case affirmative action in a police force long regarded by most people who aren't white not as a crime-fighting outfit at all, but the primary organ of social control and state repression.

My next remark is spoken with as much insouciance as I can muster.

'I don't have a car, I'm afraid. You'll have to provide transport.'

I drop the chain, swing the door open and go off in search of my keys and wallet. I call over my shoulder, 'Come in, Lieutenant,' and wonder vaguely as the words leave my mouth whether my person, the place, or both, still stink of the sweetish *dagga*. He will know it if he smells it; no copper can fail to do so in a country awash with the stuff. The invitation is superfluous for Mabaza follows anyway; he is no doubt trained to do so in case a potential witness – or suspect – goes for the baseball bat behind the door, the shotgun under the bed, the Glock under the pillow, the bottle of pills near the washstand in the bathroom or simply slings a belt from the bedroom ceiling light and jumps off the bed. I am to be delivered whole and in working order to Viljoen's office for whatever purpose the commandant has in mind. I keep my face and mind a studious blank as the uniformed officer, a holstered pistol at his waist, politely holds open the rear door of the police Ford.

My feelings towards police in general have always been ambivalent; there's nothing particularly unusual in that, but growing up in South Africa, even as a middle-class, English-speaking white boy, there was no sense of trusting the cops. If Dixon of Dock Green ever existed, it was in a vanished, romanticized Britain of which I was almost wholly ignorant until I returned there in the 1970s to the joys of televised crime drama; to me a policeman in a field-grey uniform, peaked cap or Afrika Korps-style kepi, armed with rubber riot baton and revolver or Sten gun, was a figure of both contempt and fear.

A number of anecdotes spring to mind. For example, as a junior court reporter I would join my colleagues from other papers – the *Cape Times, Die Burger,* the *Argus* – for coffee and croissants in Mark's café at the top end of Adderley Street, usually at around 9 a.m. One morning a journalist named Maggie was sitting nearest the door, her handbag next to her, when someone reached in and snatched it. There were two of them, working together and, using the handbag as a football, slinging it across to each other like a couple of rugby wingers, they raced off on foot through the morning traffic. A uniformed policeman – white, Afrikaans-speaking – was standing just around the corner, and when he saw the two 'non-whites' darting in and out of the cars, we whites in ragged and futile pursuit, already all out of puff, he tucked his peaked cap under his arm and sprinted after the thief and his partner. The two split up, of course; neither was caught and the bag and its contents vanished. The perspiring, furious cop returned empty-handed to the café.

'*Liewe bliksem*, what the hell was that about?' he demanded of the journalists. Maggie told him. The policeman mopped his brow and replaced his cap. He shook his head.

'Man,' he said, 'if only you'd told me in the first place, I would have just shot those two kaffirs.'

On an earlier occasion – I was probably four or five – my mother entered her bedroom one afternoon to discover an intruder standing on the far side of the double bed, near the window through which he'd presumably gained access, and holding an open drawer taken from the bedside table. He was going through it, looking for cash or jewellery. Her response was immediate; she did not have to think. With a howl of fury, she jumped over the bed and threw herself at the burglar, who leaped out of the window and ran off across the backyard and vaulted over the fence.

The police were called. A veteran with a sergeant's stripes was not impressed by my mother's action. What if he had had a knife? Or a hatchet? She had put her life in jeopardy by tackling him. He was nonplussed by the news that no, she did not own a firearm. He urged her to acquire a licence and pistol as quickly as possible; he recommended a short-barrelled .38 – a man-stopper, he called it. A revolver was best because it didn't jam, and it should be compact enough to fit into a handbag. 'And listen, lady. You shoot first, okay, then you fire the warning shot' – and he demonstrated, pointing his index finger at the window, then up at the bedroom ceiling. 'Bang-bang – now who's going to know which shot was fired first, hey?'

There were other incidents later, of course, much darker than either of these memories; for example, the tendency of certain black activists to hurl themselves – what other explanation could there be, after all? – through a window during interrogation in an office on an upper floor of the ten-storey Blue Hotel at John Vorster Square, otherwise known as Johannesburg police headquarters. Or from the Greys, as Security Branch headquarters was called then. It became almost a frequent occurrence, and these places gained a mythic status of terrifying proportions.

As for Commandant Jakobus Viljoen, I already knew him well, at least at a distance. He was the Clark Gable of a national police organization in transition, the public face of state coercion refocused, appearing at news conferences, and he did it so very well. A tall, well-built man in his forties, he had curly black hair turning silver at the temples, a clipped moustache and goatee, a wide, ready smile, lustrous eyelashes and large blue eyes set in an olive complexion, every inch a Latin lover were it not for the impeccable uniform – a double row of service medals complete with highly polished Sam Browne – and a record, which he always managed to let slip to newcomers in the foreign press corps, as a former Springbok centre half with seven caps to his credit; in short, a well-read, urbane and sporting patriot, the very image of every matron's idea of a Wilbur Smith hero, a Voortrekker warrior, bible in one hand, musket in the other, surrounded on all sides by shield-slapping impis closing in with their stabbing spears on the wagons.

It was a stage act, and he waged war wonderfully; not with musket or Old Testament to hand, and not on behalf of Afrikanerdom particularly, but for a newly united nation and with smooth words of reason, generosity of spirit, that humour and warmth of heart for which the best sorts of Afrikaners were renowned. He could spout the poetry of N.P. van Wyk Louw, or quote Roy Campbell to an English-speaking audience; in a word, Viljoen was a charmer. It was no less lethal a war, of course, and the battle was for the hearts and minds of the assembled hack pack, international opinion and creditor banks – and the goal: to gain time, precious time, to put changes into effect, to get them implemented before spears and much else besides were washed in blood.

Tonight, away from the batteries of television cameras and lights, he lacks all star quality; he is out of uniform and in shirtsleeves, collar undone, tie askew, the shirt itself showing damp stains of sweat on chest and shoulders. He slumps behind a scarred wooden desk piled high with brown files, a cigarette smouldering between the fingers of his left hand, the overhead light casting him as an angry and exhausted gambler out of credit and with no cards left to play. The air conditioner rumbles and shakes high up in the wall but does little more than stir the close and foetid air. Even his charm seems to have deserted him.

There are two metal chairs opposite Viljoen. One is occupied by Frances. She drops her eyes and I give no sign of recognition.

'Thank you for coming, Palfrey.'

'Do I have a choice?'

He raises his head and looks at me; those pale eyes hold mine for a moment, the mouth moves as if about to break out into one of his famous smiles, but he changes his mind and turns his gaze instead to Mabaza, who waits behind me, by the door. 'Thank you, Lieutenant.'

Frances and I exchange furtive looks.

Mabaza asks, 'Nothing else, Commandant?'

Viljoen smooths down his moustache with thumb and forefinger.

'Perhaps you could drop Miss Nqutu off on your way.'

Mabaza nods. 'Goodnight, sir.'

At least the Mabazas of this world don't say 'baas' any longer.

Frances stands up. I don't look at her. I hear her footstops and breathe in her scent as she passes behind me.

Viljoen swings his swivel chair so he sits facing the only window, his forearm along the edge of the desk. There is no view; it is impossible to tell what lies beyond the glass panes because they've been painted white.

'The duty sergeant is making tea. Do you want some?'

'Thank you,' I hear myself say, realizing that my thirst has barely been dented by the two glasses of water, and wondering at the same time whether my pupils are still dilated by the *daggazolletjie* I've smoked; I feel very calm and clear-headed, but at the same time I know the intoxication to be deceitful; it makes us feel ourselves to be a great deal more clear-headed and intelligent than we generally are, hence its attractiveness to many people who are seldom clear or smart about anything.

'You know Joshua Schuter?'

'Oh, yes. I do.'

My mouth is dry as sandpaper, but I resist the temptation to lick my lips and swallow.

'Would you say he was a friend of yours?'

Now it begins.

'I would, yes.'

'And you know Miss Nqutu.'

More statement than question.

'Yes.'

Stick to the truth as far as you can, I tell myself, and add nothing.

'How long have you known Joshua Schuter?'

All my life, or very nearly.

There have been gaps, of course, intervals lasting years, but we go back a long way, Joshua and I, to kindergarten and the innocent crimes of childhood, and later on the not-so-innocent crimes of boyhood and youth.

I remember him as a child very much like myself, only with reddish hair and blue eyes, both of us gangly with stick-like limbs, permanently grazed and muddy knees, socks neither up nor down, shoes scuffed with dirt moments after they were shined, an equally dusty face no matter how many times it was washed, a gap-toothed grin, and a generous swathe of freckles. We met at the whites-only playschool near Kenilworth; in my case delivered in an elderly baby Fiat by my mother, he driven by a uniformed chauffeur in one of Cape Town's very few Rollers.

The schoolhouse was a bungalow that sat on breeze blocks with just enough room for someone our size to wriggle underneath; a fact lost on neither of us. There was a large, sandy yard, two huge gum trees with vast, ridged roots that shot out across the ground in all directions, an enormous red box or crate, and a wonderful series of scaling nets and climbing ropes where we spent most of our free time, chasing each other up and down and emitting what we hoped were blood-curdling battlecries.

Our relationship began in a manner that was typical. Inspired by a story I'd read about Robert Catesby, Guy Fawkes and their fellow Catholic conspirators in their design to blow up Parliament by means of gunpowder secreted beneath the Palace of Westminster, I suggested to Josh that it would be a fine thing if, as the 5th of November anniversary passed, we could emulate the plotters by blowing up the school. All it would take, I suggested, were the remnants of the fireworks used to mark Bonfire Night. So many rockets and crackers failed to use up all their explosive; all we had to do was collect the stuff, cram it into a suitable container, push it under the floorboards, lay a trail of gunpowder to one of the gum trees, and retire behind the massive trunk after lighting it with a simple match.

It was just a fantasy. Usually it was Josh who was the source of such ideas, most of them impractical, foolish or downright dangerous; it would always surprise him how easy it was to persuade other people to take them seriously and act upon them long after he'd discarded them.

A few days later – and I confess I had forgotten all

about our project – Josh appeared with a box of partly used fireworks. We got rid of the paper and other detritus, compressed what seemed to be unused explosive into a biscuit tin with an airtight lid, and set our bomb right under the classroom.

The long fuse burned with agonizing slowness, characterized by blue smoke and a loud fizzing. Our absence from class was noticed immediately; one of the young teachers spotted us watching from the tree. She ran outside, armed with pan and brush, and broke the gunpowder trail; she stamped out the sputtering powder and kicked sand over the rest; we were hauled inside, roundly told off and our parents telephoned and asked to collect us. My mother was informed that I had outgrown the school and it was suggested that I move on.

It is highly unlikely that our improvised explosive device would have worked, but so it was that Josh and I were first expelled from school, aged five. I say first, because it would not be the last time in my case; Josh, however, was a quick learner. He took cause and effect to heart; he reasoned moreover that if crime was to be made to pay, it could not be achieved by trying to beat the system, only by subverting it and making it work from within. It was a lesson that would last him a lifetime, a leitmotif that helped him arrive at the apex of a bewildering mountain of companies. It would, in the end, make him a dollar billionaire, but not a happy man.

'When did you last see Joshua?'

I clear my throat before answering. 'A week ago. I was supposed to meet him today for lunch, but he didn't turn up.'

He stops fiddling with his files and swings around to face me.

'What time were you supposed to meet?'

'Three o'clock.'

I tell myself I have nothing to hide. It isn't true, of course, but I pretend it is. I don't look away, but gaze frankly back into Viljoen's eyes. I sip my lukewarm tea. It doesn't taste of anything very much, but at least it's wet.

'Can you account for your movements today, Mr Palfrey?'

'I can, yes.'

'It would be helpful.'

I say, 'What's happened to Josh?'

Silence.

I imagine the worst. A car crash. A mugging gone wrong. Suicide with one of those beautiful Purdey shotguns of his father's . . .

'Is he dead?'

'What makes you say that?'

'The fact that I'm here in your office in the middle of the night.'

It's 11.20 p.m.

Viljoen shakes his head like a man shaking off an insect. 'We would like to talk to him.'

'May I ask why?'

'You're asking me as a journalist?'

'As a journalist – and as Joshua's friend.'

Viljoen picks up his pen and taps out a tattoo on the desk.

'If you help us, Mr Palfrey, I think I can share a few facts with you. Your paper's last deadline has passed, and I don't think you can do any more damage than has already been done. But I must ask you not to share any information I give you with your colleagues until the morning.'

'An embargo until—'

'Nine.'

'I spent the morning in my office. My driver will back me up. I waited in the restaurant until around four, went out and drank a beer outside Minetti's. Josh had said he would join me over lunch. He had an hour to spare, he said. He never turned up, and he left no message. I thought it odd because he's so fastidious about such things. I wanted to pick his brains . . .'

I don't mention Frances, or her appearance at my table out on the pavement. I decide I won't, not unless he asks. It wouldn't be fair. My envy of Josh in her bed does not extend to getting Frances into trouble with the law.

'And later, what did you do?'

'I went home, Commandant. I was there until your people turned up.'

'Alone?'

'Yes, alone.'

'Can anyone vouch for that?'

'No, I don't think so. I live alone, and until Lieutenant Mabaza arrived at my door, I had no visitors. Perhaps I was seen or heard by neighbours . . . am I a suspect?'

Viljoen watches my face closely for any reaction to his words. 'Dr Cris Schuter, your friend's father, is dead. The old man was found at his house in Bishopscourt this afternoon.' Viljoen glances up at a clock on the wall. 'His death was not of natural causes, although of course, until the pathologist makes his examination and files his report, that's unofficial. That's why we want to talk to the son as soon as possible.'

Maybe my thought about the custom-made shotguns is not so far out.

I'm relieved it isn't Josh. Of course I am. But the news of his father's death comes as a complete surprise. I wonder if Viljoen has told Frances, and how she reacted. What is there I can say? In the circumstances, it's better that I say as little as possible.

'I wonder if I could ask you one more favour, Mr Palfrey, as a friend of the Schuter family, and that is to help us by identifying the remains.'

I feel a surge of adrenalin kick in.

Why me, for God's sake?

'What – now?'

The room seems more airless than ever and I'm conscious of sweat on my upper lip.

'You knew the minister, didn't you?'

They can't touch you. Not now.

I put my cup back on its saucer, an action that gives me a moment to consider my reply.

'Ex-minister, you mean. I met Joshua's father on a number of occasions – socially and professionally.'

I can't think of an excuse to get myself out of this. A journalist, a true journalist, would try to leverage his position; he'd use Viljoen's request to trade information. That is what I must do. I'm not going to do this for nothing. I'm a professional, too, in my own way. Yes, I have a job to do even if my deadlines have passed.

Do they really think that I might be involved?

Stay calm.

I say, 'Were there any signs of forced entry?'

Viljoen gives me a very level look. In my confused and agitated state (which I am still doing my best to hide), it seems to me to be a look that says Viljoen doesn't for a moment take my act as an inquisitive reporter seriously, that he thinks I'm putting it on to cover up for my own sense of . . . what? Guilt?

I am guilty, but not quite in the way he thinks.

'No,' Viljoen says.

'How did he die?'

'I'm sorry . . .'

I push harder. 'Was he shot, stabbed, bludgeoned to death?'

Viljoen leans back in his chair. 'I'm not prepared to say anything about that until next of kin have been informed, other than that we believe it's murder.'

Keep it up. Live your cover. 'Whatever was used to kill him wasn't left at the scene?'

'No, it wasn't.'

So it was a weapon of some kind.

'The ex-minister would have had licences for several firearms, I suppose.'

I know he did.

'They were kept under lock and key at his Franschhoek farm.'

I'm getting somewhere. Sometimes my role as newsman seems as phoney to me as acting on stage. It's make-believe, playing a part – an embarrassing, unconvincing one at that.

'And the dogs? At night there used to be a couple of Dobermanns on a long chain outside.'

'Poisoned.'

So whatever happened was premeditated, planned.

'And the alarm system?'

'It was not switched on.'

'Servants? Domestic staff?'

'The housekeeper heard a disturbance, let herself into the house and found the body. She called the police. It was the maid's afternoon off. The driver wasn't there. The gardener works only part time – Mondays, usually. I think that's all I can tell you now.'

I must press my advantage. I really need to take notes, but I don't dare do so for fear of Viljoen drying up completely.

'Is Joshua a suspect?'

'I can't answer that.' There's an edge of irritation to his voice.

'Would it be correct to say you expect him to help with your inquiries?'

'We would like to speak to him.' Viljoen closes files and puts them away in the desk, using a bunch of keys to lock the drawers.

'What about closed-circuit security cameras? I seem to remember there was one near the front gate, but that was some time ago.'

'Disabled.'

Josh must be the next of kin, at least in this country. There's also the sister, though I have no idea where she lives now. Josh's stepmother is resident in Switzerland, or so I've heard. She and Cris separated years ago, and she probably doesn't count as family.

'Fine,' I say. 'I'll do it.'

Viljoen nods, apparently relieved, though there can have been no question of the outcome. He gets to his feet and picks up his jacket. I wonder how much he knows of

Frances and her relationship with Josh, and what exactly passed between Frances and Viljoen before my arrival in the commandant's dilapidated office, and whether whatever it is he does know or guess has any relevance to the death of a hard-line nationalist politician, a wealthy landowner and pillar of apartheid for almost half a century.

One thing is certain: Joshua's father has never lacked for enemies, not even within his own family, and all of us know it.

Viljoen has more questions once we're in his car. I'm in the front passenger seat, he's sitting up straight, arms extended like a racing driver, both hands gripping the top of the steering wheel. He drives fast, well above the speed limit, and he glances constantly in the rear-view mirror. There's very little traffic, and I'm concentrating so hard on what he's saying and how to respond that I'm barely aware of where we are at any given moment.

'So you knew each other when you were kids, you and your friend Joshua? What about later – prep school, college?'

The city isn't really dark. There's an oily orange glow.

'Yes, we were mates then, too.'

Viljoen has done his homework, and quickly.

He starts telling me about how his view of English-speaking South Africans has evolved. How he was raised to believe they were the enemy. How untrustworthy they were seen to be, how weak they were thought to be physically, not up to much in the sports that really mattered – rugby and shooting. The notion of the *rooinek* as an inferior species of human with dangerously harmful and subversive views went all the way back to the Anglo-

Boer War because so many of the British troops sent out to South Africa had been small and undernourished. Perhaps that myth had sugared the bitter pill of the Afrikaners' military defeat.

Then, during military service, he'd met a few English-speakers and discovered they weren't like that at all. Some of his best friends turned out to be *rooinekke*.

Am I supposed to be impressed by this generosity of feeling?

'You did military service here, didn't you, Mr Palfrey?'

So that's what all this is about.

'I did, yes.'

He knows. Denying it would only make things worse.

'What was your unit?'

Beads of sweat break out on my scalp.

'I was called up into the 1st Infantry Division,' I tell him. 'Cape Town Highlanders.'

I'm not lying. It's true as far as it goes.

He glances at me and away, checking the rear-view mirror before pulling out to overtake a truck. I watch the needle swing through 130 kmh and beyond.

I find the button for my side window and lower it a couple of inches.

'Joshua Schuter was there too, wasn't he? At Oudtshoorn?'

He knows. It's just an exercise. The bastard's trying to trip me up, get me to lie. He wants to find the point of resistance so he knows where to apply the pressure. There's nothing about Viljoen or his conversation that lacks deliberation. He doesn't make small talk. I note with relief that we've slowed right down and are swinging into a parking lot. I recognize where we are – outside the police mortuary at Salt River.

He's waiting for my answer.

'Josh? Oh, yes. We were there roughly at the same time.'

I try to sound vague, absent-minded.

Roughly? There's nothing approximate about it. Who am I trying to fool? Viljoen has probably got some pal of his in the defence ministry to pull my personnel file out of a dusty vault, along with Joshua's service record.

Viljoen puts on the handbrake, kills the engine and lights.

I release myself from my seat belt, but Viljoen makes no move.

'It's a long time ago,' I mumble, my left hand feeling in the dark for the door handle.

'Ah, that's just it, Mr Palfrey, sir. We make our important choices when we're very young, far too young to my mind, and we spend the rest of our lives living out those choices and trying to rationalize them. I know I made my choices before I was twenty. I bet you did the same, Mr Palfrey. And your friend, too. Without really knowing it at the time, of course.'

I wish he wouldn't keep calling me Mister Palfrey. I think he does it deliberately, using a slightly mocking tone to annoy. I'd much prefer it if he stuck to using my surname on its own.

'What's this got to do with Cris Schuter's murder?'

Viljoen doesn't answer but unlocks the doors and we both get out.

He smiles at me across the roof of his car.

'I think you and Joshua Schuter made your choices back at that smart school you went to. Bishops, wasn't it? They say it's the finest school in the country. I wonder if that's really true. I mean about the school. Like everyone else, Mr Palfrey, I saw in the world around me what I wanted to see. I believed what I wanted to believe. It's our nature, man. It's a very human failing. In that respect, I don't think we're any different, you and me.'

Viljoen probably tells all his villains the same thing to make them feel better. He leads the way, going up the steps and pushing open the door, waiting for me to pass ahead of him, the liquid light and stink of ammonia spilling out into the warm night. My shirt is stuck to my back, but it isn't the heat.

It's panic. I don't want to be here. I don't want to answer any more questions.

Whatever the connection with the old man's killing – I can't see it but I'm sure Viljoen is several steps ahead and sees it only too well – he's taking me on a journey in time and space, forcing me to revisit memories I thought I'd left dead and buried and for good reason. I'm not a willing travel companion. It's not a journey I want to make in any circumstances, but right now, at one minute to midnight, I have little choice.

DAY TWO

TWO

TWO

The dead are different; they appear to shrink and their normal colour is drained away. In death they relax. They no longer belong to the spirit that animated them, that set them laughing, gave them pink cheeks and made them dream. Cris Schuter is no exception, for when the slabmen roll what is left of him out like a tray of ice cubes under the harsh white strip lighting in the early hours, it's as if this waxy shell is a poor impersonator of the tall, vigorous man I knew as the father of my childhood friend. My best friend.

One of the attendants folds the green sheet back a few inches at a time, revealing the body by degrees – first the mussed white hair, once a luxuriant black, then the face, ashen and almost unrecognizable, eyes and cheeks sunken, the jaw slack and, finally, below the bluish-grey chin, the fatal wound gaping wide, a bite of a killing stroke, the jagged cut so deep that the crescent of raw red flesh, that of a throat sliced wide open, strikes me as an obscenity. The French have a name for death's wide smile: *égorgé*.

There is something deeply shameful, even pornographic, about the brutishness of a slit throat.

Struck dumb at the sight of the corpse, I nod, but it

isn't enough. Viljoen wants verbal confirmation, to be followed by a signature.

Viljoen stirs. 'Well, Mr Palfrey?'

'It's him – Cris Schuter.'

Speech requires immense effort. My tongue feels too big for my mouth.

Blindly, anxious to be out of that place with its infernal, sweetish stench of body fluids and ammonia, its vase of plastic flowers and out-of-date calendar with a photograph of Swiss mountains, I scratch my name on a form with a borrowed pen, Viljoen pointing to the right place. Why Swiss, I wonder idiotically. What's wrong with South Africa's very own Drakensberg mountains? And couldn't they have combed his hair, made him presentable? My eyes water, my hand shakes, making the signature a frantic and barely legible scrawl.

Am I acting like someone guilty of murder?

I don't care – not now. All I want, all I have to have now, is the sound, the sight, the touch of the living. I need laughter, loud music, strong drink, a woman's embrace; the oblivion of appetite and the promise of imminent satiation.

Viljoen doesn't seem to notice anything amiss.

Perhaps he's used to it, unlike me. I can't wait to get out of there. Death, especially violent death, unnerves the living. Once the identification process is over in the small hours, I wring a concession from Viljoen: the promise of a personal tour of the crime scene later the same morning. He agrees with a gruff 'ja', and I ask myself whether he would have offered if I hadn't pressed him.

*

The bureau driver collects me at nine. We head out of the city, southwards against the rush-hour traffic for the sub-urbs flung like a necklace around the mountain, the beads of settlement strung along the road and railtrack down both the Atlantic and Indian Ocean sides of the Cape Peninsula as far south as Simon's Town. I sit in the back of the car and flip through the morning papers; there isn't a single paragraph about the death and there's nothing on the radio either. It makes me feel a little better – with luck I will still have a few more details than everyone else when the news does break, and I have until three to file a substantial story; it is too much to hope it will still be an exclusive by then.

From a journalistic point of view, the mystery of Josh's whereabouts is almost as important as the murder of his father. Josh is the coming man, his father symbolized the old guard. To gain any space in the paper at all, the kill-ing will have to be written up as a parable of the times, the passing of the order of tyrants, dying as they once triumphed – in blood. For that reason and for reasons of friendship, the big question is Josh, in my mind and everyone's else's; I can truthfully say he still hasn't returned any of my calls, and Frances hasn't been in touch to say if she has heard anything since leaving Viljoen's office.

I feel a strange mix of emotion as we drive under the footbridge along which I trudged as a schoolboy to see not so much Josh as his pretty sister (Rachel is married to her third husband and the mother of five children, all adults by now, and we've long ago lost touch); then we turn left up a steep and very quiet residential street lined with mansions, gated and fenced and surrounded by gardens and pools. This is millionaire territory, and one can tell from the open space before each house – a clear field of fire unobstructed by trees or shrubs that might hide a burglar or 'terrorist', for these are people with plenty to lose.

I recognize the Schuter home at once; it is third on the left, a police van parked outside in the street, and I feel both dread and excitement as we swing into the driveway lined by banks of agapanthus, the purple African lilies all in flower, the driver shifting down into first, the car climbing up to a house I have known, on and off, for the best part of a lifetime. It is so familiar, eerily so, when all the rest of the world has changed so much. Regret at change, nostalgia, the sense that the past is a better place – all this is a disease of growing old, and I try to shrug it off.

This is Viljoen's doing. He has despatched me on a mission of his own making. I am doing his bidding. A favour? I don't think so. He knows I have plenty to hide, even if I had no hand in Schuter's brutal end. I'm sure – and I don't know quite how – that Viljoen knows a great deal, but somehow he's decided I'm of use to him.

We have always been friends, Josh and I.

Despite everything.

Perhaps that's the nub of Viljoen's interest.

But what have we really in common? On the face of it, very little.

We'd more when we were kids; loneliness, for one thing. He might have had money, and might have been surrounded by its trappings, but he probably didn't notice (in fact I'm sure he didn't), and in any case, it wasn't privilege he wanted but a home; not four walls and a roof so much as a mother's embrace and a father's approval. Neither of us had that. That was the central plank in our relationship. We were loners by necessity, washed up on adjacent desert islands; the Boer and the *rooinek* might have been natural enemies, but we were thrown together out of mutual need.

I lusted after his sister, too; I could not have been more delighted to find myself sitting between Josh and Rachel on the back of the Schuters' Rolls at a local drive-in cinema watching a black-and-white World War Two movie called *Under Ten Flags*. War fascinated me, but apart from the general topic of a disguised armed merchantman that sank Allied shipping until finally brought to account, I have no memory of it; what I recall to this day is Rachel's smell, the touch of her skin, her thighs, the fine gold hair on her arms, her narrow wrists, the way her clothes clung to her, her teeth, her liquorice breath on my face, the way she wriggled when she laughed.

Her sweet, warm, animal smell.

And she quite unconscious of the priapic turmoil beside her.

I was invited back to the Schuter farm at Franschhoek, and I vaguely remember another small brown boy roughly our own age who played with us among the oaks. Our Man Friday wore Josh's hand-me-downs, but that I know with the benefit of hindsight. I didn't notice at the time, and I don't think Josh or I would have thought it noteworthy, but I am sure the recipient must have.

He was quiet, this child; watchful, biddable within reason, but I remember he was stubborn with the pride of the underdog when pushed, for pushing is what boys do to one another to establish a pecking order. This fellow let us know he wasn't part of ours. He was his own man. He would play with us, certainly, but not at any price. I wouldn't have thought to have called him Coloured. That he was darker than either of us was neither here nor there.

Not for me, and not then.

Weren't most Afrikaners tarred by the same brush?

Wasn't the first Dutch governor, Simon van der Stel, a Coloured by the sick standards of apartheid?

Children are never racially conscious until corrupted by the adult world.

I remember two more things about him: his fascination with our air guns, and his devising of a new game involving green dustbin lids. It was a smart stratagem on his part to get himself included in our games, and to lay claim to temporary use of one of our weapons. Three lids were 'borrowed' and we slid into the woods and hunted one another, firing our weapons at the lids, which we held up as shields as we crawled, slithered and ran from cover to cover. We had two air rifles, and there were three of us, so we took turns. The odd one out would use the brown boy's catapult, but neither Josh nor I could use it with the same devastating effect; in his hands it would knock the lids right out of our hands, leaving our knuckles bruised and stinging.

The sound of a lead pellet passing close by my ear, or better still, striking the ground inches from me, was hugely exciting. This, I thought, was what combat must be like. The only drawback was that minute fragments of the green paint flew off the lids when struck at short range, and some got under our skin, adding a rash of green freckles to our cheeks.

All three of us were fascinated by weapons of all kinds. That was something I certainly shared with Josh. The Schuter farm boasted several: a bayonet from the Franco-Prussian war, a French cavalry sabre with a wicked blade, a Royal Navy cutlass. There was a Martini Henry rifle, too heavy for us to handle, and a bolt-action 7 mm Mauser used by one of Cris Schuter's great uncles in the Boer War of 1899. Josh let both his friends, the pink and the brown-skinned, touch these treasures, and we took the bayonet and cutlass off to play with.

For boys of that age, edged steel and the mechanism of a firearm have a fascination that's almost sexual.

The Schuter place in Cape Town is different from the farm in all sorts of ways. It sits astride the ridge, a prime and secure location with an unobstructed view across Newlands and Constantia to Kirstenbosch Botanical Gardens and what were once the forested foothills of the mountain, the trees and undergrowth mostly stripped away and replaced with more villas of the affluent perched on stilts where Josh and I once played our games of scouts and woodsmen, of Davy Crockett and Geronimo, Wallace and Beowulf.

As the Peugeot struggles up the drive, I look out of the side window to my right, for there is the pond into which Josh and I poured bags of horse manure and then persuaded all twenty-two of his friends at his ninth birthday party – both boys and girls and none of them brown – to take their shoes and socks off and wade around in the soupy muck on the grounds that ripe horse shit did wonders for one's health. He and I, of course, stood on the sidelines, our mirth suppressed, urging the others on, our feet still shod and quite dry. I don't recall what this prank did to the goldfish, but I do remember the stinging smack on the back of my legs from my mother when she found out.

The carpet of tough, spongy, bright green kikuyu grass rises to the blue, glittering plunge pool, the very sixties sliding glass doors that run along the entire north-western wall of the open-plan living area, and the magnificent view of the mountain from the south; a view that is never the same from one day to the next; sometimes the ramparts are so close and clear I feel I can reach out my hand and touch the cliffs. The very next day Table Mountain will seem to have moved away in a sulk, turned in on itself, its majestic outline indistinct, its cliffs and gorges wrapped enigmatically in mist and cloud, streams of water pouring like tears down its rock face.

Today police tape surrounds the entire house, the outer cordon keeping people like me away from doors, windows and flowerbeds.

I don't try to go in; I walk around the house and stand at the edge of the pool in the hot, crystalline sunlight and look at the mountain as I used to, only the slim Rachel with her short golden hair is no longer lounging by the pool in her black bikini to share the panorama. It is a view like no other in the world and it provokes memories I never knew I had. Standing there again, I think the same thing Josh and I discussed at the same spot all those years ago. No longer aged nine, it was a dozen years or so later; he was a student and I was a junior reporter on the local morning paper; we were in our early twenties and we drank beer out of cans taken from his family's huge American fridge after our customary five-mile run.

I said, 'We're lucky.'

'How's that?'

'We're so lucky, Josh, and we don't even know it.'

'What are you on about?'

'We're male. We're white. We went to private schools. Not just private schools, but the very best private school.'

'Ja. So?'

A man of few words, Josh.

'So we don't have to be smart. We don't have to compete. We don't have to work hard. We don't have to be talented. We don't have to be good at anything very much. All we have to do is wait – and keep our minds closed and our mouths shut.'

'Wait for what, man?'

I stretched my arms out wide, embracing the view before us.

'It will come to us, all of it. Wealth, power, prestige, leisure, a long life. With your money you'll live here on the hill, just like your dad before you. You'll probably own the paper I'm working for without even being aware of it. It'll just be one of your majority holdings in your portfolio, that's all. I'll be the editor, of course, and I'll live further downhill as befits a professional. We'll both marry Herschel girls, and with a little luck their daddies will be rich as well, and we'll get together for a drink at the club occasionally, and when we're too old for sailing or cricket we'll join the local bridge club with our wives. If we die of anything it will be sheer tedium.'

'You know what, Seb? You're a bloody cynical bastard.'

Bloody was one of his favourite words back then.

'The secret to our success is to ignore the fact that the system that puts us up here on the hill is the same system that keeps them breaking stones on Robben Island, that the Rule of Law is being whittled away with each day that passes. We can join the Progressive Party and hold up placards protesting about racism, and feel better about ourselves when we smell a whiff of police tear gas, but when all's said and done, we are beneficiaries. When we feel guilty about it, and the rest of the world points an accusing finger at us, we can turn around and blame the government.'

I dropped my arms and turned to him.

'Isn't that what being a liberal is? Isn't that what you are, Josh?'

'That's fucking Commie talk, Seb.'

Little did he know.

He didn't actually say fucking but fokking. His accent was strong in those days, guttural and thick, his tone high-pitched just like his dad's.

'It's true, though.'

Josh laughed; it was all too serious. In later years he would use his skills as an equity investor, hedge fund manager and venture capitalist to build a wall of wealth that would shelter him from unsavoury realities. It was his bulwark against the truth. He threw his head back, shook his long red hair out of his face, put the beer can to his lips and said nothing more.

Roll on the good life.

I wondered then at his offhand reaction; whether he had already decided where he stood. Had he made the calculation that his interests were already such that he could not allow himself to be drawn into the battle? Are not most people similarly inclined in that they only take a stand when their interests are threatened? Joshua's interests – his inheritance, in other words, and what he planned to do to expand the Schuter empire – surely depended on maintaining the status quo, albeit a reformed one.

Bishops had taught him he could be critical, but remain one of the *manne*, the boys. That was the nub of it. He wanted it all. Well, fair enough. If he had already arrived at that conclusion, I had to admire him for his clear-sightedness and his courage in facing it, even if we were to find ourselves on opposite sides. It takes as much courage to do wrong as it does to do right sometimes.

Or to do nothing.

A degree of self-deception was inevitable for any enlightened Afrikaner willing to swallow the lie of racial 'separate development'.

It would give anyone monumental moral indigestion.

Maybe that was why his laugh sounded so uneasy.

In those days, Buchanan of Buchanan's Biscuits lived directly opposite; he was another contemporary and fellow Bishops boy. It was in his living room that I had my first long, fascinating, arousing, deeply shocking sight of a vagina. It belonged to Buchanan's snooty yet coldly desirable girlfriend, aged no more than sixteen, and was revealed as she sat at his feet on a Persian rug. She had turned slightly, pivoting on her left buttock, lifted her right knee, letting her short skirt ride up her tanned thigh, and looked up into Buchanan's face as he talked, making sure he saw nothing, demonstrating to me that she wore nothing beneath. It occurred to me only later that she had quite deliberately shown me the goods – the extraordinarily ugly yet succulent and, from that angle, hairless oyster of womanhood – as if to say, This is what he gets tonight; your daddy isn't rich enough, you don't have a sports convertible, you don't live in Bishops-court and you're far too serious and boring. All true, of course.

Isn't that what they called me at school? The white kaffir?

The left-hand property, a mock-Tudor affair plastered inside and out with fake black beams, had been the home of the Bauers. The father was an industrialist and some-thing big in pharmaceuticals, the boy had merely been an acquaintance, although also at Bishops, and someone I remember as having a reputation for an inappropriate interest in his fellow pupils' genitals – a passing phase, apparently, as he was to marry later and produce his own brood of little Bauers. The Hendersons were over to the right, or used to be; the two sons had gone to St Andrew's, the daughter to Herschel's, like Bishops a single-sex church school, exclusively white and exclusively gentile – unless, like the Bauers, one's Jewishness was discreet, secular and outweighed by great wealth and influence.

The only brown or black boys here would have been the children of servants, and they would have been neither seen nor heard.

*

Here I am, the prime suspect back at the scene of the crime.

Is that how Viljoen sees it?

I walk back around the house to the front door and notice – I don't know how I missed it when I got out of the car; it must have been the distraction of the mountain – the two police patrol cars, the three-car garage, its swing doors open, revealing men in white noddy suits, gloves and hats like shower caps, their backs turned, working at a trestle table, and the wrought-iron gate leading to the servants' quarters.

A uniformed policeman seems to be waiting for me; I imagine that the scientific people working in the living area must have seen me hovering about outside through the big plate glass doors. I am told I can't enter the house without Viljoen's permission; the commandant is in charge and should be here any time soon. I am happy to wait; I tell myself that to some extent the process of identifying the body of the late Cris Schuter has prepared me for what is to come.

I'm wrong. Nobody, not even the murderer, could count himself ready for the sight of that living room.

I wait about thirty minutes in the shade of the front porch before Viljoen arrives at the house, looking harassed and wearing a sports coat, grey flannels and no tie. He has pulled his shirt collar out so it lies against the lapels of his jacket – a habit of rural Afrikaners generally and police and off-duty military in particular. He nods without smiling, says nothing, and vanishes into the garage to consult his colleagues, the crime scene manager, forensic investigator and pathologist.

When he emerges a few minutes later, he is stuffing paperwork into his briefcase. That done, he gives me a tour of the crime scene. Even now, neither of us says anything. He ducks under the tape, and I follow. I don't tell him that I can find my way blindfold around Cris Schuter's Cape Town residence.

A set of mobile aluminium steps, a miniature step-ladder, has been placed over the entrance. A uniformed sergeant, the crime scene officer, stands back and lets us pass.

The front door opens on to the hall with its cream Chinese rug. It looks so normal, so familiar, but for the duckboards that have been laid down across the carpeting.

'Blood behaves in a strange way when it comes to carpets; it can work its way underneath and you see nothing on the surface,' Viljoen says, adding that I should not stray from the boards at any point. 'But if the killer stays around too long, and he steps on the carpet, his footsteps will push the blood to the surface, leaving us a very nice print.'

Is there a point to his telling me that?

What is he suggesting?

The door immediately to the left I know leads to a visitors' washroom. The foyer branches off left and right, east and west; Viljoen takes the right-hand corridor first, and we pass two bedrooms on our left. Both, I know, are of a good size and both have views of the mountain. I resist the temptation to tell him the first used to be Josh's room, the second his sister's, and I don't ask who uses them now. Directly opposite on the right-hand side of the corridor is an opulent family bathroom complete with jacuzzi, power shower and two washbasins, next to it a separate lavatory and, at the very far end, Cris Schuter's master bedroom en suite. It has views of the mountain as well as the distant peacock sea.

The colours are pastel; inoffensive tones of cream and beige, white and gold for the bedroom itself, blue tiles in the family bathroom, the palest green in the en-suite facilities.

Viljoen stops before the kingsize bed, the embroidered maroon cover thrown back, the white froth of duvet tumbling to the floor, the plump, lacy pillows disordered. At the foot of the bed is a big plasma television screen, still a rarity in 1994. I can smell French linen water. A woman's room, I think, but when did Schuter last have a woman in it?

'He was sleeping; he was disturbed by a noise and woke to find an intruder in the house – maybe even standing over him right here, like this.'

Viljoen doesn't look at me; he stares at the room as if trying to bring to mind the old boy's last moments. A young man wearing white overalls, with latex gloves on his hands and holding a miniature vacuum cleaner, scrambles up off his knees and nods respectfully at Viljoen, muttering something about having just finished the room. Viljoen gives no sign of having noticed his presence any more than he would have a housemaid.

I ask, 'How do you know?'

'The maid made the bed in the morning – he must have taken a nap. According to the housekeeper, Schuter slept irregularly. An insomniac, he took catnaps, and it was not uncommon for the maid or the housekeeper to make up the bed two or three times in the course of a day. He often worked all night, apparently. He seldom ate cooked meals – he lived on dried fruit and nuts, or so she said.'

'You have their statements already?'

'Last night – or rather, early this morning, after the identification.'

How terrified the servants must have been by these midnight raids; the orders shouted in Afrikaans, the thumps on their doors, the powerful torches shining in their faces as they cringed in fear. They must have thought the bad old days were back.

An alcove off the dressing area with its floor-to-ceiling cupboards and rows of suits contain a modern adjustable desk with a melamine top and ergonomic chair. I could move closer, passing unobserved behind Viljoen, but I would have to step on the carpet and this I cannot do. This is presumably Schuter's study, but there are no papers of any kind that I can see, only large volumes piled on a single shelf that reflect his main interests in old age: architecture, animal husbandry, viticulture and oceanography.

'What was he working on?'

'His memoirs.'

They should make for interesting reading.

'Where are they?'

'Being dusted for prints.'

Viljoen is watching me. Does he expect a reaction? If so, he must be disappointed.

We turn and make our way back, passing the young man with vacuum cleaner, this time taking the left-hand corridor, Viljoen still in the lead. It is very warm. The air conditioning is off and I wonder why. To our left is the

left is the big kitchen, recently refurbished with steel fit-
ings from Germany and extensive enough for a trio of
cordon-bleu chefs to prepare a three-course meal for a
hundred covers. It is immense, extending almost half the
length of the entire house. Opposite, on our right, a door
leads to the dining room, with a wall of glass opening
out on to the lawn and pool, the omnipresent mountain
shrouded in heat haze beyond.

Viljoen seems to know what I'm thinking. 'We don't
change anything – we didn't put the AC on because that
disturbs the dust and fibres.'

He walks on, looking neither left nor right.

'We placed acetate sheets under the windows, dusted
them with powder and applied an electrical charge – you
can pick up quite a detailed footprint on an otherwise
unmarked carpet.'

Maybe, I think, he is telling me this out of pride at his
team's scientific approach. Or is he trying to throw me
off balance, make me slip up, reveal something that will
implicate myself in the killing?

Once again we come to the end of the corridor. There
is a small landing, a wrought-iron balustrade, and four
wooden steps in a half-circle down to the living area. The
entire facing wall is glass, and it seems as if the main
occupant of the room is Table Mountain itself, a slumber-
ing giant.

'Ja, this is where he died.'

As an observation, it's entirely superfluous.

In one way the place hasn't changed in forty years, not
since Schuter approved the plans and supervised the building himself. He wanted a city home that was, in the
sixties, the epitome of modern style. Everything in

the living area is white, from the grand piano to the immense shag-pile carpet, set off by the kitsch brass portholes set in the left-hand wall.

There has been no attempt to update the decor.

The piano is still there and the white carpet too, along with the huge swordfish on one wall, the shelves crowded with silver trophies, large and small, won in big-game fishing contests in the Florida Keys, grass tennis tournaments in France, golfing competitions in Taiwan and international skeet championships in California, even a bronze Olympic medal for trap shooting. He went everywhere in that diminishing world where a South African could still get a visa. At least he left the stuffed animals' heads, his hunting trophies, behind on the farm.

Schuter's own attempts at watercolours decorate the walls along with photographs of the notorious, all shaking hands with a beaming Cris, a parade of self-satisfied smirks to the theme that big crimes do pay, and well. I recognize Kissinger and that scoundrel Nixon, separate portraits of Golda Meir and Moshe Dayan and below them the unsavoury trio: Salazar, Franco and Trujillo. All were helpmates to white-ruled South Africa in her years of international isolation. The last tier is closer to home: here are the faces of Hendrik Verwoerd, the architect of apartheid, his grim successor, John Vorster, and a signed portrait of the self-obsessed conservative Zulu leader, Gatsha Buthelezi, in traditional tribal gear, a leopardskin cap set at a jaunty angle and a fly whisk in his right hand.

The only difference I can see in Schuter's shrine to himself now is his own blood, and a great deal of it. It looks as if someone has drenched the living area with it. It's everywhere.

'He was a very fit man for his age,' Viljoen says with what I take to be some admiration. 'He fought back hard.'

Certainly the place and manner of his killing have a sacrificial quality. I wonder if Viljoen sees the symbolism: a wide semicircle of the white carpet below the sporting trophies and photographs is soaked a deep crimson, and where the shag pile ends, the blood lies thickly like oil in a pool on the parquet flooring as far as the sliding doors. It is on the walls, even the ceiling. It is starting to dry and turn a dark reddish brown, crusting on the surface.

I can smell it from where we stand.

'That's the carotid,' Viljoen says, as if following my gaze. 'It has terrific force, man. The first cut just nicked the artery, so it came out under pressure, just like a spray – you can see from the perpendicular drops on the ceiling.'

The first cut.

There is more than one.

'The blood loss can be measured by multiplying the quantity of blood in the heart with the heart rate – so if we talk about 100 millilitres in the ventricle, and we assume that the victim was struggling, and we can say that his heart was beating around sixty-five times a minute, we're looking at six and a half litres lost every minute. So he would have lost consciousness in forty seconds – less, perhaps thirty.'

The outline of Schuter's body has been pegged out in police tape on the blood-soaked carpet, right below the photographs and trophies.

'No one saw or heard anything?'

Viljoen does not answer directly.

'We think there were at least two assailants,' he says.

'They held him, ja, from the back. One sat on him and the other grabbed his hair and that was when he managed to rear up as the second one used a knife or razor. That's why you see the blood has spread so widely. He was fighting as he died, but it was not for more than a few seconds. His killers must have been covered with his blood. He was drained of it.'

Viljoen takes my arm while I wonder just how much he knows but isn't telling.

'I want to show you something, Mr Palfrey.'

We head back along the corridor, this time to the kitchen, and stop in the doorway, passing another plain-clothes officer clutching a video camera.

Viljoen points.

'Look – you see?'

There are footprints, bloody footprints, leading across the black and white tiles to the big metal sink and workspace below an open window. I count three – two of the right foot, one of the left. Whoever it was was barefoot, making big strides, in a rush for the exit.

'One of them was thoughtful enough to leave us a little present, you see. He ran up the stairs to the dining room, crossed over to the kitchen, jumped up on to the sink and went out of the window. The stupid kaffir left us his calling card. We think he takes a number ten shoe and is around five-eleven – when he wears shoes, that is.'

Some things haven't changed one bit.

'It's blood?'

'I don't think it's fruit juice, Mr Palfrey, but we're testing samples we took right now.'

It is Viljoen's attempt at a joke.

'Why not use the front door? And there are no foot-prints on the carpet in the corridor . . .'

'Maybe he thought there might be a pressure pad under the carpet. It was just a step across to the kitchen from the dining-room door. And maybe that's how they got in – through the same window. I don't know if you noticed, but it's the only window that isn't barred, maybe because it looks out into the walled courtyard and the servants' rooms.'

But hasn't he just said the house alarm wasn't switched on?

I look back over my shoulder. Sure enough, through the open doorway to the dining room is a footprint on the wood floor, next to the captain's chair at the head of the stinkwood table.

He says again, 'You see?'

'Yes,' I say. 'I see.'

For all his press conferences and racist remarks, Viljoen is no simple-minded matinee idol in uniform, a ventrilo-quist's dummy. He's in charge of the Cris Schuter murder investigation because he has the experience, the skills and he is no fool. He is leading me – and I've no idea yet where or why.

For a moment the image from the front page of that morning's *Die Burger* returns: the swarms of bluebottles on the bloated corpses sprawled in the alleyways of the mining towns of the Witwatersrand, the grim harvest of in-fighting between ANC activists and Buthelezi's war-riors, the last wild and savage toss of the dice by covert *verkramptes* to divert the ANC from its road to power – using blacks to kill other blacks to throw the elections off track. Those anonymous victims of the ethnic power struggle will receive no such attention by police investigators, let alone ones as high-ranking as Viljoen. For them it will be a mass grave and quicklime.

I say, 'How do you know it's more than one?'

'I don't, Mr Palfrey. It's speculation. But you said yourself that you knew the old man, did you not? He might have been seventy-nine, but do you really think you could overpower Schuter and cut his throat all by yourself, especially if he managed to break free after the first attempt and you had to subdue him and cut him a second time?'

I must have nodded.

'You are right-handed, aren't you, Mr Palfrey?'

Mister Palfrey.

'Yes.'

'Whoever did this was right-handed. His second effort was more determined. He used his left arm to hold the victim's head, and then he held the weapon in his right hand and stabbed him in the vicinity of the carotid, using the point of the weapon to penetrate the neck and then dragging the blade across, left to right, making sure. We say "he" because it would have required some considerable strength and size, although the artery is very close to the surface – you can feel it yourself.'

Viljoen smiles for the first time this morning, but there's no humour in it.

'Anyway, that's the pathologist's view.'

Viljoen turns to me in the hall.

'What was he like, this Cris Schuter?'

I'm being tested again. Viljoen knows perfectly well. I

say, 'Schuter Senior was old school and proud of it. He walked barefoot to the village school. They say he rode a mule or horse bareback long before he owned a bicycle or drove a car.'

'A country boy.'

I shrug. 'The papers say he could shoot with rifle, shotgun and pistol by the age of ten and spoke Xhosa as well as he did Afrikaans; I'm sure he would've been subject from a tender age to fire and brimstone sermons of the predikant.' There would've been the lessons from the Old Testament (hence the names chosen for his own children). He would have said grace before every meal, dressed in black for services on the Sabbath. He was a member of the most fundamentalist of the three Dutch Reformed churches – the Gereformeerde Kerk.

Viljoen will empathize with this purist world.

Staunchly anti-British and anti-liberal, he was a man for whom 'Communist' was an epithet that applied to anyone deemed ungodly in word, thought or deed, a broad concept of evil embracing miniskirts, the Rolling Stones, the Western press, premarital sex, drugs, the African National Congress, the South African Communist Party and Prime Minister Harold Macmillan's 'winds of change' speech.

And yet, I say, he belonged to a tiny nation whose overriding characteristic has been its adaptability. The world's first heart transplant operation was carried out by an Afrikaans surgeon at a time when one of the world's pre-eminent ballerinas was herself an Afrikaner. Afrikaners have produced a steady stream of poets, novelists, artists, philosophers and scientists, out of all proportion to their number.

Keep talking.

Schuter Senior qualified as an architect at Stellenbosch, studied business management in the United States and spent two years in Australia to absorb modern methods of wine-making. He played tennis like a demon. He could have turned professional had he not already been so busy transforming his Franschhoek vineyards' sour, thin yield of vinegary wine into something very special, and, by keeping prices down (through the use of cheap labour thanks to the apartheid laws he helped uphold), he'd been able to invest in a redesigned label, swapping an ugly two-litre flagon for an elegant bottle fit to grace the finest table, together with some astute marketing gimmickry in Europe to persuade supermarkets to buy in bulk. He'd won his country's top export award for three years in succession and, incidentally, turned himself into a millionaire.

'Did he live here permanently?'

I get into the swing of it, happy to show off my knowledge and momentarily ignoring the possibility that Viljoen is simply playing one of his deceitful mind games.

Cris Schuter had come off the farm and into the city, and this bungalow – its steeply pitched roof of grey slate reminds me of a church – is a monument to his financial success, to modernity; to me, the virgin-white living area with the silly fish on the wall and silver-plated cups is like a narcissistic sepulchre to his achievements up until that point in his career.

It was at a time when the Afrikaners were making their third great migration in their short history. First, in the early nineteenth century, they trekked in their wagons out of the Cape Colony, out of reach, or so they hoped, of the iniquitous British, pushing aggressively inland, thirsty for land and labour. Then in World War Two, Afrikaners were the main beneficiaries of rapid industrialization, emerging from rural obscurity into rapidly growing cities like Johannesburg, their nationalist leaders using new-found trade union muscle to achieve political power in 1948. Finally, in the 1960s, as they put in place their grand racial ideology, the lie of separate development, they moved boldly into the world of capitalist finance.

With such cheap labour – forced labour in all but name – what could not be achieved?

Viljoen is still playing the innocent. 'You saw him as a hardliner, then – a *verkrampte*?'

I don't think it's that simple. The old boy was no blinkered Transvaaler. He had imagination. Living in the Cape it must have been impossible to ignore change, so it was only natural that if he gave his son and daughter biblical names, he should also prepare them for the new reality by sending them to the best English-speaking schools; they should in his view straddle both worlds, not only as the inheritors of Afrikaner language, culture, faith and tradition, but able to take their rightful place in the international community, knowing not merely which fork to use, how to greet a princess and dress for the opera, but how to discern a Pollock from a Lichtenstein, a Bach sonata from a Bruch cantata, a limerick from a villanelle.

Poor Joshua. Poor Rachel.

How could they live up to such ambition thrust upon

them by a father who demanded the impossible of himself?

The first time Cris Schuter and I met it was by accident.

He made a strong physical impression on me; he was tall, tanned and very dark. He smiled easily. He could have been an Italian from Calabria or perhaps a Syrian. He had the most extraordinary eyebrows, bushy and untamed like those of Nietzsche, and they joined in the middle, a sign of bad temper. The first time I saw him he had just come off the tennis court; he carried two rackets under his arm, and his shirt was heavy with sweat. He wore sweatbands around each wrist and his head. His hair was black as a raven's wing, and worn fashionably long. He looked to me like a dark Visigoth, a warrior chief.

The second time he was out by the pool in Bishops-court, relaxing, stripped to the waist and wearing a pair of baggy yellow shorts, lovingly cleaning a matched pair of English-made over-and-under twelve-bore shotguns. I don't think he knew who I was or why I was there. He didn't ask. To me, an only child with an absentee father who boarded at school and spent his holidays with his grandparents, Cris Schuter had immense appeal as a role model. His lack of questions was in itself refreshing; most adults seemed to think interrogation a compulsory preliminary to asking a strange child to tea.

He put out his hand and I took it firmly, the way I'd been taught.

'How do you do, sir.'

I knew how to play the respectful Bishops boy.

'I'm Cris Schuter. You're . . .'

'Seb Palfrey.'

'An English boy.'

He had a high, cracked voice, not at all what I expected.

'Yes, sir.'

I was proud then to be thought of as English or British.

'Call me Cris.'

'Yes, sir – I mean, Cris.'

'You go to Bishops?'

'Sir.'

'Do you speak Afrikaans, Seb?'

'Yes, sir. Cris.'

'This is an English shotgun, Seb. The best. Have you seen one before?'

I could not take my eyes off it.

'No, Cris.'

'Take it – here – hold it like this.'

He showed me how to open the breech, how to carry it safely, let me peer through the shiny, smooth barrels. He instructed me on how to bring it up to the shoulder, to swing it through the imaginary target, to squeeze the trigger as the barrel obscured the duck or partridge, to follow the swing through.

I was in ecstasy at that moment.

I was too young to distinguish between indifference and tolerance. He must have assumed I was just another of Josh's many school friends, and that I would help myself to food or drink if I wanted it. I simply don't think he drew a line between children and adults; to him they were just people. He drew lines elsewhere. There were white people and black people, there were clever people and stupid ones.

The only discordant note in this picture of healthy

63

physical prowess was his surprisingly high-pitched voice; he seemed well aware of it, for he spoke quietly most of the time, only letting it rise to a falsetto in private or when he forgot himself, as he did all too often at the podium during political rallies. This squeaky voice was a trait Josh inherited; to the chagrin of both it might have been the only one that passed from father to son. In all other physical respects Josh resembled his dead mother, from his blue eyes and sensitive skin to his shock of red hair.

The mother. The natural mother. To begin with it never occurred to me that the dark-haired and elegant woman I occasionally encountered in the Schuters' Bishopscourt home or glimpsed behind the wheel of the Silver Wraith (she liked to drive herself around town) was not the mother of either Rachel or Josh. I had passed into adulthood and both Josh and I had completed our military service by the time I learned that Thérèse, Josh's real mother, had died in childbirth in their Franschhoek home, that Rachel was Josh's half-sister, the fruit of a second marriage that ended in divorce, and that Marika, the woman who shared Schuter's bed in the days when both children still lived in the house on the hill, was the third wife, the daughter of a Dutch Reformed Church dominee with no money but a strong political pedigree and all the right National Party credentials.

It was she who had sat in the front seat of the Rolls with Cris at the drive-in cinema while I tried – unsuccessfully – to grope Rachel by stealth in the back. The Afrikaans-language press adored her, comparing her favourably with Jacqueline Kennedy. Magazines like *Huisgenoot* and the colour comics that accompanied the weekend papers were seldom without her portrait at some function or other, a charity concert or a polo match, perhaps; she was invariably pictured smiling, hanging on Cris's arm, and, to the hacks of hyperbole, Marika was the perfect hostess, the perfect partner, the perfect mother, the sweetly more than acceptable face of Afrikaner-dom's ruling elite. She was certainly tall, pretty, silent, beautifully dressed and very nervous of children. With hindsight I realized she did not really know what to do with Josh or Rachel, or how to talk to them. She treated them warily, the way some people can't find it in themselves to cope with cats and dogs or horses. And like household pets, children are messy, noisy, needy creatures that require feeding and cleaning and much besides, the most important single element being attachment, and the second, unconditional love.

Marika, poor dear, did not know where to begin, and neither did they.

When we go outside again the heat is ferocious. I put on my sunglasses while Viljoen slips off his jacket and slings it over his shoulder. From a tolerably cool start, the morning has become oppressive in less than an hour; some people complain the Cape isn't really African at all, that it lacks soul, but the summer sun definitely is: it sucks the colour out of everything, and the life out of me.

He tells me something of the investigative techniques. How the police scientists taped up the windows, switched on ultraviolet light and sprayed something called Luminol into the rooms – evidently it will immediately reveal tiny traces of blood that might otherwise have be missed on walls, ceiling or floor.

And have they found any? Viljoen doesn't answer. He puts a finger in his mouth as if extracting something from between his teeth.

He says, 'How well did you know Dr Cris? I mean, once you were older and working as a reporter. Were you friends?'

I look for my office car; then I see the police have moved it back down the hill and out on to the street. I'm annoyed. The unfortunate Potgieter, my driver, will be roasting down there without shade of any kind. They wouldn't have told him to move if he was white, or if I'd been present; it is just the propensity of these officious people to order Coloureds around for no other reason than that they are 'non-white'. As if it was a God-given right.

That will change, is changing, has to change.

Friends? Hardly. I know now what Viljoen is looking for.

In a word, motive.

I look at my watch before replying. 'We're different generations,' I say. 'I used to bump into him at party rallies in the election campaigns. I was invited with other members of the foreign press to his place in Franschhoek for the annual tastings. I don't know that he knew who I was particularly. Perhaps there was a vague recognition on his part, but I'm pretty sure if he came up to us now he wouldn't know my name. He'd nod and smile and welcome me and look to you to make the introductions and then he'd say, "Of course, it's Seb Palfrey, isn't it? You used to be a friend of my son."'

I'm talking too much again.

'Why used to be? Aren't you still?'

Viljoen isn't stupid.

Does he really think I killed Schuter, or organized his assassination?

No. But he does know enough about me to make me feel uncomfortable.

Maybe I'm being paranoid, but I sense he already knows who killed the old man, and that he's simply using the crime scene to unnerve me, to get me to talk. As much as I'm playing the interested newsman, he's pretending to help the foreign reporter.

He's waiting for my answer.

'He would have remembered me as a childhood friend of Joshua's, Commandant. I don't think he or Joshua got along terribly well in later years and I doubt whether their social diaries and invitation lists overlapped much, so he wouldn't really have known one way or the other.'

'In other words, neither you nor Joshua are regular visitors to Bishopscourt?'

'Good Lord, no, not now, but I can only speak for myself.'

'But there were differences between father and son?'

'Political differences, certainly. Joshua is what passes in this country for a liberal. I don't know about personal. Aren't all fathers and sons rivals in some sense or other? It's natural.'

I'm in danger of overdoing it. I remind myself not to elaborate.

'Didn't Joshua Schuter confide in you as a friend about his relations with his parents?'

'His mother died when he was born.'

'I meant his father and stepmother.'

'He didn't volunteer much, Commandant, and I didn't

think it diplomatic to press the matter. I didn't discuss my parents with him as far as I recall. I don't think it's something boys do. Sometimes friendship is a matter of not poking one's nose into personal matters. These things are best left to a therapist or priest.'

We leave the shadow of the eaves and stand out in the sun, the tar in the driveway softening in the heat and already sticky underfoot. Sweat under my hair begins to run down to my collar. I'm uncomfortable. I want to walk down the hill. I want to write the story. I'm always fidgety before my daily fix of filing copy to the rag. It's not that I have a deadline to worry about – that is some hours away – but the story is taking shape in my head and I need to get it down while it's still fresh. I don't have to think much about what words I'll use – by now my brain does all the selection and processing by itself. All I have to do is write it.

'Thanks for your help,' I say. 'I appreciate it.'

I'm acting the role of appreciative British newspaper correspondent.

'There'll be a press conference at three,' Viljoen says, playing the helpful cop.

Three. I will have filed by that time; I'll have a lot more than my competitors, and they'll have no time left for the first editions. I look forward to the expressions of annoyance on the faces of the other British correspondents when they receive callbacks from their offices on my story: the obnoxious little shit from the *Telegraph*, Hawthorne, for whom Mandela is still a Communist terrorist, the large and slow-moving Fenner of *The Times*, a kindly Yorkshireman who's worked his way up from copy boy on the *Yorkshire Post* and who seems glued to the bar at the Pig and Whistle and counts off the days to his pension, the impossibly young and simpering Sinead Cogan of the *Gazette*, a blonde with smelly feet who's slept with practically every male member of the foreign press corps, myself being one of the exceptions, and of course the dull, baby-faced Reuters man, Viggers, who always wears a suit and tie and who spends most of his time filing economic news for screen clients from the comfort of his office, and who proclaimed within my hearing only last week that South Africa is no longer a political story – it's only financial news that matters now.

I don't offer my hand to Viljoen because my palms are damp, and he doesn't offer his.

'One thing more, Mr Palfrey, if you don't mind.'

I stop and look back up at him. I put my hand up to shade my eyes.

'Do you know, in your capacity as a journalist, someone called Maqoma? Or did you know anyone of that name?'

'Maqoma?' I pretend to think for a moment. It is part of his history, mine too. I frown, look down at the ground, then shake my head.

'I don't think I do,' I say at last. I have always tried, with mixed success, to avoid telling outright lies, and as a reporter I have always sought to avoid helping the authorities with names or information of any kind. I'm no copper's nark.

'Or anyone known as Maqoma – perhaps known to you by another name.'

I smile, turning my palms up in a gesture of helplessness.

Viljoen is close. He has touched a nerve. This is the

crux of his questioning, I realize now; it has all been building up to this moment. Clearly, Viljoen knows he is on to the track of something a good deal more than the who, how and why of a murder.

He wants me to know, too.

Cold droplets of sweat run down my spine and my heart beats double-time.

'Sorry,' I say. I make an effort to smile, take a step backwards, then turn and begin walking down between the massed ranks of agapanthus and through the electronic gates to where Potgieter waits for me in what little shade he can find next to the office Peugeot. I half expect Viljoen to follow, or call me back a second time. I don't look back, though I feel his eyes on us until we drive away.

Am I going to be arrested?

Not a word said about Frances.

And where is Josh?

As we head back to the city I replay our conversation. Did Viljoen believe me? Could I have handled it differently? Could I have handled it better? I could have fudged my answer to Viljoen's last question. I could have said Maqoma was the name of one of several Xhosa chiefs who for a time successfully resisted the white settlers' conquest of their land and people (true enough; Hintsa was another), but that would have stepped dangerously close to the bone. It wasn't the settlers but the British Army who finally smashed indigenous resistance.

I could have tried to drag Viljoen down a blind alley by prattling on about history, adding that the Schuters were descended from the Germans, mostly single males, who settled in the Cape in the eighteenth century and who were assimilated into the Dutch settlement, speaking the rough dialect that was to become Afrikaans, and putting down roots in the Stellenbosch and Franschhoek area. The Schuters were originally artisans, their lives back home disrupted by the impact of the Thirty Years War; like many early Afrikaners they may well have intermarried with mixed-race people of Khoisan descent, adapting to the Calvinist religion and taking to cattle breeding and trading as Europeans spread inland in search of land and slaves.

Would Viljoen have been diverted? I doubt it.

I'm sure he knows as well as I what was omitted from the history books used to teach us children, from the venality of Jan van Riebeeck, who arrived in the Cape in 1652 as head of the first Dutch East India Company settlement, to his lust for 'employing' indigenous people gullible enough to approach his men. Within thirty years there were more slaves than settlers – most of them imported by ship from West Africa. If we had gone outside to the pool and looked hard enough, we might just have been able to see what remained of the huge bitter-almond hedge that continued to seed itself over the centuries; van Riebeeck had planted the barrier, enclosing about six thousand acres of the original settlement, to keep out leopard and lion.

Unfortunately it failed to keep the settlers in.

I have many unanswered questions as I sit down to write my story; the most pressing is why Commandant Viljoen has taken the trouble to give a *rooinek* newspaper correspondent an exclusive tour of the crime scene. The Palfreys might be among the oldest of South Africa's white families, but to some I will always be a *rooinek*, and it isn't just my birth in Cambridge, my years abroad, my British passport or the rag that employs me. So why not *Die Burger*'s police reporter? Or the domestic news agency, the South African Press Association? Is it simply because I agreed to identify the body late at night?

Did I have any option?

No. Viljoen owes me no favours.

So why me?

There can be only one answer.

I'm Viljoen's stalking horse and our journey has just begun.

THREE

I've barely pushed the 'send' button on my story and stretched back in my chair, luxuriating in the afterglow of a job well done, when a worried Potgieter peers around my office door, holding a cup of coffee like a peace offering and bearing the news that the Peugeot has a puncture and he hopes I won't be needing the car for another thirty minutes or so. I say I won't and not to worry. I take the coffee, but he lingers, twisting his mouth like a disapproving sommelier and trying to summon up the courage to say something. There is more: a Security Branch officer is waiting outside. He is demanding to see me, saying it is urgent and can't wait.

I have a scoop. It isn't yet two – a whole hour before the news conference and the rag's first deadline. Nothing is going to spoil my euphoria. The hack pack is north, some in Gauteng and others in Natal, reporting the continued clashes. I have caught them all on the hop, with the possible exception of Fenner. It has been the same story for weeks – the elections are approaching and the violence is worsening. How often can one take the risk of exposing oneself to danger, of writing the same thing, and for how long, before news editors and readers alike tire of it? I have a new angle on an old story, which is what my trade is all about. For the reporter, there's nothing new in this world – with the possible exception of the Second Coming and Armageddon. In the first instance, there will be a good deal of trouble sourcing the story (no one will believe it); in the second, there'll be nobody left to broadcast it, let alone read it. I feel pleased with myself; so much so I decide I will treat myself to lunch once I have sorted out whatever this is.

'Well, show him in and bring some more coffee.'

When Mabaza enters I'm taken aback. Obviously I didn't examine his warrant card carefully enough when he held it up for my inspection last night; perhaps I was too stoned.

'Lieutenant, I thought you were investigating Cris Schuter's murder.'

'I am, Mr Palfrey.'

'But you're not homicide, Lieutenant.'

He smiles, showing very even and very white teeth; he doesn't wait to be invited but sits in the only other chair and accepts a mug of Potgieter's revolting instant, which I can tell he doesn't really want but thinks it rude or impolitic to refuse outright. Have the two of them played a trick at my expense – Viljoen pretending to be the white boss, and Mabaza playing the black subordinate? Or is it hard man and soft man? Why bother? Everyone knows Security Branch outranks all other police departments, but I do wonder whether a black Security Branch lieutenant can tell a white commandant from CID what to do. It's an interesting point in 1994.

'You know better than I that Mr Schuter was an important figure at one stage,' Mabaza says. 'He was a very wealthy man and also a Nat politician. It's a joint investigation.'

That's a diplomatic way of putting it. I can see now why Lieutenant Mabaza has been selected for higher things in the new South Africa that awaits us all.

'So you don't take orders from Commandant Viljoen and he doesn't take orders from you, Lieutenant.'

The smile stays in place. 'We work together, Mr Palfrey.'

'Ah – colleagues in the new non-racial police service.'

He isn't sure if I am taking the piss, but he doesn't rise to it. He looks at me steadily, waiting to see if there will be more of the same. I want to ask him where he is from, how old he is, and whether he was a student at the time of the township revolt in '76, whether he remembers it – the 'necklacing', the placing of car tyres around the necks of alleged police collaborators, pouring petrol into the outer tubes and then setting them alight. Or maybe the Sebokeng township rebellion in '86, a twenty-one-month-long orgy of killing that spread like wildfire all along the Reef and beyond. I don't ask, though; a white man's questions put to a black man can seem intrusive, unfriendly, or downright patronizing. I especially do not want to be misunderstood by a Security Branch officer.

I say, 'And this is why you're here?'

'Yes, sir, it is.'

Has he talked to Frances?

How much does he really know?

Mabaza is so tall that, sitting in the low armchair I keep for visitors, his knees are in the way of his arms as he tries to reach forward to make space for the mug on my chaotic desk. That's why I chose the chair – it's very comfortable, but it also puts people at a gravitational disadvantage. They are below me and it is difficult to climb out of the chair once in it. Much easier, then, to submit to my questions than try to escape – that's the theory, at any rate. Don't dentists and members of the psychiatric profession use similar methods? It was during a particularly unpleasant root canal operation on one of my most inaccessible wisdom teeth that the idea came to me. It isn't having the right effect on Mabaza, however; he is perfectly at his ease, looking at everything, taking it all in – the spiral notebooks and grey cardboard files, the stacks of old newspapers, my ancient Rolodex, the computer monitor held together with masking tape, the grimy keyboard that has swallowed more than its fair share of spilled tea and coffee, the printer, the facsimile machine, the map of the republic across one wall and, in the corner, next to a metal filing cabinet, a shredder.

'How can I help, Lieutenant?'

'Do you know the current location – ' here Mabaza breaks off for a moment to glance at a small notebook in his lap – 'of a Miss Frances Nqutu? She and the deceased's son, Joshua Schuter . . .'

I finish the sentence for him, which is what I presume he wants. 'Are an item,' I say. 'In fact, they are more than that. They are engaged. Miss Nqutu told me – only yesterday, as a matter of fact, while we waited for Joshua – that they are to be married.'

If I am bitter, I hope I don't sound it.

Mabaza makes a swift note, like someone ticking off a box on a form. Perhaps he knows shorthand or one of its variants. It wouldn't surprise me.

'And do you?'

'What?'

'Do you know where she is?'

'No, I don't.'

'Do you know where she might be?'

'Maybe her parents' place, or her sister's.'

She has a mother in the Transkei and two sisters. But I'm not going to tell them that.

'Have you tried to contact her?'

'I phoned her a number of times. I left messages. She has not returned my calls.'

'So you have not discussed the murder?'

'We've not had an opportunity to do so. I assumed she had done so already – with Commandant Viljoen.'

'When did you last see her?'

'Last night. Late. In Viljoen's office – you were there, remember? Then you were asked by Viljoen to drop her off. Presumably she still lives in a rented flat in Observatory, near the station. We were on our way to identify Cris Schuter's remains in the mortuary at Salt River. I assumed she'd already made her statement . . .'

Hasn't he read it? Or has there been no statement? Or is the cooperation between CID and Security Branch not all it's cracked up to be? My money is on the last option. Mabaza makes another note, then closes the pad and slips it into a side pocket of his navy suit jacket. Mabaza's attitude towards Viljoen has been deferential, as one might expect of a mere lieutenant towards a commandant. But then he is Security Branch . . .

I sip my coffee. It is truly awful. 'Is that it?'

'No, sir. Not quite.'

He reaches inside his jacket and takes out two documents

and offers them to me. They are similar, roughly A4-sized and folded down the middle. They look official.

I hesitate.

'Please,' he says.

I keep my hands folded in my lap. 'What are they?'

Mabaza leans forward a second time and puts them on my desk as the telephone begins to ring. He isn't smiling.

'They are search warrants, Mr Palfrey, signed by the chief magistrate. One for your residence, the other for these premises.'

Frances. Frances of the close-cropped hair, the high cheekbones, the copper skin, the long, straight Nubian nose, the wide, sculptured mouth that reminds me of a pharaonic queen, Nefertiti perhaps, the unfathomable eyes like dark pools, the legs to die for. Josh and I were together when we first met her. That was twenty-five years ago, but I remember every detail.

I jumped off the bike and pushed it through the gate in the wire fence. Josh followed. Someone was guiding us, but all I could see was the back of a stranger's sweatshirt.

We tugged off our black balaclavas and gloves – worn not against the cold, but to avoid being identified as white by any police patrol on the way in – and gazed about us. There was nothing to see. The night enveloped us in black velvet. There were no street lights, no trees, no vegetation to screen us from the road. I felt very exposed despite the darkness. I sensed we weren't alone by any means, but I couldn't make out any faces. There were just the shapes of men, the sound of their low voices, their feet moving in the sand.

I told myself, not for the first time, that there were bound to be informers.

'Over there,' Josh said.

We parked the bikes behind the battered Datsun pickup that had guided us in.

We walked up to the kitchen door. Someone was leading us to it, and he hammered on it and shouted something I didn't understand. There was a muffled response, and the door opened a crack, a golden lance of light flung across the dusty yard. A rapid-fire exchange followed and the door was thrown wide.

Light blazed out like a beacon, accompanied by a barrage of noise, the noise of hundreds of people making merry.

'Come on.'

My fingers were squeezed and crushed. Hands pounded my back and shoulders. I was hugged, kissed and passed from one person to the next, pushed and pulled, tugged and patted. I felt like an overlarge Christmas parcel. A portly, beaming woman I took to be the shebeen queen embraced me, then, with an almighty shove, almost threw me out of the kitchen and through the crowd into the tiny sitting room.

They made way for us. The embarrassed white visitors fell over their own feet, their red faces a sheen of sweat in the sudden heat.

Welcome, white men.

Welcome to our netherworld.

Bottles and glasses stood everywhere. People – men and women, young and old, smart and poorly dressed – sat, sprawled, knelt and leaned. It was like trying to walk through a London tube station at rush hour, but in this case Josh and I had to find our way through a fug of cigarette smoke, deafening laughter, squeals and shouted conversations. No London Underground carriage was ever crowded with so many happy boozers, some of them canoodling in dark corners.

And there she was.

Sitting bolt upright, in a clingy red dress, sporting a big sixties Afro hairstyle, in the centre of a broken sofa, holding court. She was the centre of it all without even being aware of it, or she seemed unaware of it. Every man in the place – and there must have been a hundred or so – paid her attention whether they wanted to or not. They couldn't help themselves, and neither could I.

She seemed to exude an electrical field of her own.

She had presence.

Frances Nqutu.

Model. Mistress. Farmer's daughter. Sometime Resistance runner.

The face that adorned a thousand posters in fifty townships.

A cold beer was pressed into my hand. Someone offered me a cigarette and I took it without thinking, accepting a light, still staring at this vision and, when her eyes settled on me, I looked away quickly, overwhelmed by shyness. People squeezed up so I could sit down. They introduced themselves, shouting in my ears, taking my arms and squeezing them.

The black Nationalist handshake.

'This your first visit, man?'

I nodded.

'You like Soweto?'

I smiled and nodded vigorously.

'You crazy fucking white man. You don't have to fucking live here.'

This was followed by a friendly punch, a burst of laughter and then a hug.

In swift succession I was introduced to a trumpet player, a poet, a furniture salesman and a garbage collector. We all talked at once and I don't think anyone could hear anything anyone else was saying. But it didn't seem to matter.

Josh stood over her. She glanced up.

People moved up so he could sit next to her.

Damn you, Joshua Schuter.

You always get the prettiest ones.

And you a Boer, too.

The shebeen queen waddled in to present the two oddball whites with more cold lagers.

All it took was a glance.

From that instant – Josh taking the beers absently, not even saying thank you or looking up, his attention fixed exclusively on the woman next to him – I realized the rest of us did not exist for either of them. They weren't aware of where they were, or who else was around. They existed solely for each other. We might as well have been on the moon for all they noticed or cared.

I never witnessed two people drawn to each other so quickly, or so completely. It was recognition, an instantaneous ignition. It might have been hackneyed at another time and in another place; in Orlando West, one of the twenty-seven townships that make up that great urban sprawl known as Soweto, like a collar of black servitude flung around the mines and banks of white Johannesburg, the risks of such an alliance, the illegality of it, the wide gulf that, superficially at any rate, separated them, made it anything but prosaic. It wasn't just race. It was origin, it was culture, it was wealth, it was expectation. Above all, it was the fact that they inhabited entirely different, mutually exclusive worlds. Perhaps that was part of the attraction – the sheer impossibility of it, giving the finger to both communities, to the government, to respectable opinion everywhere, and not least to Joshua's father. I cannot pretend to have known Frances sufficiently well then or later to make up reasons for her wanting him, but I can claim to have known Josh well enough over the years to see the attraction he felt when faced by the unobtainable. It was like presenting him with the north face of the Eiger; he was unable to resist.

He could have everything and everyone else; he had the power, the money, the conventional male charm of his world. He had so much to offer, and it was a lot more than Buchanan's convertible, a house in Bishopscourt and a bored teenager without knickers on a Persian rug. In a word, it was his sensibility. I thought then that women saw the sweetness of the untamed child in him, the neediness in his face. They wanted to mother him. But all that counted for nothing in Soweto. Reputation, influence and privilege in the sense that Josh's people knew them had no value in those dark streets. He was weak like everyone else, only more so because he and I stood out. Our whiteness would not save us from whatever *skollies* lurked out there, a downward chop of a panga, a sharpened screwdriver up under the ribs. There was no reason why it should. Our pink skin had no value – rather the reverse. His own society could not protect him. He was naked; just a man like any other, flesh and blood, and his vulnerability broke all the rules of white conduct. Appearing weak and defenceless was unpardonable. What they were contemplating, what they saw in each other, was beyond conventions of any kind. There were a thousand reasons why he could not have Frances. That was why, perhaps, he had to have her, and she him. It was dangerous for both of them in every way imaginable.

I drank my beer and made the best of it.

Josh smiled and talked, giving her his full attention, gesticulating wildly as South Africans do, giving Frances the full treatment with those blue eyes, flipping his long hair back from his face with an almost womanish jerk of the head, his long legs folded up at an awkward angle, knees protruding like a couple of telegraph poles.

I wondered, how did Josh really feel? Was he simply a voyeur, titillated by the underside, amused by the antics of the downtrodden, apartheid's day-tripper? Was it really love? Could either of us, at that age, distinguish between the real thing of the heart and simple lust?

At that age I was ready to fuck just about anything, but such sinuous beauty shamed my aimless want.

When we met in the shebeen, or illegal drinking den, it was 1969. As dens go it wasn't at all bad; by Soweto standards it was quite a desirable home with a tin roof, a yard, two bedrooms, a tiny hallway, a kitchen and bathroom. There was running water and the place was simply furnished. The property was fenced. It looked neat inside and out. Not only were there no street lights or trees – every tree planted by the white municipal authorities was torn down at once – but there were no street names either; it was as if the Soweto toughs had decided that they could no longer endure any visible evidence of white control and patronage. Why should they?

We'd arrived on the outskirts just after the brief African sunset and were swaddled in the murk from four hundred thousand coal fires and dust raised by a couple of million feet tramping home from white-owned factories, mines and offices; in the complete darkness that followed so swiftly I had no idea where I was. Perhaps Josh did, but I doubt it. We were entirely at the mercy of our hosts and our friends, whether it was getting in or out again, or in moving from one place to another.

It was also a first in another sense. It was my first visit to Soweto, that secret gateway barred to whites that led to the turbulent, fervid world of Africa, the real Africa; its fast, colloquial, detribalized city patter, its laughter, its art, its jazz, its classlessness, its football, its generosity of spirit, its warmth, its wit, its sensuality and its violence – all of it on the move, thrown into rapid change like some molten, subterranean and fast-flowing river heading only God knew where, quite unstoppable, and hidden from view by a cold scab of ignorance, a static veneer of indifferent white 'civilization' that seemed unchangeable, unchallengable. My world – the world that Josh and I inhabited – was only a couple of dozen miles away in leafy suburbs with half-acre plots, five-bedroom villas and pools behind infrared alarms and electrified fences on the other side of Johannesburg, but in every other respect we seemed to have embarked on a perilous adventure, a journey to the centre of the African magma that would last us – each of us – a lifetime.

Josh and Frances were oblivious to everything and

everyone around them, unaffected by the music, the shouted conversations, the passing backwards and forwards of bottles and glasses, the sudden bars of light projected on the walls as headlights swept passed, the sound of dogs barking in the yard outside, the squeak of the gate, tramp of feet, a door slamming, the danger of a police raid.

They heard none of it.

They seemed to synchronize their movements. Unconsciously they copied one another. If he touched his ear, she touched her hair; if she crossed her legs, so did he. They looked at each other often. When they kissed, they seemed to know when to turn and when to offer their mouths; the one was not more forward than the other, nor the other more reticent. And neither missed, kissing an ear or a cheek instead of the intended target. This loveplay was almost balletic in its instinctive choreography. One would speak, then look to the other for approval or support, and of course it was there, always.

Frances was seventeen and just starting out on her career as a model; I'd seen an outsize image of her face adorning a billboard straddling the railtracks and potholed road on the way into Soweto; she was helping to sell creams and shampoos that promised to make blacks whiter. The creams were supposed to whiten the skin, the shampoos to achieve the well-nigh impossible straightening of African hair; objectives as pointless as they were – to me, at any rate – undesirable. But it paid well in an expanding black cosmetics industry, kept her many relatives afloat and financed her part-time studies for a degree in politics and anthropology. And it was just the beginning.

I was right opposite them, a coffee table piled high with empties separating us, but the two of them paid me no attention. Five people were crammed on to a sofa meant for two and I was engaged in two conversations simultaneously, one with the very serious poet and the other with the worldly furniture salesman in flashy shirt and tie and two-tone shoes who spoke out of the corner of his mouth, a caricature of a hip dude. A woman squeezed past, then flung herself down almost in my lap. She held out her hand; she introduced herself as Constance, she was a colleague and friend of Frances. Did I mind? Too bad if I did. She was already pressed against me. We were thigh to thigh. Above the waist she was an ebony swan. I could feel her right breast against my ribs. She wore a pink angora top and from what I could see and feel nothing below. Would I please fetch her a gin and tonic? It would be my pleasure. Ice and lemon? As I got up, despite a crippling hard-on, it occurred to me that this might be the first time a white bastard had bought Constance a drink, got up to get it in the kitchen and then brought it to her. A little later on, after we had had a couple more, her hand caressed my knee and she playfully bit my earlobe and then put her tongue into it; had I a car? Was it outside and did I have the keys? Her fingers played with the hair at the nape of my neck. No. She leaned over and asked Frances something, leaning with her forearm on my crotch, hardly subtle but most effective. Frances looked at her, at me, and said something into Josh's ear. Josh shook his head at me. I leaned forward, annoyed at the interruption. What was all this about?

He shouted his reply.

'She wants to fuck you, Seb. She likes you and she wants to fuck you in the back of Frances's car. Or she wants Frances to drive you to her place. It's not a good idea, man. I mean the car.'

I knew what he meant. He was right. We were illegals. We were whites who'd entered a black area without a permit to be there, and in my case on a Triumph 650 cc motorcycle without licence or helmet. When blacks were found in white Johannesburg without a pass, they got a good kicking, were thrown into a police van, beaten some more and left bruised and bloody in a ditch on the edge of town.

The alternative was getting banged up for thirty days and probably losing a job that kept an extended family just above the poverty line. Or a thirty rand fine most couldn't afford.

The kicking was obligatory.

After another hour we left for the only nightclub, the Green Door, Constance still in tow, though by this time much the worse for wear. I'd never heard jazz like it. But then I'd never heard the name Hugh Masekela or Dollar Brand, either, up till that point. Constance danced with me for a while, during which she still attempted to persuade me to go home with her. As gently as I could I tried to explain that although I found her very attractive and would like nothing more than go to bed with her (true enough), there could be problems for us both if were caught by the authorities. Informers were everywhere, weren't they? After a while she went outside and was violently ill in the privy and eventually passed out and was taken home by friends.

The visit ended dramatically in the early hours with

Josh and myself being arrested – by a black Security Branch officer. We were held for a couple of hours in a police station. As we waited, wondering what would happen, some faces appeared in the doorway that I vaguely recognized from the shebeen and the nightclub. There was one in particular that stood out – he was of medium height, about our age, quite light-skinned, and he had a goatee below intense hazel eyes. Someone told me he was a photographer, and the local ANC heavy. He was called Zakaria, or simply Zak.

I forgot all about this until some weeks later.

We were let off with a small cash fine – small to us – and we rode back along a deserted highway on our bikes to that other, sterile Potemkin village of a white world as dawn was breaking. For me, nothing would ever be quite the same. I had had my first glimpse of Africa, something denied to most whites. I had seen what the future would be. I didn't attach any particular importance to the appearance of those men in the police station until my journalism course drew to an end. I don't think Josh had noticed, and the name, when I mentioned Zak, meant nothing to him. Apparently their presence – they had leaned nonchalantly against the counter, Zak speaking in a low voice to the plain-clothes cop – had spelled out a clear message: these are our friends and you will please treat them as such.

The fine had been a compromise to save face.

Neither the arrest nor the fine could dim my excitement at having seen Soweto for the first time, and not from an official tour bus laid on by the government for student journalists; for Josh, of course, the visit to Orlando West had been a *coup de foudre* of a different order.

I never saw Constance again; I was to see Frances often, sometimes smuggled into the northern suburbs under a blanket in the back of Josh's beat-up old Volkswagen beetle, a peace symbol spray-painted on the boot. That was Joshua Schuter's image in those days: long hair, pot, bikes, Deep Purple, a dilettante interest in Buddhism, a habit of reading Herbert Marcuse and Marshall McLuhan aloud and an obsession with a beautiful black girl.

And yes, all right, I admit it: I was envious.

To the casual observer at that time, it must have seemed as if I were Joshua Schuter's acolyte. He was loquacious and demonstrative; I was silent and still. He was tall and red-haired; I was short and dark, a Sancho Panza to his Aryan Don Quixote. He liked to cut a melodramatic figure in the centre of things; I preferred the shadows, the sidelines, even then. He used me, of that I have no doubt, and he knew it. He needed an audience and I was it when no one else was around. I was also part of the natural camouflage of friends and acquaintances that wittingly or otherwise assisted in disguising his illicit romance with Frances.

Perhaps she spoke to him about it, or maybe it was out of guilt over the role I played in facilitating the logistics of moving Frances in and out of white areas that he told me one day that he would find me a nice black Sowetan girl. Perhaps he feared the *ménage à trois* was too much for me and I would move out of the cottage we shared, and he would have to find someone else to help pay a share of the rent and lay false trails for his nightly shenanigans. In any event my response was typical: I did not require a pimp and I was quite content as I was, thank you very much. I was as much offended by use of the word 'nice' as the suggestion that I could not pull successfully without his help. I was contemplating a move, certainly, but there were two good reasons for staying on. The first was my curiosity as to how this affair with Frances would progress, and the second was – and here I confess it must sound pathetic – that I didn't want to stop seeing her, even if it was only on her way to or from Joshua's unmade bed.

There was a third, darker reason, of which more later.

Josh did not realize the extent to which he and I had grown apart; he thought we were still close friends bent on mischief. I think he was genuinely hurt when I started staying away at night; he must have realized I had a girl somewhere in downtown Hillbrow, but he would sulk like a jealous lover whenever I came back after three or four nights away on the trot. I never explained that my absences were dictated by the shift system of cabin crews on South African Airways flights and my corrosive envy at his trysts with Frances. Why should I have? I was not a talker, and liked talking about myself least of all. But I don't think even Frances listened as patiently as I did to his latest whimsies, his talk of Dr Timothy Leary's advocacy of hallucinogenic drugs, his passing interest in Zen and then Taoism, his use of the I Ching, his sudden fascination with the Cabbala, his grandiose plans to save mankind, the environment, the very planet.

My task, as I saw it, was to let all this second- or third-hand claptrap wash over me and pick out any useful nuggets for future use. I knew what I was looking for. I had been well briefed. I don't think it ever occurred to him that I was anything but simply a friend who could be trusted to listen attentively to every confidence. There was really no reason for him to think I was markedly different in any way from our other mutual friends: Bridgeport, for one, Riley for another. And Van Reenen. They all fell under his spell.

He was quite capable of turning their heads around three hundred and sixty degrees without ever seeming aware of it until the damage had been done. He could, within the space of a week or two, persuade all three to take up socialism or vegetarianism or Shamanism; by the time he noticed the effect he'd had on them, he'd already moved on to something else. Josh was the perpetual seeker, the advocate of other men's ideas, and he left a trail of confused converts in his wake.

Did he suspect a sinister motive on my part?

With him it was still horseshit in the goldfish pond, but he still never got his feet wet. I seldom disagreed with him or challenged him; on the one hand I couldn't be bothered, and on the other, I had my own agenda. Unlike Josh, I didn't talk about my allegiances, my affairs, the relationship I was having at that time with the flight attendant whose name was Annette du Preez, a tanned twenty-two-year-old honey blonde with cornflower-blue eyes from Potchestroom, a *ware* Afrikaner whose remarkable physical assets and sexual tastes and stamina helped me forget all about Frances for days at a time between Annette's return fights to Luanda and Lisbon.

We had both attended Monterey Preparatory School. I was a boarder, Josh a day boy. That drove the first wedge between us: day boys weren't taken seriously, they were merely daytime visitors, albeit delivered by a Rolls. I forged new partnerships; in particular I was won over by the place itself.

It had been the home of an eccentric industrialist of eclectic tastes who'd long since died. The school covered around sixty acres, forty of which were given over to a forest in which we were allowed to play more or less unsupervised. We built tree huts – not just tree huts, but veritable fortresses. I had my own gang of insurgents and every spare moment was spent in combat with rival clans of muddy-faced nine-year-olds.

To begin with I found it hard; for the first months I was a habitual sleepwalker and bed-wetter, and I had recurring nightmares. Eventually things improved. Children are flexible, adaptable creatures. By my second year I found myself in heaven. I had never been so happy. My father had long since left home and my mother was by now unwell; it meant I spent many weekends and half-term holidays at school and special events were laid on by bachelor masters for we dozen or so semi-orphans: we climbed the mountain, hiked the contour path or played my favourite game in which two sides defended footballs filled with lead – medicine balls, they were called – and attempted to seize the opposing forces' balls, no pun intended. The game involved a series of raids and counter-raids fought out over woodland and thick undergrowth. To disable an opponent, one had to muster a superior force and ambush him, pinning him to the ground and forcibly removing his trainers ('tackies' as they were known). It was tactical training, and my favourite method was to leave no one at all in defence, but strike fast, first and hard, using all available manpower in one massive, make-or-break frontal assault.

It usually worked.

The school itself became the home I'd never had. The main house was a mock Tudor mansion with a baronial hall, a minstrel's gallery, and an enormous panelled library with the complete works of John Buchan, Sir Walter Scott and G.A. Henty. My dormitory was the garden room, its walls still covered with handmade French wallpaper, the en-suite bathroom had a marble basin and floor and Delft tiles on the walls – the real thing.

I did as little work as possible. I read widely. I grew wild and learned to use my fists.

Josh, by contrast, studied hard. He pleased his father by coming top in maths and the sciences, and, quite naturally, he was fluent in Afrikaans. He captained both the First XV and First XI whereas I just made the Second XV and got nowhere at all in cricket. He became school captain in his eleventh year, and captain of his house, Hawks. Somehow, possibly because the head had a soft spot for me, I was appointed head of the rival Peregrines. I knew I didn't deserve this elevation and I certainly didn't seek it; I was never on the side of law and order. I was a lazy ruffian, a poacher to Joshua's gamekeeper. His uniform was always impeccable; my threadbare blazer was shiny with age, and jam from countless doughnuts had worked its way into the lapels to defy the most thorough dry-cleaning.

It was a pattern that was to repeat itself at Bishops. Josh sailed through his Common Entrance *magna cum laude*; his sporting achievements alone would have sufficed to win him a place. I scraped through the exam, and the only reason they took me at all, I was told, was because the Monterey head had written a note of personal recommendation. As for my friendship with Joshua, it was all but forgotten. We seldom met, and only then by accident. I was always being beaten for one crime or another; I don't believe he ever felt the cane on his honourable rump.

The key to being beaten was never to show pain; it was a point of honour never to weep, and always to thank the tormentor afterwards with the words, 'Thank you, sir.' My first full six with the housemaster's cane was at thirteen; it was my punishment for bunking out to meet a girl at her home. It wasn't worth it, of course; we'd sat demurely on the edge of our chairs in her parents' drawing room drinking tea and making small talk when I suspect what we'd both fantasized about was a good snog at the very least. It was just that neither of us had any idea of how to precipitate the natural course of events we had so long desired.

White boys aren't supposed to cry.

Later on I was thrashed for smoking, then drinking. The centrefolds of *Playboy* with which I decorated my study in the sixth form were repeatedly torn down by prefects and masters alike, and were as quickly replaced. By this time I'd found what I was looking for at a girls' orphanage a few streets away, and I was a frequent if unauthorized visitor. But for me the most significant event occurred during a routine French lesson one steamy summer afternoon. The teacher, a diffident Englishman named Foster, mentioned the words 'dialectical material-ism', and I asked him to repeat the term. He did so, and wrote the magical words on the blackboard, giving us a quick explanation of what the phrase meant.

Nothing would be quite the same again after that, at least not for me. It was as if a shutter had been raised and I could see the world beyond the end of my nose for the first time.

Josh, meanwhile, had filled out. By sixteen he was positively sleek with new-found authority as school head. He chaired the debating club, the foreign affairs society, the chess club. He took to sporting a red silk handkerchief in his breast pocket and saying a very long Latin grace on punishment nights, the candlelight in the White House dining hall sparkling on the gold blazer badge worn by all school prefects.

> *Benedic Domine nos et dona tua,*
> *quae de largitate tua sumus sumpturi,*
> *et concede, ut illis salubriter nutriti,*
> *tibi debitum obsequium praestare valemus,*
> *per Christum Dominum nostrum.*

Josh was head inquisitor.

It was a ritual designed to intimidate rule-breakers like myself before the post-prandial ordeal of accusation, tribunal and beatings began. I could see where Josh was going in life, where he fitted in and how, and I hated him for it. I think I despised him for trying so hard to impress his formidable father, and it was made worse by the fact that my own father – someone I adored, admired and had sought to emulate – was in reality a violent drunkard who'd scarpered.

Didn't he sense any irony in an Afrikaner's blatant attempt to assimilate himself into the English-speaking elite? Apparently not, but this was the country's top

Anglican school – a school that preached Enlightenment values, that taught us about equality, sacrifice and suffering, about democracy and freedom; a school founded by Bishop Grey in 1849 to carry on the work of imperial rule; a school modelled on its nineteenth-century British counterparts, complete with corporal punishment; a school open to the male offspring of parents who could pay the steep fees, but one that was barred to all non-whites without exception, and where Jews could be counted on the fingers of one hand. Of Muslims and Hindus there were none.

We were being trained to rule a world across which the sun had long since set.

To me, then, in 1966, with a second-hand copy of Marx and Engels's *Communist Manifesto* in my greasy blazer pocket and Spengler in my bedside locker, Josh in all his glory was nothing short of loathsome for his complicity. What was empire anyway but robbery with violence?

The telephone is ringing. Mabaza is out of the visitor's chair and on his feet, moving behind me. Just outside my office door, I hear what I assume are more police coming out of the lift and into reception, Mabaza issuing orders on where to start their search.

I wedge the receiver under my chin to free both hands and open up a new file on my computer; I have very little time before they turn off the power or seize the hard disc. Three or four paragraphs will be more than enough, but I must work quickly.

'Palfrey.'

'Hey, how you doing, Seb? It's François.'

François Malherbe is the local stringer for the *Washing-*

ton Post, and one of the best informed of the local press corps. He has always found time for me in the past; now he calls in a favour I do not know how to refuse.

'The cops are searching my office, François, and my home.'

'Right now?'

'As we speak. I've just been shown the warrants.'

'Why?'

'It's Security Branch. I think they're mad at me for a piece I filed earlier about Cris Schuter.'

'That's why I'm calling, Seb. People are already getting callbacks on your story and I wondered if you could tell me what you know.'

The rag must have put a shorter version out on its website as a teaser.

'Sure,' I say, listening to the thumps and bangs in my office behind me. I tell Malherbe the basic facts as I know them – that Cris Schuter was murdered in the living room of his Bishopscourt home sometime yesterday afternoon, that I have identified the remains, that he had put up a fight, that an edged weapon had been used. I tell him about the footprints. In any case, I say, there is supposed to be a press conference in a few minutes.

'It's been cancelled.'

'Any reason?'

'I don't think they've managed to inform next-of-kin, but they've not said. But why are they searching your place?'

'I think it's the usual turf war between CID and Security Branch.'

Malherbe asks, 'Can I quote you on what you've told me?'

'Of course.'

Mabaza is next to me, hovering.

I say, 'Got to go.'

'Thanks, man. Do you mind if I include the police search in my story?'

'Be my guest, François. It might even help get them off my back.'

'You're not a suspect, are you?'

'God, I don't think so, but I suppose anything's possible. It hadn't occurred to me.'

Oh yes it had.

'Have you spoken to the son, Joshua?'

'No. I've left messages—'

'You're friends, aren't you?'

'We were at school together.'

'Bishops.'

'That's right.'

'Is he still seeing that black chick – the ex-model?'

Is there anyone who doesn't know about Frances?

I say nothing. That's one story I'm not going to give away.

The police are carrying out bundles of documents taken from the filing cabinet; a lot of good it will do them.

'Well, here's a tip for you, Seb. One good turn and all that. They've issued an arrest warrant. They're saying over at CID they want Joshua Schuter's help with their inquiries into his father's murder. How's that, huh?'

'Don't they know who he is?'

'Times are changing, Seb. Maybe that's the point.'

My reference books, atlases and video cassettes are next, piled up on a metal handcart with rubber wheels. The Security Branch have come well equipped.

'Joshua a suspect? You're joking. What's the motive?'

I try to sound surprised. I twist round in my chair and look up at Mabaza, but his expression gives nothing away.

'Apparently the forensic people found something today up there at the house . . .'

'Mr Palfrey.' It is Mabaza this time. 'Mr Palfrey, we need access to your desk, and I must ask you to let us have your computer hard disc and any back-up files . . .'

He looks over my shoulder as I press the 'send' button for the second time that day. He peers at what I've written, and I know by the time he's finished it will already be on the foreign desk's screens in London. There is nothing either of us can do about it now, for better or worse. It is already as good as tomorrow's fish and chips wrapping. Then I hand over the keys to my desk.

If Malherbe is right, I have to hurry.

> The office and home of veteran correspondent Sebastien Palfrey were raided by South African secret police on Thursday, hours after the British journalist broke the news of the murder of a right-wing Afrikaner politician.
>
> Lieutenant James Mabaza of the Security Branch served warrants for the search of Palfrey's Cape Town residence and office while he was investigating a possible political angle to the assassination on Wednesday of Dr Cris Schuter only weeks before South Africa's first non-racial elections. The election campaign has been marked by a

bloody feud between the African National Congress and fighters loyal to conservative Zulu leader Gatsha Buthelezi. Hundreds have died in clashes in Kwa Zulu and Gauteng.

'I think the fact that I have been selected for this privilege reflects growing strains in a police force struggling to redefine itself in the transition to majority rule,' said Palfrey, aged 44. 'But it does not bode well for freedom of speech in the country.'

Schuter, a wealthy businessman, former junior minister and staunch supporter of white supremacy for half a century, was hacked to death by an unknown assailant or assailants on the living room floor of his Cape Town home in the exclusive suburb of Bishopscourt. He was 79.

At the time of his death he was thought to be working on his controversial memoirs.

Dr Schuter leaves an estranged wife and a son and daughter.

For the full story on the murder, see page —.

I shut down the desk computer, turn it off, push myself away from the desk, get to my feet and pick up my jacket. I'm going to leave them to it. My presence won't change anything. I should hide my laptop somewhere; perhaps Potgieter can look after it for me. No, I have a better idea – I'll secrete it away in the Peugeot in such a way that neither Potgieter nor the cops will find it.

'Go ahead, Lieutenant. Be my guest. Help yourself to whatever you want.'

The phone on my desk rings again, but this time I ignore it. Let Mabaza explain himself to my foreign desk. He can do it so much better than I. He thinks he has all the answers, doesn't he? If it is the rag, they can always get me on my mobile. That's what it's for.

I walk out without looking back, trying not to hurry, leaving the office door open and taking the stairs. I pass three police officers in reception; they are carrying out my map, neatly rolled up, along with two framed photographs of Cape Town pre-1900, one showing a tangle of masts in the dockyard, the second Table Mountain swathed in cloud. I half expect a restraining hand on my arm at any moment, and to be told I'm to be detained for questioning, but somehow it doesn't happen. Not yet.

I tell myself that by now they will have found my dope in its hiding place under the parquet flooring of my bedroom. Will they prosecute, or try to use the evidence of one of my few remaining vices as leverage? What will Viljoen have to say about it?

I'm not going to wait around to find out. Someone, perhaps Mabaza or Viljoen, has been following the traces back and they've come up with me. I want to know how. It isn't the murder; I'm certain they can't pin it on me. No, it's that they believe I know where Joshua is, and I'm not telling, and I don't think the opinion is based simply on knowledge of our friendship. By this time Joshua has a great many friends, a lot of them more influential than me. He could go to any one of them.

So how do they know?

Has Frances talked?

I'm hungry; there's a new sushi bar which colleagues say is quite moderately priced in trendy De Waterkant. I've been looking forward to it, but now there is no time for such indulgence. I have to know whether or not I have a police tail. If I do, that'll be confirmation that they expect me to lead them to Josh.

I feel like a puppet, legs jerking involuntarily into forward motion, the invisible strings pulled by Viljoen and Mabaza.

FOUR

I'm playing one of the oldest games there is.

It is deceptively gentle, fought out like croquet, in slow motion. I'm on the run, but I must make it look casual. No panic. No haste. No sudden movements. Nothing furtive or underhand.

Evasive action, but it has to look anything but.

I always enjoy visits to Willaston's; it's a department store that reminds me of old black and white films because it seems locked in a time warp about fifty years behind the rest of us, at least until the ramparts of apartheid started to crumble and South Africa caught up with itself. It carries stuff on its shelves no one born after 1950 could possibly want.

Maybe I like it because it reminds me of my boyhood, or because it's the place my grandmother would meet her friends from their bridge club in pre-war days – driving up from St James in her immense black Buick, decked out in gloves and stockings and smelling of 4711, a little cloche hat pulled down over her curls, sipping tea and munching on cucumber sandwiches served up by deferential mixed-race girls in starched white aprons and caps, some with their front teeth missing because, contraceptives being neither cheap nor widely available, it was thought to promote and enhance oral sex as an alternative to the risky business of full intercourse. Those affected spoke with a lisp as a result, saying, 'Yesh, medem,' to every peremptory order, every whim.

Madam would have been horrified. She would never have understood. In any event, to her, sex – any sex – was a vile and painful event imposed on married women by their menfolk and to be endured for the sake of procreation if it couldn't somehow be avoided altogether.

Somewhere in my study there is to this day a large album packed with black and white snapshots of the family in the twenties and thirties; it seems to have been a tidy, comfortable world oblivious of the cataclysm that would shortly overwhelm Europe, and, back then in South Africa, race simply wasn't an issue: it was all about the competition for power between English-speakers and the Boers. The blacks were an invisible mass, without an effective voice, off the political map, and kept that way by means of the *sjambok*, the pass laws, the South African Broadcasting Corporation's policy of refusing to report 'extra-parliamentary politics' and by the diktat of that secret society, the Broederbond.

I'm not buying anything today, certainly not cucumber sandwiches.

A big store has always been ideal for checking to see if one has a tail of any sort. It offers vertical and horizontal movement, and as far as trade craft goes, it's an environment that favours the poacher over the gamekeeper. It's as easy as riding an escalator up from one floor to the next, taking a lift down, then switching to the stairs, or moving into the far corner of the women's department, thus exposing a *borselkop* plain-clothes man, caught red-faced between racks of perfume or lingerie and buffeted by black tannies from Langa and Guguletu townships.

I wear khakis, short-sleeved shirt and deck shoes, a daypack over one shoulder; a tourist looking a little lost. I spend ten minutes moving around at a leisurely pace, inspecting cheap glassware, linen and cutlery for no good reason, then take a lift back down and nip smartly out again on to St George's Street, slipping on sunglasses and a ridiculous sunhat, its floppy brim hiding much of my face.

There is no telltale sign of a mobile team hurriedly reforming around me; I tell myself they probably don't have the manpower. Doing the job properly is expensive; it requires no fewer than five people and as many as eleven, a radio car and ideally a bike to do a thorough job of surveillance. My guess is that these days, with the kind of unrest they have to contend with, the secret police must rely on static posts, clocking their quarry in and out and depending on a snowstorm of paper chits to compile a pattern in the mark's movements.

The best of British luck to them.

When I left for work this morning there was an innocuous four-door Ford parked opposite with two people in the front seat. Whether Security Branch or CID, there was no way of knowing.

I know they were police because of their unnatural stillness, their way of deliberately not looking in my direction.

No bumper stickers.

Two rear-view mirrors.

Concealed radio aerial.

Viljoen's boys.

I stroll towards the foreshore, hands in pockets, the hat pulled down firmly on my head; a southeaster is steadily gaining strength, howling between the office blocks, whipping up paper and dirt into tiny whirlwinds. I turn my face aside to guard my eyes, pretending to window-shop, staring in through the plate glass of banks and airline offices, cupping my hands to block out my own reflection, moving again, hesitating, walking backwards a few paces, stopping, but always in a general, crablike, sideways drift against the tide of humanity moving up Adderley Street.

And there it is: a battered yellow cab drifts past as if looking for custom, slows, then stops.

Am I imagining it?

No one gets in or out.

I have a tail, certainly, but it isn't the cops.

At the city railway station I meander through the concourse to a newsagent's stand, buy a selection of the morning's English and Afrikaans papers, and settle down over a cappuccino. Fifteen minutes and I'm on my feet, hatless, and, by a circuitous route, sauntering, hands in pockets again, towards the ticket machines.

I gave Potgieter a long weekend off; as I paid him his week's wages I told him I was taking a break. I'd be back on Monday afternoon and wouldn't need him or the car until Tuesday. I couldn't face the mess in the bureau or my home. They hadn't broken anything – they'd just left both in a shambles, ankle-deep in books and paper, magazines and pictures taken off the walls and out of their frames. They had been thorough, I'll say that for them. (And yes, my grass had vanished from its hiding place, but I didn't tell Potgieter that.) I seemed to be missing a pair of shoes and a hairbrush, but that was all.

In any case, I said I'd been working too hard for too long, and I planned to relax on the beach. I have my mobile if he needs me for any reason. I am fairly sure all this will find its way back to Viljoen or Mabaza, or both. I don't begrudge Potgieter telling tales; for his kind, even now, in 1994, four years after the ANC was unbanned, it might be a matter of survival, of keeping a job for which the main qualification is not a clean driving licence but a willingness to inform on the foreign journalist. I can't blame him for exercising the skills of self-preservation as a copper's nark, and I've always taken care to save him from the embarrassment of being lumbered with any information that could be of the remotest use to the security forces.

'Hey, mister . . .'

I don't notice him because he's so small; he can't be more than nine or ten and the top of his head fails to reach my waist. He wears filthy shorts, a torn T-shirt and a pair of sandals made out of car tyres. He watches me warily with old-young eyes and holds something out to me in his grubby paw. It looks like an office file.

I look past him, to the station entrance, to the bright splash of sunlight where people hurry past on foot, the stalls selling cheap clothing, shoes and pirated CDs.

'Mister—'

The child pushes the folder at me and I take it. With my free hand I reach into my pocket and hand him a two-rand coin.

The boy grabs it and is gone, sprinting away.

The yellow taxi stands at the kerb; the brown face behind the mirror sunglasses turns my way and the driver rests one hand on the top of the steering wheel, his other arm dangles limply outside. Perhaps I imagine it, but the driver appears to give me a nod; then he turns away and the taxi accelerates out of sight.

I tuck whatever it is under one arm, buy a first-class return to Simon's Town, then walk over to the departures board, and from there to platform five; the train is waiting and I slip aboard moments before the doors slide shut on a blast of the conductor's whistle. With a few jolts and a lot of metallic squealing, we roll out into sunshine, heading south, a journey in time and space, only backwards, casting off years and throwing out memories like discarded baggage as we clank over the points.

The first stop is grimy Salt River – coal dust, ozone off the sea, a mass of pylons and overhead cables. There Cris Schuter lies in his police ice box, awaiting the undertakers; then Observatory, where I once shacked up with an American student drop-out; Woodstock and an illicit nightclub of transsexuals and transvestites of all colours; Mowbray where Frances lived; Rosebank, where I smoked my first joint. Familiar names appear on the station platforms every two or three miles, as the train rattles slowly around the mountain, its horizontal crest buried in its white tablecloth of cloud. At Rondebosch I gather up *Die Beeld* and the *Cape Times* and get out. Two other people leave the train, both middle-aged women carrying shopping bags. I let them go ahead of me; they walk out through the small gate that will take them into the village and the university, or, if they wish, all the way up to Bishops and Rondebosch Common where Josh and I used to start our afternoon cross-country runs.

I take the steps down into the subway and emerge on the far side, on the platform for trains going back to town. I put my papers and bag down on a green wooden bench, put up my right foot and retie the laces. There is nothing to worry about, I tell myself: there is no anonymous green car with two watchers in the parking lot; no hapless plain-clothes types hanging about on foot, trying too hard to look nonchalant.

No yellow cab.

Fifteen minutes later I cross back again and board the next southbound train to Simon's Town.

The journey throws off the years.

Newlands and the cricket grounds where I wrote my first news story as a cub reporter on the *Argus*, and the rugby stadium where as a schoolboy and to my secret joy (along with the very public delight of those in the non-white stands) I watched the Lions thrash the Springboks; Kenilworth where Josh and I attended kindergarten; Claremont where I first had sex with a 'Coloured', a servant (who had kept her teeth), a relationship that lasted weeks until the mutual fear of being caught broke us up; Plumstead where white schoolgirls from the local state school used to wear such delightfully short uniform skirts that they left nothing to the imagination; Muizenberg and the beach where Buchanan and I went on the last day at Bishops, giving prize-giving and the final school assembly a miss in favour of a little *zol* and more interracial tussles, sandy groping, salty licks and multi-lingual moans of pleasure behind the whites-only bathing huts; the twee St James, a copy of a Cornish resort with its tidal pool and British-style pebble beach, final resting place of the notorious Cecil Rhodes, and where my grandparents' house still stands, its bay windows looking out over False Bay to the hazy Hottentots Holland mountains, beyond the gigantic Scots pine planted by my godmother; Fish Hoek's wide sweep of white sand and the catwalk where I played as a toddler. The further south we go, the younger I seem to be, the older the memories, until, finally, we reach Simon's Town, where I am not yet even a glint in my seventeen-year-old mother's eye.

Out of the suburban time machine at last, I dump the papers and stroll down the main street of the pretty whitewashed town named after the Cape's first Dutch governor, Simon van der Stel, past the imposing gates of the South African Navy's submarine base (it had long belonged to the Royal Navy, but once the country was declared a republic in May 1961 the triumphant Boers used acetylene torches to cut down the coat of arms as a detested symbol of colonialism – and who could blame them?) and make my way over to a line of shops. I need a few supplies and a gift or two of a practical nature. I also need drinking water.

More memories, more stories, are stirred up like dust at every step. It was in Simon's Town dockyard that my mother and her sister worked during World War Two on leaving school, debriefing Catalina flying boat crews on their return from hunting U-boats in the South Atlantic, and, in between patrols, rolling cannon balls from Nelson's navy along the wooden floors of the verandas of Admiralty House in impromptu and thunderous games of bowls, their thirst assuaged by lashings of pink gin. Boys they dated, boys they danced with, boys they kissed, boys not much older than themselves donned their flying suits the next morning and said their goodbyes. Some never did come back.

It was where my uncle by marriage, a Royal Navy Reserve lieutenant of destroyers, fought off a Great White in Simon's Town harbour, using an oar and standing up in his dinghy to do battle. The sharks were emboldened by the war at sea, and encouraged to vary their peacetime diet of seals by the predation of U-boats. Militants of the pro-Axis Ossewabrandwag would light brush fires along the mountain's contour path to help the U-boat commanders spot the outline of convoys rounding the Cape through their periscopes; on one occasion Afrikaner nationalists seeking a Nazi victory managed to maroon the two Catalina squadrons based at Seakoevlei by digging a ditch that drained the lagoon, leaving the aircraft stuck fast in the mud and the convoys without air cover.

The sharks must have dined well in those dark waters that week in 1941.

During the Cold War, Simon's Town's role as an intelligence listening station – the mountain had been tunnelled out for the purpose of concealing a nuclear-proof headquarters – was thoroughly exploited by the Nationalist government to keep its lines open to Washington and London notwithstanding apartheid, casting itself as a champion of the so-called Free World, only to discover in the twilight of the Soviet Union that the South African base commander and his wife had worked for many years as Soviet illegals – moles, the press called them.

Enough. My destination is fourteen miles further south, at the entrance to Africa's most southerly game reserve at Cape Point.

Unless you are quick and know where to look, you'll never see it from the road, or at least not from a passing vehicle. Even on foot, the place isn't visible from the verge until the pedestrian has passed on and then stops at the outermost point of the next headland and looks back and down, right down, at a steep forty-five-degree angle, to the boulders at the foot of the cliff. Only then will he or she glimpse one or two small shacks jutting out into space, the roofs outlined in black against a shimmering silver ocean.

That's Smitswinkelsbaai, anglicized to Smitswinkelsbay.

Literally translated it means the Bay of Mr Smith's Shop.

God knows why. There is no Mr Smith or any shop I know of.

I walk all the way, quickly easing into my stride, getting used to the heat and only stopping twice for a gulp of water and splashing it over neck and shoulders. It might seem an odd thing to do for someone of my middling years to strike out in the afternoon heat for a fourteen-mile hike when I could have employed my office driver, or taken a cab from Simon's Town station, or from anywhere else in the Peninsula for that matter. The reason is simply that I want to do this alone, without prying eyes, without word getting back as to precisely where I am headed; when all's said and done, it is to protect Josh. And yes, I must admit I am reliving the past. In any case, I know where it is as long as I am on foot;

I know it from the shape of the hills, the curve of the coastline. I made this same pilgrimage dozens of times as a youth. It's impossible to explain where it is exactly, but the terrain, the lie of the land, is embedded in my memory. I tell myself I will know it when I see it, and I'm right.

I make it in three hours and twenty minutes, and by now have politely declined offers of a lift from two of the four cars that have passed me in all that time. I check my watch and see it is just after seven in the evening as I stand where the path begins and peer down between my sore and dusty feet. Nothing can be seen except the thick, chest-high fynbos on the cliff, and then, hundreds of feet below, the rocks and the surge of the sea itself, streaked grey and white as it flings itself against the invisible shoreline, clawing at the rock pools and beds of kelp. No human habitation is visible. To the casual hiker it won't seem possible: there is nothing there but a wild, precipitous and inaccessible coast. There just isn't room for a hut. It's too steep. Even the path is invisible – unless one knows it's there.

Josh sees me coming.

About fifty paces downhill, on the second of the many zigzags, holding my arms up to avoid the brush that grows thickly over the track of burning sand, I can see most of the huts by now. I recognize Josh standing in the grassy backyard of his wood and tar-paper shack – he peers up, watching my approach, hand up to shield his eyes from the sun. He has a fire going, and as I get closer I can see he is cooking his supper, the fruit of his afternoon's dive off the rocks.

Crickets rasp, birds dart up, herring gulls wheel overhead

and the scent of wild flowers and thyme take me back to our childhood; to the girls we pursued in this remote place, dragging our mattresses outside and spending the nights snogging under the stars, listening to the crash of the waves, in the mornings watching the seals or Southern Wright whales coming in close to calve, setting up bodysurfing contests in the afternoons. There is a beach, but it isn't always there. After a particularly wild storm it sometimes vanishes altogether, hundreds of tons of sand swept away only to return in calmer weather.

His first words: 'We're running out of paraffin.'

No greeting.

'I brought candles.'

I can see the disappointment. He won't say it, but I know he's been hoping that I'd bring Frances. Or that she knows where to come, drops everything, and comes running. Alone. The last person he wants to see, apparently, is his old pal, Sebastien Palfrey.

He has taken three large *perlemoen* – abalone, crustaceans the size of soup bowls – from the rocks, diving down, holding his breath, gripping the rock with one hand to prevent the swell dragging him against the barnacles, and with the other levering the creatures off the rock with a screwdriver or something similar. He scrapes out the flesh with a diver's knife, slicing it into strips, and prepares to grill it, leaving the shells empty, their interiors smooth and bright with mother-of-pearl. Three. Three meals. But one guest is missing.

The taste reminds me of smoked ham, only better.

'I've got some wine to go with this,' I say, and open my backpack to extract a bottle of South African Riesling.

'You can put it in a bucket of water.'

We are like a couple of strangers at a bus stop, exchanging platitudes about the weather.

We say nothing about his father's murder.

There is running water, very cold, taken directly from a spring that serves all the beach shacks. An eighteenth-century municipal by-law that provided for the provisioning of passing sailing vessels with water from that same spring has succeeded in preventing anyone building anything permanent in the bay, from putting up a hotel to widening the coast road or indeed establishing any settlement save these flimsy weekend structures.

'I brought you some milk powder, olive oil, coffee, soap, a bottle of brandy and – let's see – your favourite cigars.'

He doesn't thank me; he doesn't say anything. He bends to his cooking, using hot stones to grill the food, flavoured with the bay leaves and oregano that grow around us. I dump the provisions inside the hut, glancing around quickly, relieved to see how little has changed in all the years since I was last there, then pull on my swimming shorts and venture out to help. I pick a bunch of wild rocket and wash it under the tap, add chopped onion and a pinch of sea salt, balsamic vinegar and the olive oil. We eat the abalone with our fingers, in silence, drinking the wine from tin mugs. It reminds me how we used to gather pine nuts on the mountain when we were boys, eating them by the handful.

We don't talk; we look up at each other now and then.

Josh glances at the path. It's empty.

Does he think I was involved?

That I ordered his dad's killing?

That I've stolen his girl?

I am not going to mention his father until he does.

He'll have to ask. I'm not going to volunteer anything.

There are things I could say. I could say he made the wrong choice. He played the liberal, the *draadsitter*, the man who stays on the fence and who waits to see what will happen, who pockets his profits from the system that makes them possible. That the gold school badge of his, along with all the other rewards that have come his way over the years, turned his head, dulled his sense of right and wrong. At least his father had the courage to act according to his convictions, and probably died for them. It's something I can respect. What has Josh ever done but pose with his lefty books and second-hand ideas while accumulating more wealth than any one person has a right to?

I don't feel very sympathetic.

And when he did come down off the fence it was not by deliberation or conviction; he fell off, took a tumble all those years ago into the darkness that held us all in thrall.

What has changed since we last shared a meal on this shore?

We are men. I have just turned forty-four, and Josh is a few months older. He is a captain of commerce, an extremely wealthy man, someone whose gross income probably exceeds the GDP of several Third World countries combined, and here he is, living like a beach-comber. Here, his army of servants and business associates are of no use to him. His state-of-the-art home cinema, his heated swimming pool, his computers and cellphones, his fast cars, his stock holdings, his personal bank accounts, his directorships, his London tailor and bootmaker, his memberships of Boodles in London and the City Club, and the array of interlinked companies he controls – out here, none of it counts for anything. His empire can't protect him.

What is he when all this is stripped away?

He can't call up his executive jet and hide in his Houghton mansion in Johannesburg's northern suburbs; his holiday home fronting the Knysna lagoon in the Eastern Cape is an obvious place for the likes of Viljoen to look. So too is the Franschhoek farm, and the Cape Dutch farmhouse near Stellenbosch University, his alma mater. There are presumably the homes of his various women friends, but they too will be on someone's list; perhaps even now Mabaza is accessing the data from the National Intelligence Service in Pretoria. Of course the airports will be watched. He can't vanish abroad, drive over the northern border at Beit Bridge, or hide in some long-forgotten fuckpad in Monaco or Mayfair. Josh is too well known.

Am I sorry for him?

Not at all.

Viljoen can't seriously imagine that Josh cut his own father's throat. I don't believe it. I can't believe anyone does. It's inconceivable. So why the arrest warrant? And why has Josh obliged the likes of Viljoen and Mabaza – and the media – by making a run for it, by disappearing?

What is Josh up to?

I'm missing something. Viljoen probably feels the same way.

There is a pattern and it has to be right in front of me, but so close I can't see it.

I have to ask myself the same question the police must have pondered: who stands to gain from Cris Schuter's violent death? Josh will inherit, of course, but he is already immensely wealthy in his own right. He would have inherited anyway, presumably, even if father and son were disaffected. Blood is thicker etc. And if the motive was to smash the Schuter financial empire, then Josh must also be a target. Removing the father isn't going to be enough. Is that why Josh has decided to disappear – because he's next? That can't be it, either. It would be easy for him to step up the level of protection, to move the target beyond the range of the mysterious assassins. He can afford to take avoiding action.

South Africa has already changed; the old order is on its last legs.

I have to rule out a political assassination, too.

The taxi driver in the mirror-shades knows something I don't.

Is it revenge?

It is true Josh and I are both killers. It is the one thing we have left in common.

Apart from Frances, of course.

We both have blood on our hands – and I don't mean Cris Schuter's. It is the only thing that binds us together as friends after all this time. The tie of a lifetime's friendship is reduced to shared guilt, to complicity in state crimes. Josh and I are united by our shame, by our acts of omission and commission. But it has nothing to do with the old man's murder, not directly.

Right now there seems to be only one thing on the fugitive's mind.

He speaks with his mouth full. 'Where is she, Sebastien?'

*

Rewind. Go back.

After those years of estrangement at prep school and then Bishops, we had found ourselves thrown together again as nineteen-year-olds, myself at the Argus School of Journalism in Johannesburg and he a student. By sharing the cottage, smoking dope and getting drunk our friendship was renewed, and cemented further with the illicit nocturnal visits to Soweto. Even so, the irritant, the destructive energy undetectable on the surface – like woodworm – was once again burrowing into my mind. It was the poison of envy, this time not of Josh's pre-eminent role as sportsman or academic, or what I had fondly thought of as a solid home background, but of his relationship with Frances.

I tried to deal with it. I examined it, turning the issue on its head. For one nasty moment I could not help wondering if I would have been so captivated by Frances if she and Josh had not been lovers; would I not have seen her as she was, my view of her unclouded by my desire to have, and to be, everything that came so easily to Josh? Would she have seemed so insanely attractive, so mysterious, so amusing, so lively, so utterly irresistible? Would I have wanted her at all? Was she really so special? Weren't there scores of leggy, long-thighed, high-breasted, bright young black women like Frances? Soweto's Baragwanath Hospital was full of nurses only too willing. What was the fuss about? Wasn't I happy with Annette? Of course I was. And was it really Josh that I resented – not Frances, for taking away my best friend, distracting him, diverting him from paying me attention?

It was a guilty thought, something deeply distasteful, a

notion I would have preferred not to have thought about at all. I wanted to push it away, but couldn't help myself wondering. Back then the notion was just too repugnant to contemplate; it was what my parents would have said was 'dirty'. I don't think that back then I would have known or understood the term 'homoerotic'. It was certainly too much at variance with my fragile adolescent idea of my masculine self. It was altogether too unmanly, too confusing, too unsettling to deal with.

It was after six or seven visits to Soweto that the first approach was made, and it was quite unexpected. It was January 1970. I don't recall the date, but I do remember it was late afternoon in downtown Jo'burg and I was emerging from the Argus premises at the end of the working day. I was alone. It was still very hot, cumulus piling up like whipped cream in the blue sky. The city was in for an hour or two of thunderstorms and heavy rain – a typical Transvaal summer day.

'Hey, Seb – how you doin', man?'

It seemed like a chance encounter at the time, but thinking back on it, I realize he was probably waiting for me.

'I'm Zak – remember?'

He pumped my hand, African style, grasping fingers, then thumb and finally pushing our fists together. He steered me along the pavement, one hand on my back, always talking, keeping up the friendly patter, imitating an American drawl as so many people did in those days; and just as I was on the point of accepting his invitation, there was the car and I was climbing into the front passenger seat without really thinking about it while a smiling Zakaria Wauchope trotted around the other side, jumped in behind the wheel, reminded me to use the safety belt and, still talking away, pulled smartly into the traffic. We headed north, along Jan Smuts Drive.

There was something about him that reminded me of somewhere or something in the past, but I couldn't identify it. And I didn't mean our visit to Orlando West.

He was talking about his work as a senior photographer on the *Star*. He was from the Cape, he said, and he was classified a *Kaapse Kleurling* – he laughed loudly at this and looked at me out of the corner of his eye to see what impression it made – and went on to talk about how dangerous it was covering the townships as a photographer when things got rough. As a Coloured, he was in the middle, distrusted by the white cops and the black activists. Like other photographers, he had to get close, very close. Reporters could get away with not being there at all, or at least keeping out of the range of stone-throwers. Hadn't I noticed during my nocturnal visits how it was that some nights the police were out everywhere in force, and how on other occasions how the Comrades seemed to be running things? He said it was the unpredictable nature of the violence that frightened him more than anything else.

As we passed the zoo he turned to me.

'I want to ask you something, Seb – and you know a car's about the safest place for confidential talk. You knew that, didn't you?'

No, I didn't.

Zak explained. It was hard to monitor a conversation in a moving vehicle. It took lots of people to follow a car around the clock, and while one could expect the phones and all other electronic communications to be bugged, a conversation in a moving vehicle was about ninety percent safe, especially if the car was borrowed or rented, and never used again for the purpose. So we'd talk business in the car, if that was all right with me, then we'd have a drink or two, and he'd drop me off at my place or wherever I wanted to be.

I digested this and was going to ask what it was he wanted to say when he glanced at the rear-view mirror and said, 'We've been keeping an eye on you, man, you know?'

'We?'

I had a pretty good idea who it was he meant, but he didn't reply. He watched the mirror a lot and he kept switching lanes, slowing right down, then speeding up again. I belatedly realized this was a technique Zak used to identify any followers.

'You remember that time you and Josh were arrested?'

'Sure,' I said. 'I'm not likely to forget it. It was my first visit to Soweto.'

'Did you see me?'

'In the police station, you mean? Yes, of course. I did see you, but I didn't know who you were back then.'

He turned his head and grinned at me. 'We like your style, Seb.'

We?

'How do you mean?'

'You're quiet. You don't show off. You keep your views to yourself. You're modest. You don't lose your head. I haven't seen you drunk, and you're careful around women. You're sensible with money. I like that, man. You're also pretty smart – for a white boy who went to Bishops.'

He found this very funny. I didn't so much, so I smiled.

By now we were well into the northern white suburbs. I looked out of the side window at the high walls, the remote-controlled gates, palatial villas, swimming pools and lawns, and I thought that Zak, as an accredited press photographer working for the country's biggest circulation daily, would not have to worry about being caught in the wrong place. He didn't have to worry about the pass laws. In any case, he didn't look very black. He was unlikely to be stopped at random.

The car slowed and Zak spun the wheel; I recognized the district known as Blairgowrie.

Somewhere less like Scotland would be hard to find.

'Will you help us, Seb?'

'Us?'

'The Comrades. Will you help us?'

So that was it. My heart beat faster, my mouth dried up.

We pulled up at a pair of white metal gates. Seb didn't get out. He just sat and waited, looking at me, wanting a response. I was very aware of the possibility of entrapment, of Zak being a provocateur. And even if he was genuine, who was to say whoever he worked for wasn't one? Ever since Sharpeville things had become a lot tougher; by 1963 the deaths had started, prisoners flew out of windows, they were found dead in the showers of police stations and prisons, or they just 'banged their heads' somehow and died of it. Inquests and inquiries glossed over the evidence. Time and again, the police got away with it. People could be locked up without trial, first for ninety days, then 180, and finally, as long as the Security Branch wanted, on the whim of a mere sergeant. In the name of national security, of fighting terrorism.

'Doing what, exactly?'

'Hey, don't worry about it. I just want to know if you're interested. If you'd like to help. You're not going to be planting bombs or shooting people, if that's what's bothering you. We want to use you in more intelligent ways. My people want to make use of your talents.'

Whatever they might be.

'How do I know this is on the level, that I'm not being set up?'

Someone had come out of the house, a middle-aged man in white shirt and tie. An office worker who's just got home, I thought, and has had to come out and let us in himself because the servants have already gone off duty.

'That's why I brought you here, Seb. To meet Dr Stanko. That's him over there. He's a good friend. You can trust him. He wants to meet you. I made the recommendation, as a matter of fact. He'll tell you himself everything you want to know. But I need to know first if you want to get involved. If you don't, man, that's fine by me. It's no problem, really. No one's twisting your arm. We'll have that beer, you and I, and then, as I said, I'll take you wherever you want to go. And we'll both forget all about it. Deal?'

I thought to myself that whoever they were, these Comrades, they'd done their homework. I was more than ready. I had been ready for years. But how did they know what my personal views were? I'd mentioned them to no one I could think of. And what could a middle-class white kid just turned twenty do for the Cause? More to the point, was I really up to it?

It was one thing to have views, another to actually do

something about them. Did I have the balls for this undercover stuff? When it came down to it, was I prepared to take the risk of spending a lifetime on my knees scrubbing toilets with a toothbrush in the white section of Pretoria's maximum security prison, or kept naked and manacled in solitary for months at a time? Terrorism was a crime punishable by death, and terrorism meant anything the authorities wanted it to mean.

Stanko was a large man with a paunch and dark, receding hair. He wore glasses. I put his age at around fifty, old enough to be my own father. He looked pleasant enough. He had a careworn look – he was clearly a professional of some kind, a bank executive or university lecturer, neither rich nor poor. Anonymous. Middling in every way. The streets of London or New York or Paris were filled with men like this, I thought: married, middle-aged men, over-weight, with forgettable, plain, worried faces, men with families and mortgages heading to and fro between the office and home in the suburbs, equipped with briefcase, umbrella and *Daily Telegraph*. In a word: innocuous.

Dr Stanko just stood there in the gravel drive, waiting.

I felt like a high-diver on the edge of the board, the pool far below and as small as a postage stamp. I leaned forward, let gravity take over, and listened to the sound of my own voice. I was dizzy with the excitement and fear of the moment. I was sweating, and my blood thundered in my ears.

'All right, Zak. I'm interested. I make no promises, mind, but I am definitely interested. Let's have that beer.'

'Hey, fucking great, man, I thought you would be,' Zak said, and we drove in the through the gates, Dr Stanko moving past down the drive to close up after us. As I undid my safety belt and got out of the car I had a strong sense that I had just taken an irretrievable step, and one I might easily regret in the months and years ahead. But it did seem then to be the right thing to do. I wasn't committed to anything. All I had to do, I told myself, was listen. I could always say no, just back out and apologize and say it wasn't for me. No one was going to force me to do anything.

I was left alone in the sitting room. Zak said he was getting the beers, but I was sure he was talking to Dr Stanko while doing so, briefing him on what had been said. I stood at the window and looked out; a big acacia spread its branches wide and I watched a pair of hoopoes swoop back and forth, feeding on insects. Beyond the tree was a kidney-shaped swimming pool, a rose garden and a rusty child's swing. The sitting room was typical of its kind, reflecting the European tastes of its white residents: a mock Adam fireplace, a Caucasian rug, floral loose covers on the settee and armchairs, a framed Delacroix print on the wall, a well-thumbed copy of *Newsweek* and *Vogue* in a magazine rack, a set of family pictures in silver frames. I moved closer and examined the faces; Dr Stanko's was not among them. I was thinking to myself that maybe Frances would pay me more attention if she knew I'd signed up for Resistance work when I heard a car start and saw Zak at the wheel, driving out of the gates, Stanko closing them behind him once again.

He came into the room, hand outstretched.

'Zak has some business to attend to – he apologizes, but he'll be back later.'

Stanko's smile was welcoming, his handshake firm. He

poured a can of cold lager into a glass tankard, carefully placing his thumb under the point of impact to minimize the frothy head, and handed me the glass, then helped himself. He indicated we should sit opposite one another.

'Your health, Mr Palfrey.'

We drank and watched the world darken as the first heavy raindrops fell.

He had a mild South African accent, probably Eastern Cape, I thought, a descendant of the 1820 English settlers brought in to places like Queenstown as a buffer against the Xhosa. Yet the name Stanko carried a Balkan ring to it.

Maybe he was a Yugoslav Jew who'd managed to get out ahead of the Nazi invaders, or perhaps he'd been a pre-war refugee from Lithuania or Latvia. It was hard to tell, but he had the look of a survivor.

'You can call me Stanko, though it's not my real name and I'm not a medical doctor. I have a doctorate in ethnology. This isn't my home. I borrowed it for the meeting. We call it a safe house – somewhere where we can occasionally meet without fear of being compromised. We won't use it for any other purpose, and it has an exit at the back on to the street at the rear – I don't know if you noticed, it's on a corner, and it was chosen for that reason and because we trust the owners not to ask any awkward questions or take any suspicions they might have to the authorities.'

'We?'

It was a term I had heard more than once before that afternoon, and I wanted to know what I was dealing with. If all this cloak-and-dagger talk was meant to impress, it wasn't working.

'Zak didn't say?'

I shook my head.

'I'm sorry. The ANC is a broad church,' Stanko said, 'of which we are a small but active component. That's all I'm prepared to say at this stage – until we get to know each other better.'

A banned part of a banned coalition, in other words.

I said, 'How can I possibly help? I have no special skills. I'm white. I'm middle class. I'm as far removed from the struggle in the townships as it's possible to be. I might as well live in Oslo or Rio de Janeiro for all the good I can do.'

I was conscious of waving my hands about too much.

It was nerves.

Stanko handed me another beer.

'We'll be the judge of that, Sebastien. What I want to know is whether you don't feel you'd be compromising your integrity as a journalist, right at the very outset of your career, by taking sides?'

I had the answer ready.

'We all take sides, Dr Stanko. We take sides when we do nothing. We take sides when we emigrate. We take sides when we close our ears, when we decide which newspaper to read. We take sides a thousand times every day with the smallest acts of commission or omission. And right now, with around a hundred and ninety items of law that inhibit or proscribe free expression, talking about the integrity of a journalist's career in this country is a spurious luxury – it simply doesn't apply. It's a matter of responsibility.'

It was what he wanted to hear.

Josh would have answered differently yet no less forcefully. He would have said a journalist's course was to fight his professional corner, to seek the light between the bars, to circumvent the rules, to fight the good fight with the pen and not the sword, to agitate with a truth, to stay within the bounds of the law, no matter how compromised.

Josh was a liberal and could afford to be.

We talked for an hour. Among other matters, I mentioned my two-year deferment of military service, and asked Stanko whether, from his organization's point of view, I should submit to national service or leave the country. He said he would take advice, but his immediate reaction was that it would be useful to have members with military knowledge, particularly from inside the combat arms of the South African Defence Force.

It was, in retrospect, a form of verbal seduction, a judicious use of gentle praise and apparently genuine interest on the part of a practised case officer in a rather lonely young man who craved attention. That, together with the perceived power and prestige the clandestine life seems to offer those of poor self-esteem, was the bait that won me over into agreeing to become a probationer on the books of the South African Communist Party. I didn't put up a fight; I was a pushover. I was gagging for it. I didn't need convincing. I'm sure, with the benefit of hindsight, that they saw this clearly in me. Ideologically, I had already bought the whole absurd bag of bones. Emotionally, I had long thirsted for a cause I could identify with, ever since that French lesson at Bishops. I left Dr Stanko's safe house, after the thunderstorms had passed, walking on air, breathing in the smell of newly-irrigated earth in a state of elation, driven home by Zak and quite oblivious to his amiable chatter. I was on a high. It was better than grass. It was almost as good as sex. I, Sebastien Palfrey, had signed up for the Resistance. It was the biggest single act of my twenty years.

And yes, Zak must have sensed my mood on the way home because he took the opportunity there and then to sell me an 'arm' of *dagga* – an arm was a package as thick as man's forearm and extending from wrist to elbow – for the enormous sum of two rand, or about a pound at the exchange rate at that time. He had several kilos of it stuffed inside the spare tyre of his car. We had a drink after the exchange, and he dropped me back in Hillbrow, though not too close to my girlfriend's place. Henceforth Zak became my personal supplier whenever we were in town at the same time.

It wasn't just a drug, it was a symbol. Boys and girls across the colour bar were making contact to buy and sell grass, and they smoked it together to township music. It was but a small hole in the apartheid wall, a symbol of quiet revolt in the sixties and early seventies, and everyone under thirty was doing it.

Well, not everyone; but most young English-speakers, certainly.

'Do you remember the farm, Seb?'

Zak smiled at me, waiting for my response. We sat in the car and shared a sample of his *zol*. He called it customer relations.

The farm? Of course I did. The moment he mentioned it I realized I knew him from childhood. Looking at him I saw the boy in patched khaki shorts down to his knees, the catapult in his hands, his eyes alight with mischief.

'I do now,' I said, speaking through a spiral of smoke, feeling the pot kick in hard. I felt as if I was being lifted off the face of the earth into weightless orbit.

'We had lots of fun in those days, didn't we, hey?'

'We did, yes.'

I slipped the brown paper package into my jacket pocket and opened the car door. I was perfectly steady, but my inhibitions had been reduced, and I was feeling more reckless than usual.

'Can I ask you a question, Zak – and will you answer it honestly?'

There was just the slightest hesitation.

'Sure, man.'

'Can you ever trust a white man one hundred per cent?'

He looked at me hard for a moment.

'No.'

'Not even a white Comrade?'

'One hundred per cent?'

'Yes.'

He shook his head.

'Not even him – Dr Stanko?'

'Nope. No offence, but you did ask.'

'None taken. It's what I thought. It's how I'd feel. Thanks for being so frank about it.'

He shrugged. 'It's nothing.'

'See you, Zak – and thanks.'

'Wait a moment. I have to explain something to you. White liberals are part of the problem, man. You know that. They're fooling no one but themselves. As for the very few whites who join the Communist Party – present company excepted – they still think they can tell the

Comrades what to do because they have Marx and Lenin on their side. They know better. It's still paternalism, man, just with a red flag, a different ideology. But it's a white man's ideology. You get it?'

'I think so.'

'We have to find our own way.'

'I understand.'

'I hope you do, and that you don't forget.'

He reached over to pull the door shut.

'*Totsiens, ou maat.*'

Zak clenched his fist and shook it. An ironical salute.

I watched him drive away.

What Zak, Stanko and their masters in exile didn't know was that the clandestine power I courted was my way of balancing the books with Joshua. He might have millions and the charm to go with it; I told myself I would use all my dark powers to unseat his kind, bring the established order down, topple the state and all who sailed in her. It was my own Faustian pact. Yes, liberals were very much part of the problem.

At twenty we all want to change the world, don't we?

What I didn't know then, of course, was that I had been selected, watched, recruited and set in motion, not because of my idealism, my political conviction, my brilliance (anyone who knew my school record would have known otherwise) or the fact that I was launching myself on an unsuspecting world as a junior newspaper reporter, but simply because I had access. Access is what every intelligence service strives for. It is the alpha and omega of the covert world, and in my case it was access to the family of one Joshua Schuter.

From the Party's point of view, that was all there was
to it.

I was a means to an end.

Scroll forward again, twenty-four years, to Smitswinkelsbay: tonight Josh and I drink cognac and listen to the
wind coming off the sea and the crash of the waves on
the rocks below, sitting opposite each other at the wooden
table, feeling the shack heave and shake at each banshee
howl as if the structure has a life all of its own and is
trying to tear itself free of the cliff.

An unsmiling Josh allows himself the luxury of a
cigar, tearing off the band, biting off the end and lighting
it with a guttering candle; he is dressed in ragged pull-
over and shorts, unshaven; his feet are bare, his hair is
windblown, the candlelight turns the thick ginger hair
on his forearms into spun gold. He looks like a schoolboy tramp, someone who can't quite resolve the state of
his mind with the advancing age of his physical being, a
middle-aged child with millions in the bank, a warrant
out for his arrest and what is left of his dad in a police
morgue.

I raise my mug. I say, trying to be cheerful, 'This brings
back memories.'

He doesn't respond. He doesn't even look at me. He
keeps his arms folded on the table and his eyes down,
staring into his own drink.

'She won't come here,' I say. 'Forget it, Josh. She won't
come for the simple reason that she's afraid they'll follow
her and she'll end up compromising you.'

'You made it, though.'

133

'Perhaps she cares for you rather more than I do. She's certainly selfless in a way I could never be.'

He makes it sound like an accusation. How come you, and not her? Ah, yes, of course. Frances certainly does not lack for courage, but she isn't rash like me. She is careful. I have had some training and experience in detecting whether I have watchers on my back, and I know how to throw them off the spoor if I have to. We probationers were forced to practise it constantly. We were always taught during training in Tanzania, later East Germany and finally at 'finishing school' near Grozny in the USSR itself – where I was selected to take yet another step deeper into the craft of espionage – that if you have a tail, you don't shake it off unless it's absolutely essential.

Standard operating procedure is to behave normally, as if you've noticed nothing amiss; it's invariably better to duck the rendezvous, to clear the DLB – acronym for dead letter box – another time. There is always a fallback time and place. In its heyday, Moscow was unparalleled in its teaching of trade craft; there was no one who could better their spymasters, not even the Chinese or Israelis. The British and Americans were rank amateurs by comparison. I can still hear the words of the cheerful instructor, a diminutive ethnic Yakut and major in the GRU: Don't let the bastards know you know they're there at all.

Let the fuckers live with their illusions.

I go outside, pulling the door shut behind me, and head around the shack and stand out in front on the grass verge. I can't see where the land ends and the sea begins. I can't even see the ground I stand on; all is darkness, save for the rash of stars revealed in the cloudbreaks, so bright away from the city and its suburbs. The wind tears at my hair, tugs my T-shirt, pushes and pummels me. I feel the thunder of the sea through the soles of my feet, the ground vibrating all the way up through the cliff from the beach some three hundred feet below. I know, though I can't see, that the ground falls away right in front of me to what we used to call the garden; it's a small grassy depression surrounded by a broken drystone wall, the thick, serrated blades of aloes providing an effective if hazardous barrier. I decide to sleep out there: I'll fetch a mattress, drag it down with a couple of blankets. It is out of the wind, and it will not be at all cold. It will indeed be like the old days, and after the three-hour hike in the sun, the sound of the wind and the sea will send me straight to sleep. Tonight I will need neither brandy, *daggazolletjie* nor sex to subdue my unquiet mind.

My nightmare will stay in its lair.

It's a sensible precaution, too: if I am mistaken, and they do after all know where we are and raid the place in the early hours of the morning, they will with any luck miss me altogether as they pound down the hill and force their way into the shack. I'll have a chance to slip away.

The head agent's safety is paramount.

A Communist without the Party is a priest without his church.

Bereft, and in permanent mourning.

'Will you tell me about it?'

I've gone in again to get the mattress, the blankets and a pillow. Josh seems to have woken from his daze; he is looking at me with an expression of bafflement.

'Tell you what?'

'I'm sorry. I'm not myself tonight. Tell me what happened to my father. Tell me what you know.'

Now it begins.

'I can do better than that.' I drop the bedding and go over to my backpack and open it. I pull out the file the street kid gave me, walk over to the table and drop it front of him.

'What's this?'

I am a coward; I want him to extract the facts from the officialese. I do not want to have to spell it out and watch him while the details sink in. So Josh sticks what remains of the cigar in his mouth, squints through the bitter smoke and turns the file around. He flips it open.

I go back to the door.

'Where'd you get this?'

He waves me back.

'How did you know I'd be here?'

'I tried to put myself in your shoes, Josh.'

I take a step towards the table.

'So what the hell is this?'

'It's a copy.'

He scans the pages, frowning. 'I asked where you got it.'

'I'm a reporter, Josh. A reporter has sources, contacts. Someone owed me a favour or did me a good turn – what does it matter?'

He knows it's a lie, and he knows it's pointless asking for a name because I'd never give it to him.

He looks up. 'Did you have anything to do with it?'

'Me?'

'Did you?'

I sit down opposite him.

'I know what you were, Seb,' he says. 'Maybe you still are. I know all about you.'

'I'm not sure what you mean.'

'She told me, Seb. Frances was Zak's woman, you know. In the beginning, before we met. She did some work for him – afterwards, too. He would tell her things. She picked stuff up. I'm talking about MK. Zak was MK. Spear of the Nation. And she told me all about you, too.'

'And you think I'd do something like that?'

'Not personally, maybe. But you could have organized it.'

'Don't talk balls.'

'Is that all you can say?'

'Why, Josh? Jesus, why would I do something like that?'

'You hated us, you bastard.' He flings the words me, his voice high pitched, breaking like Chinese crackers over the howl of wind. 'All of us. All the time you were pretending to be my friend you were spying on us. You're a fucking spy.'

He is breathing hard, trying to control himself. He clutches the report with both hands and is back at the start, reading more carefully.

I say quietly, 'The war's over, Josh. It's finished. Whatever happened to your father, it had nothing to do with us. Believe me.'

'So what's with the arrest warrant?'

'I'm sure it's very simple. The cops look at everyone with access to your father, they look for opportunity and means – and then they eliminate every name on the list, one by one. The police are very systematic that way.'

'And you, Seb?'

'I'm on their list.'

'But it wasn't you?'

'Christ, no.'

'It wasn't the Party? Or your masters in Moscow?'

'No,' I say. 'It wasn't.'

Josh is reading again.

He jabs a forefinger at the page.

'It says here there were two or more assailants.'

'Yes.'

'One of them was barefoot.'

'Read further. I think you should read all of it before you jump to conclusions – the media made the same mistake. The papers made a big thing of that. They immediately assumed it was a couple of *skollies*, black or Coloured. The usual racial stereotypes always seem to come to the fore immediately a white's blood is spilled – and of course they didn't have this report.'

Josh says, 'Nothing was taken.'

'That's a statement or a question?'

He looks at me, scowling. 'A question.'

'I wouldn't know. They didn't say.'

'And this?'

'It's an initial crime-scene assessment by the scientists, Josh. It wouldn't include that kind of detail.'

'Why do you think they've fingered me?'

'You had your differences, you and Cris, didn't you? Political and personal – and let's face it, most murders in normal societies are kept in the family, or among friends. Your dad didn't spend much time with you and Rachel when you were kids, and your stepmum even less. The odds are heavily in favour of the murder victim and the killer knowing each other.'

Josh shuts his eyes, the fingers that turn the pages of the report closing into a fist.

'Don't every father and son have their differences? That's not a motive, for fuck's sake. Do they really think I'd – God, cut my father's throat? Hold him down, and . . .'

'I don't think the police seriously do think you had anything to do with it. But they can't make assumptions about what went on between you in private, behind closed doors. I think they're going through the motions, following procedure—'

He pushes himself up on to his feet, bends over the table, his weight on his hands. His head goes down so I won't see his face, but I do see the tears splash the pages of the report.

'Fuck you, Palfrey.'

It comes out a mangled yelp of pain.

'If I were you, Josh, I'd go to the nearest police station and say you've heard they're looking for you and you decided to come in straight away, that you were fishing off Cape Point—'

'You're not me.'

What I want to say is that I haven't come all this way to act as his judge and jury. I'm no moralist. My job isn't to sit in judgement on his relationship with his father or the lack of it. It is true that when I arrived he didn't appear particularly grief-stricken. He was in control. He didn't have the shakes. There seemed to be no sense of horror at the terror, pain and desperation his father must have endured in his final moments; even if father and son had never rubbed along very well, they were of the same flesh and blood. The first thing Josh wanted to

139

know was why Frances wasn't there. Hours passed before he showed any curiosity about what had happened in Bishopscourt. If I'd been in his place I would have been full of anxious questions at the outset. I wouldn't have stood there, silently cooked and eaten supper and waited until after dark to speak. I would have paced up down, trying to decide what I ought to do. I would have asked for advice, argued the toss, changed my mind and probably ranted and raved, and shed a few tears as well; tears of sorrow, of regret and, yes, of self-pity.

That doesn't mean he killed his own father.

He wipes his face with the back of his hand and sits down heavily. He goes on reading, ignoring me, trying to make sense of the technical jargon. The mask of self-control is back in place. At that moment, and it is only fleeting, I feel sorry for him.

I pick up the bedding and struggle over to the door, get it open and use my foot to stop it banging shut again as I push the mattress out ahead of me. I do the same thing with the blankets and pillow because I can't get through the door while holding them, not with the wind pushing me backwards.

''Night,' I say.

He helps himself to more cognac.

'Seb, were you ever really my friend? Or were we enemies from the very start?'

I can almost picture Viljoen's smile. It's as if he's there at my shoulder, waiting for my response, willing me on.

I don't reply. I don't reply because I don't know the answer. I toss the blankets and pillow into the darkness and slam the door shut behind me.

DAY THREE

FIVE

The wind has died by morning. The South Atlantic's rage has turned to a whisper, its tongue of froth lapping at the beach. I roll out of my blankets and run down, the path still damp from dew, watching where I put my feet in case of thorns. When I used to come here as a boy I didn't worry about such things; I could put out a cigarette on the sole of either foot and wouldn't feel a thing. The storm has left the usual jetsam in its wake: shark eggs like elongated leather purses, black and red strands of kelp, salt-bleached pieces of wood like old bones.

I strip off and hobble on my soft feet over the pebbles and shells and wade in up to my chest. Floating flat on my back, I can see the cliff, the white stones that mark the edge of the road, the beach shacks. I see Josh emerge and walk down slowly, a towel around his neck. There is no other movement, no smoke, no one up there watching us.

After our swim we sit bollock naked on a flat rock, drying off in the early morning sun.

'You didn't answer my question last night.'

I pretend not to remember. 'Which was?'

'How you knew I was here.'

'There was nowhere else, Josh. It was a process of

elimination. Your house in Jo'burg, the family farm, the holiday home in Knysna, the place in Stellenbosch – they'd all be visited by the police. You're too well known to just buy a ticket and fly out of the country. I assumed this was where you'd be because it's the only place left where you can lie low.'

'You walked all this way on an assumption? You must be bloody sure of yourself. I'm sorry, Seb, but I just don't believe you.'

He is right, of course. He has had all night to think about it. I wonder how much else he's managed to work out for himself. In any event, what he dislikes most is my presumption. Who the hell do I think I am?

'Suit yourself,' I say, turning around to warm my back. 'I need a break anyway.'

'Who told you, Seb?'

'Who told you to get the hell out in time?'

'A mutual friend – probably the same friend who told you this was where you could find me. Am I right?'

I don't answer.

'Our old friend Zakaria Wauchope. The *Star* photographer who got us both off the hook in Mamelodi. The kid we used to play with.'

'I thought it was Orlando.'

'Wherever. He came up to me at a reception for young Cape Town artists in Constantia. He'd done some of the photography for the catalogue. I didn't recognize him. He was wearing a suit. Very dapper. He'd put on weight and lost some hair. I guess we remember people the way they used to be, but never see the changes in ourselves because we feel pretty much the same as we always have. He came straight over, stuck out his hand and introduced himself. He told me he had a photography studio in town, and had turned commercial, and if I ever needed any work done, I should check his place out. It was quality, or so he said, and because we were old friends he would give me a very competitive discount. He specializes in portraiture and landscapes. I thought he was a cocky little bastard and I was about to tell him what he could do with his studio when I realized all this was being said for the benefit of anyone overhearing us. Then he pressed his business card on me, giving me a sly wink.'

That much is true. Stanko approved start-up capital from Party funds to set Zak up with a front company. A photographer's studio was perfect; there were always people going in and out. He also had his own cab company – again, a useful front for Party activity.

Josh says, 'He put his hand on my arm and then he said, very quietly, leaning up against me because it was noisy, "Mr Schuter, please listen. This is for your own good. Your friends are concerned about your welfare. Get out of town. Someplace you can hide. Somewhere they won't look. Take a few days' leave. A week, max, okay? Do it this weekend. No family, no staff, no car, no calls. Do yourself a favour." Then he smiled at me, grabbed my hand and shook it, said loudly how much he appreciated meeting me, what an honour it was, and moved away.'

'He said nothing about your dad?'

'No, nothing at all.'

'So you took him at his word – though you haven't seen him all these years.'

How could Zak have known what was about to happen? There is no reason to think he did. Maybe the warning was entirely unconnected – though with the benefit of hindsight, it seems highly unlikely.

'Next day Zak called me on my mobile – God knows how he got my number; I thought then it might have been you – and said simply, "Get out now." I tried to trace the call, but I couldn't. He didn't give his name, but I'm damn sure it was him.'

'You took it seriously?'

'I had to.'

That I find hard to accept. 'Why? You've all the protection you need. You have bodyguards when you want them and an armoured Mercedes. You can buy information. You can buy off most of your enemies if you have to. You can hire the best lawyers in the country. Why take him seriously?'

'Because I knew what he was back then in Soweto.'

'You never told me.'

'It never came up.'

'We used to talk about everything, Josh.'

'And you spied on me. You weren't exactly frank, were you?'

'So?'

'Zak has emerged as a powerful figure, man. I don't mean in business. I means he runs what is in effect his own private army. He's a force to be reckoned with in the new order of things. His people are better armed and better paid than the army or the police. I thought you knew. I felt sure you did. You seemed very pally.'

It sounds accusatory. Josh gets to his feet and starts pulling on his shorts. His movements are forceful, and he dresses quickly. He is angry. I notice that the mat of hair on his chest has turned almost entirely grey, and what looks to me like a varicose vein zigzags down the back of his calf muscle.

'You knew Zak long before I did, Josh.'

He doesn't reply.

I think: we're older than we know, older than we want to know.

'I never liked him, Seb, if you really want to know, but in these changed circumstances I felt I had no alternative.'

Never liked him? It simply isn't true, and it's unkind.

'You were at this art show with Frances?'

I realize at this point that what Josh hates most is the powerlessness of his situation; the political uncertainty means he can no longer predict the outcome of his actions, that he has to take decisions based on the advice of people like Zak.

'Why do you ask?'

I take that as a 'yes'.

I say, 'Did she and Zak give any sign that they knew each other?'

Of course they know each other; I want to know if they are willing to be seen to do so in public.

Josh doesn't reply. He just looks at me. He says, 'Let's get some breakfast.'

Back in 1970 I was placed on probation, in a Marxist-Leninist limbo, but no one said as much and it was only later that I realized I was on trial, facing a set of tests. My first assignment was easy enough; and I can see, looking back, why they chose the British consulate in Cape Town and the embassy in Pretoria. They saw me as a possible

British plant; how better to test my loyalty – to the Resistance or to Her Majesty's Government – than to pitch me against the people I might be working for?

So it was that at Dr Stanko's instigation I became a cultural neophyte; I started taking an interest in the workings of the British Council, I attended British Council film shows and UK-sponsored art exhibitions and theatrical productions, I listened to unknown British literati bore the pants off uncomprehending audiences of three – me, a semi-conscious wino, and a student who'd entered the wrong door – with readings of their latest books. My efforts were rewarded with invitations to embassy functions for South African journalists, local worthies and British residents, and in attending them I befriended a dysfunctional family named Kingsley-Clarke – David Kingsley-Clarke, former captain of the 17/21 Lancers and his rather manly, tennis-playing wife, Manda. David I took for a snob; Manda wore the breeches and roundly put him down in front of guests, using sarcasm as her weapon. I tried to imagine them in bed together – and failed. They had children, though, a boy and a girl, both away at boarding school in England, their fees paid for by the taxpayer. David was commercial attaché working out of the consulate and Manda drove around in a huge Land-Rover, carrying out research, so she said, for a guidebook on the Cape winelands.

Dr Stanko was pleased. He told me some months on that it was believed that the Kingsley-Clarkes were both working for the Secret Intelligence Service. Manda was the more senior, a deputy to the Chief of Station, yet despite her relative seniority she had not been declared to the authorities and did not have diplomatic cover – all the better, Stanko said, for running agents under deep cover – while David was a talent-spotter; if any attempt were made to recruit me, I should hesitate, show some resistance (my ambitions as a journalist, my future as a South African), but I should allow myself to be bribed. The British, Stanko said, were happiest when they recruited for money – they were uncomfortable with idealists. They liked to find a weakness they understood and could exploit; it gave them control. They tended to trust the corrupt and the impecunious a good deal more than the politically motivated agent, or so he said, and I believed him.

Funny how spies have a mirror image of their rivals.

I provided Stanko with pen portraits of both David and Manda; I drew diagrams of the consulate and the Pretoria embassy; these were followed by details of other staff, diplomatic and locally engaged, and nothing was too humdrum, no one too lowly, for Dr Stanko's ceaseless quest for information, from ex-directory telephone numbers to the registration, colour and type of unmarked embassy cars, the location of security cameras, the love life of Sandra, David Kingsley-Clarke's plump and friendly secretary.

There were often specific questions, with a deadline.

Did the embassy use a specific travel agent?

Where was the facsimile machine in the military attaché's office?

Where was the consulate's switchboard located? What type was it? Who staffed the switchboard? Was there a switchboard staff roster and, if so, would I obtain a copy, please?

Was it true that the First Secretary (Trade), Justin Wells,

was having an affair with the French consul's wife, Solange Dubord?

Describe the locks on the embassy's internal chancery door.

Would I please 'borrow' an embassy pass – just for an afternoon?

Dr Stanko explained the way it worked to me one humid afternoon, as we drank cold lager again in another borrowed location, this time a Sea Point flat in a street of high-rises; if one leaned out far enough over the edge of the balcony one could just glimpse the sea at the bottom of the hill. He and I stayed indoors, the curtains drawn, the air conditioner throbbing away on high. It wasn't just the heat; Stanko said it would help distort our voices in the event of anyone across the street using a laser to monitor the pressure waves our words made on the window panes, processing the vibrations back into dialogue. The drawn curtain would help, too.

I had managed to get my hands on a Ministry of Defence assessment of the importance of the Cape Sea route to NATO member states. It was classified secret and had been distributed three weeks earlier to Britain's allies. I had found it on David Kingsley-Clarke's desk (not something one would expect among a commercial official's papers), took it to the bathroom and photographed all eight pages with my little Leica before putting it back.

'It's like a business,' Stanko said. 'We trade with our friends. They have information of no use to them, but which we can use. We have material of no immediate application in the Struggle, but which might be useful to them in their fight against imperialism. It's a matter of common interests. Or maybe it helps us obtain equipment we cannot afford to pay for – we can buy it with intelligence instead. Intelligence is a barter economy. You see?'

It was called Third Country intelligence-gathering.

The requirements list was growing faster than I could find answers.

So my stuff was going to Havana, East Berlin, Prague or Moscow.

He meant to be kind. He wanted to reassure me that my work was worthwhile (though I would realize later they had the answers to many of the questions they posed). For security reasons, our meetings were rare events. Dr Stanko knew the pressures on someone working alone, unable to share the burden of knowledge with anyone else. After a few months it had become quite a weight to carry all by myself – and he knew it. At the same time, he was exposed to high risk whenever we met, and he had a great deal more to lose than I did if we were picked up; he had to weigh the pros and cons very carefully. This time, though, sitting on an ugly leather sofa in the afternoon gloom, he had real news, and he wanted to deliver it personally.

'The Party has instructed me to pass on to you their congratulations, Seb. This is from the top. Your work has been successful; you have passed with flying colours. The Central Committee offers you full membership. It asks if you are ready to enter the Struggle. Do you feel ready, Seb?'

I was no longer adrift in purgatory.

I said I was ready. Definitely.

What clinched it was my report on the Schuter family holdings abroad; its findings would be drip-fed via the

Comintern to the anti-apartheid movement, little titbits emerging over time, filling in gaps on fake end-user certificates used in illicit South African arms deals involving Nigerians and Taiwanese officials, front companies set up in Tel Aviv to launder sanctions-busting cash payments, a string of bank accounts from Belgrade to Lichtenstein and Jersey in the Channel Islands, and implicating one large British high street bank.

Dr Stanko shook my hand, and we drank whisky and soda to celebrate.

'They want to meet you. They want to thank you in person, and mark the occasion of your joining our ranks with a dinner. They suggest you take a break, and once you're rested, add on a short period of training – so it would be a mixture of business and pleasure. The Party will take care of everything. The timing is flexible, but we're looking at the end of next month. How would that suit you, Seb? What answer can I give them?'

They liked my methods, Stanko told me. He said I was a natural at the business. Some standard operating procedures, it was true, seemed second nature. For instance, I never answered the phone the first time, and if I wanted to speak to someone like Stanko and I had to use the telephone (it was discouraged), I would use someone else's line, or a payphone, and I would never ask directly for whoever it was I wanted to speak to. I'd ask for someone else, a mutual friend or partner, and when they answered, I would make small talk for a few moments and then ask if the doctor was available. Whenever meeting a sub-agent, I'd arrive a few minutes late and we'd always leave separately, a few minutes apart, and preferably through different exits. I would always be the last to go.

Minor details, but they mattered, especially to Moscow.

They particularly appreciated my arrangements for my 'holiday'. I flew with sweet, unsuspecting Annette on a regular flight to Luanda. She was working, but managed to find the two minutes it took us to join the mile-high club, in those days still a rather daring accomplishment; two days followed in which we never left our hotel room.

We lived on prawns and several bottles of Mateus Rosé, and our time together was given greater piquancy by the fact that I knew I was off into the bush and that we might never see each other again. She knew none of this, and, little shit that I was, I had no intention of telling her. This cruel deceit had its own aphrodisiac effect. I realized then that I obtained pleasure from lying, from the illicit, from hurting others. Perhaps we all do. Or maybe it is a vice peculiar to the male sex.

In any case, Annette, my perfect cover, flew to Lisbon and I went out to the airport with her to say goodbye, holding her close, feeling the little South African Airways badge through my shirt, kissing her on the lips, smudging her lipstick, smelling her smell, wanting her again, badly, making her laugh with my improper suggestion, then stepping back and letting her go, watching those legs and the flash of blonde hair until they vanished into the front cabin.

Her scent remained with me for days.

I had said I was taking the next flight to London. I told her I would do a little shopping and visit family up north.

I had the booking and ticket to prove it, too. But Annette, bless her, never questioned my honesty.

We married the following year, in 1976, a hasty affair in a Johannesburg registration office. A spur-of-the-moment thing, and probably the only decent act of my first three decades. After a strained but thankfully brief meeting with her family (they were remarkably tolerant of a *rooinek*, but insisted we were far too young, and they were right, of course), we flew to the Seychelles for ten days of sun and sea. Then we went home to live the dream of domestic bliss. It was bliss and it lasted three months. I did love her. I know now she loved me. The reason we fell apart and turned on each other with cold, bitter fury was the issue of children. She wanted them. I dared not have them. How could I, being what I was? I couldn't tell Annette that, of course.

Her suspicion helped poison what we had. I couldn't blame her. Strange people would approach our front gate late at night and ask for me. She'd beg me not to go, saying it was dangerous and I'd be mugged or worse. Telling her not to be so silly, I'd walk down the drive and talk for anything up to an hour; or on a shopping trip I'd take a little diversion and, asking her to wait, wander into a field and exchange packages with a Comrade. Or I'd run out of the house, wearing a suit, and return in the early hours, stinking of Scotch. Then there were the mysterious phone calls. No matter what cover stories I prepared, no matter how ingenious they were, she didn't believe me. She was convinced I was up to no good.

She was right, but it wasn't another woman as she thought it was.

Face it: I used my wife, just as I had used everyone else in pursuit of my clandestine purpose. The Party used me as its instrument, and I was not a slow learner. I think she sensed that. She said I had no idea how to live with another human being. I took it as an insult, but she was right. Nothing in my childhood had prepared me for such intimacy, for feelings.

What a terrible waste.

But I didn't see it that way, not then.

At one point, just before we parted, I suggested to Stanko that I recruit Annette as an unwitting agent; he ruled it out, saying she was more useful as part of my cover, and that sex and espionage didn't really mix. It wouldn't have saved us. It was too late.

My Afrikaner Snow Queen and her Red Dwarf.

Darling Annette and her very own *soutpiel*.

Then I disappeared from her life for good.

Back again, to the summer of 1971, a few weeks after my twenty-first birthday. I stood with a thousand men in the square of the star-shaped Cape Town Castle, one-time headquarters of the Vereenigde Oostindische Compagnie, its pretty Dutch balcony known as the Kat leading to reception areas where the gentleman-settlers had danced with their wives, the orchestra drowning out the groans and cries of manacled captives in the dungeons below – by the time of my visit, a picturesque tourist attraction.

It was also the headquarters of the regiment to which I

had been assigned. We wore civilian clothes, our bags at our feet while perspiring Afrikaner NCOs ran about with clipboards, shouting at us and at one another. Our names were called, and we shouted back 'Present!'. P was just before S, but I was day-dreaming when I heard the name Schuter called, and Joshua's answering shout. I didn't turn. I knew enough about the military to know when to keep still and look to my front. After all, I had been to Bishops and was right-hand marker in the school cadet force's demonstration drill platoon. I told myself this would be easy-peasy.

We boarded four-tonners for the railway station, then packed a special troop train bound for Oudtshoorn, a desert town known for its ostrich farms and limestone caves. There we were marched, a civilian rabble, through the streets to our lines: a vast sandy plateau, a square of wire containing hundreds of khaki tents in rows, a cook-house, a hall, a medical centre, a guardhouse and a church. There was no greenery, nothing but white sky above and desert below.

Nothing much happened for the first ten days; we waited for our uniforms and equipment, which was handed out bit by bit – first overalls, mess tin and boots, then webbing and helmet, then the FN self-loading rifle known as the R1, magazines and bayonet, and finally the uniform, the brown infantry beret with Springbok badge.

This from our drill instructor on the very first day: 'You are here to learn to kill the fucking kaffir, the fucking Jew and the fucking Englishman.'

It was reassuring to know I fell into at least one of those categories.

Reveille was at three a.m. and the day started with a

run of three miles, gradually extending to five, followed by kit inspection. We worked until two p.m. This consisted of six hours of close-order drill, PT and running over the assault course, lessons on tactics, camouflage, fire and movement, and finally shooting practice on the ranges. Basic training focused on three aspects of a soldier's existence: physical fitness, group discipline and weapons handling. The afternoons were spent cleaning equipment, washing and ironing our uniforms and preparing for the next day's inspection. I was in my pit and asleep by nine after a round or two of poker; very occasionally there was a film. The food was uniformly awful, we were jabbed for hepatitis and various other possible illnesses, we gave blood, we attended church by denomination. We read. We grew bored.

It was just like school, though not as brutal. There were simply too many of us for it to get personal. I told myself I could survive anything the instructors threw at me because I'd been through much worse. One hundred press-ups, corporal? My pleasure. I hardly broke sweat. Over that wall, sergeant? No problem.

I knew not to call my rifle a gun, to have it with me always, to make sure it was clean at all times; we Bishops boys were well suited to this life. We knew how to snap to attention, how to bone boots until they gleamed like mirrors. We knew how to obey. And just like at school, Josh and I would spot one another from time to time. He was in a different tent, a different company. He'd taken to smoking a pipe.

Perhaps three weeks later, the entire training battalion was ordered out of camp at a brisk jog, platoon by platoon, company by company. We were in fighting order

– webbing, water bottles, ammunition, helmets, bayonets and rifles. After about three miles we were halted, told to sit. It was barely eight o'clock, but the ground was already too hot; we either squatted on our heels or sat on our helmets. I heard the sound of engines; moments later, four C-47s droned out of the eastern sky, and men tumbled in a stream from each aircraft, their parachutes popping open.

A paratroop captain strode among us; volunteers should step out and gather at one side.

The NCOs started their usual yelling and out of the corner of my eye I saw Josh on his feet. The Party wanted me to gain military experience, to learn how the system worked. Why not? It might even be fun.

Perhaps two hundred riflemen from the 1st Infantry Division volunteered for the 1st Parachute Brigade that morning.

A sergeant barked, *'Sien jy daardie boom? Jy's terug!'*

It was hardly a tree – a scrap of thornbush a thousand metres away on a horizon shimmering with Karoo heat haze.

We paired off. One carried his mate at a run to the tree, the two then swapped around and returned. I'd done this before; a costly private education had a purpose, after all. It was a matter of using the fireman's lift, positioning the point of the shoulder in the passenger's gut, distributing the weight across one's back, the passenger taking both rifles.

Another NCO stood at the thorn tree to ensure no one cheated by stopping short.

'Jou bliksem,' he screamed at one pair of errant riflemen. *'Jou ma se moer!'*

They took the first forty to return, including Josh and myself.

At Voortrekkerhoogte army base near Pretoria, there was another rudimentary selection process: all Stellenbosch and Pretoria University students to step out of the ranks and form up to one side. They would be taken off for officer training; the rest of the paras were to stand fast. We English-speakers simply weren't trusted.

So it was that, six months after being called to the colours, Lieutenant Joshua Schuter and his platoon were dropped at an altitude of a thousand metres by Dakota at first light half a mile from the banks of the Palmiet River in the Eastern Cape. His platoon sergeant, the last out of the aircraft, was none other than myself.

We were to form an ambush position on the edge of the river, grid number such-and-such. All I knew was that this was no drill; it was a combined counter-insurgency operation involving the local police force, the Security Branch and Military Intelligence. The enemy was out there somewhere, and was expected to attempt to cross the river in our grid. Why, no one said. Where they were going, we weren't told. And who was the enemy, exactly, sergeant?

Stupid question.

They were Communist Terrorists. CTs.

Like me.

The operation was organized along the lines of a pheasant shoot on a Yorkshire moor: the beaters – the police – would drive the quarry into the killing zone and up to the guns. All we had to do was wait, then squeeze our triggers. As I went around checking each position and my men's equipment, I prayed – yes, prayed to a God I didn't believe in – that our quarry would slip the net and melt away.

Call it destiny, call it any damn thing, but it didn't happen that way.

The Palmiet flowed quiet and deep. Its smooth, calm surface was deceptive, for the waters moved swiftly between sandy banks crowded with undergrowth that stooped down to the surface. The sinuous, muscled water itself was clear and dark brown like Newcastle ale, unbroken even around the boulders and islands; river weed could be seen fifteen, twenty, thirty feet down, flowing like long hair in the current. It made my mouth water just to look at it; I think all of us wanted to strip off our sweaty, coarse combat smocks, unclip our halters and belts of green webbing, drop our grenades, knives, trenching tools, throw aside our helmets, tug off our jump boots and leap in. No such luck; instead, thirty men wordlessly dug shell scrapes in the afternoon heat, covered their tracks, drew camouflage netting across their sandy pits, and vanished into the landscape like sand fleas. Weapons were checked, belted ammuntion fed to the LMG; I moved from one position to the next, setting out overlapping fields of fire for each team, sighting the weapons for one hundred metres. Josh and I went down to the river together and silently inspected the likely route of the enemy.

The enemy. I loved the term. It reduced everyone and everything to that-which-must-be-destroyed. Instant dehumanization by semantics.

Save for a narrow path beaten by cattle and their herdsmen, the brush on either side of the river was impenetrable; it exuded a heady smell of vegetation and rang to the sound of cicadas. There was only one way they could come: a series of submerged boulders would allow them to ford the river at the depth of a man's thighs at the point where the trodden-down bank offered the one way through the thorns and aloes.

Josh left the platoon's disposition to me. It was a simple matter, and the terrain dictated the terms of our deployment. We lay inside an elbow of the river; whoever emerged dripping from the water, clawing up the bank and through the gap in the brush would find himself in an open space of sand and grass. Looking left and right he would see that the ground undulated, rocks protruded from the surface and shrubs and grass grew in irregular clumps. This was our killing ground; the enemy would be directly opposite the centre of our position. I placed two sections across the elbow, the left-hand section and the right-hand section in a line, the killing ground dead ahead and our flanks protected by the river. Each section comprised nine men; I divided them into three fire teams. The LMG I placed on the extreme left flank, ensuring that fire from the two flanks converged midstream in the centre of the ford so there could be no retreat once the killing began.

The platoon commander and his signaller lay just behind our line in a scrape of their own. To the rear, facing south, was the third section in two foxholes; it was the reserve, but it also provided all-round defence for I did not want us to be surprised by a counterstroke; I was determined to be ready for the unexpected.

How did I feel?

To be honest: nothing. I was engaged in a militarily

professional task. We were not dug in with overhead cover for I did not anticipate the enemy would have artillery of any kind, and I had concealed the platoon and prepared it so it could receive a force much larger than ourselves, a company or two at least, and absorb whatever they threw at us across the river. It was textbook tactics. If I'd thought about it, of course, I would have told myself we faced amateur enthusiasts, Comrades poorly armed and trained and presumably betrayed at the outset, or we would not have been so precise in our preparations. Someone had talked, and those poor devils were walking to their deaths. But I still did it by the book; I was that kind of NCO, I suppose, but my punctilious approach was about to be shattered in spectacular fashion.

Perhaps I knew one or two of them; it was certainly possible. Maybe we'd shared the same pot of maize together, fired our AK-47s next to each other, been bitten by those same hordes of ferocious mosquitoes, suffered heat rash under those awful, itchy blankets, sunk up to our waists in evil-smelling mud, endured a week of torment as our water ran dry.

Once I settled down, drank from my water bottle and prepared my own weapon, the sun was starting its swift descent in the west. We would stand to for thirty minutes at last light, and thirty minutes from first light; I had the sentry roster worked out; it was simplicity itself – half the men would sleep, half would remain awake and I myself did not expect to get any rest at all. I took it all personally as a sergeant of paratroops should. From 1800 Zulu plus one we would observe complete radio silence.

I crawled over to Josh and his signaller for a whispered

Order Group for the section leaders; after ten minutes we crawled back to our respective positions, using branches to sweep the sand clear of our tracks, a painstaking task that meant the sun had vanished by the time we dropped into our firing positions. I gave orders for dry rations to be eaten; no soldier was to leave his position – plastic bags or tins must be used for urinating or, *in extremis*, defecating.

A quarter moon rose at 2130; Cape wild dogs howled somewhere ahead of us. I felt the damp rise from the river, bringing with it mosquitoes and a swampy smell of mud and decaying vegetation. I tried not to stare at the bushes on the river bank; look at something too hard for too long at night and it seems to change shape, to move. The temperature plummeted and dew settled on my clothing; I ate the last of my chocolate, drank some water and looked back – all I could see of platoon headquarters was a dark patch of sand and rock.

I comforted myself with half-waking dreams of fettucine carbonara and wine, of hot baths and scented candles, of ground coffee, of luscious Annette; at 0130 the soldier immediately to my right poked me in the ribs. I was going to snarl at Trooper Van Zyl for his clumsiness and his damned insubordination; then I saw he was pointing at something directly ahead. We lay at the very centre of our line, opposite the trail that led up from the river on to the bank. I thought he was mistaken. Try as I might, I could make out nothing unusual. He had his rifle in his shoulder, but had stretched out his left arm, hand held out with the fingers stiff, together, like a blade.

He put his mouth next to my ear.

'Twelve o'clock, *sersant* – forty yards.'

Damn. Still nothing.

I blinked, looked away, then back again.

I bent my head and took aim along Van Zyl's arm. Then I saw it. It was if the shapes of vegetation along the bank were moving apart, grey shapes splitting and splitting again. My brain finally caught up with my sight and processed the images – people were emerging up the bank, then moving into the open.

Three.

No, four.

Van Zyl turned to me. He was grinning, excited and pleased – pleased he had been the first one to spot the enemy's approach. He held up one hand; five, then five again. And again.

Fifteen altogether, standing in a huddle, right in the centre of our killing ground. The range was indeed about forty metres.

Something, though, was wrong, very wrong. There were no weapons I could see. Three of the figures appeared to carry loads on their backs which they then dropped at their feet, but I looked in vain for the outline of a rifle or sub-machine gun. I heard low voices; they were talking to one another and someone struck a match and lit a cigarette.

Was that a woman's voice? Was I imagining it?

Van Zyl slipped off the safety catch on his R1.

I heard a slithering noise. Josh bumped into me. He was furious, breathing heavily and hissing at me through gritted teeth.

'What the fuck are you waiting for?'

'They're unarmed. They're civvies.'

'Open fire, Sergeant. *Verstaan my?*'

He dug his fingers into my shoulder and shook me violently.

No way. Not without a warning.

I ignored him. I shook him off and raised myself on my knees.

'Hands up – or we shoot.'

The silence that followed – and it could not have been more than a moment – seemed to stretch out into infinity. I broke it once again, repeating my order in Afrikaans.

'Staan still – of ons jou dood maak.'

The figures had frozen, as surprised as the platoon by the sound of my voice.

Firing erupted right behind me, three rounds cracking past my head and making me flinch; Josh had taken matters into his own hands. He was firing into the crowd of human shadows, using his R1 on single fire, two rounds at a time, double-tapping the targets.

At once the LMG on the left flank opened up, firing bursts of three, then the first two sections joined in. I watched the figures; five went down quickly, a sixth moved off to the right, then either took cover or was hit and went down too. Others turned tail and fled for the river, and these were the targets the LMG crew engaged.

Josh was on his feet right behind me, yelling out orders no one could hear, still firing. His blood was up. In the flickering light of the muzzle flashes he looked demented.

The shooting was continuous, ranging up and down our line. The LMG's tracer wasn't necessary to pinpoint the enemy; the targets were so close we could have thrown sticks at them. The entire platoon, except for the reserve section, was blazing away at the human shadows. The bushes shook as if attacked by a sudden wind.

I grabbed Josh's arm, but he pulled away.

'They're civilians . . . cease firing.'

He took no notice. More likely he didn't hear.

There was no return fire.

In less than half a minute it was all over; we advanced cautiously to the bank, but we needn't have bothered. Whoever they were, they posed no threat to us, and never had. A trooper shouted to his section leader; he'd spotted one survivor, clinging to the foliage at the far side, whimpering in pain and terror. It was a woman. It had to be; no man could make a noise like that. She had been hit and at any moment I expected her to be swept away; she couldn't get through the undergrowth on to dry ground and she could not come back this way, across the ford. She was stuck. A trooper put a flashlight on her. Josh raised his rifle and fired twice, taking away the back of the woman's skull.

What was left of her disappeared. I dropped to my knees and threw up my rations.

That changed something. Without being ordered to, the paratroops fixed bayonets; they formed a ragged skirmish line and started stabbing at the undergrowth with their rifles. The mood was – yes, I think I would call it feverish. It was the mood of hounds as they close in on an exhausted fox.

'You've got to stop them,' I told Schuter.

He turned his back and walked back to his scrape.

The sound of moaning, the crying and keening of the wounded, gradually diminished, overtaken by the laughter and shouts of the soldiers as they found one survivor after another and finished them off.

They turned the killing into a game.

Soon there was silence except for the sound of digging.

I went after Josh. He collected his kit, then ordered his signaller to contact company headquarters.

'It's murder,' I told him. I spoke quietly, trying to keep my rage under control, but I was shaking as if I was having some kind of fit.

'Another word from you, Palfrey, and I'll have you on a charge. You'll sort out the burial party and make sure you get rid of that lot.'

It was his coldness, his self-control, his indifference. I lost it. I jumped down into his hole and started hitting him with my fists. I knocked Josh down and jumped on him. I sat astride his chest and kept hitting him. My knuckles were wet with his blood. I couldn't recall later what I'd said. I was dragged off, finally, kicking and shouting, and someone used a rifle butt. I lost consciousness for a moment or two. I realized I had lost two front teeth, the exposed nerve in one making any movement of my tongue extremely painful.

Eight CTs had been killed in action. They were members of the Hintsa Brigade; it was a logistics unit, part and parcel of MK – acronym for the ANC's military wing, Umkhonto we Sizwe, and carried supplies for the main body. That was the substance of the report that went from battalion to brigade and on to army headquarters. The fact that the dead included five women, an eleven-year-old boy and his nine-year-old sister was not mentioned; nor was the fact that there was no evidence that the party was linked to any armed group, and that they had neither weapons nor ammunition. I saw for myself that their pitiful belongings consisted of blankets, cooking pots and a suitcase of clothing. They were squatters seeking a place to live and work, terrified into fleeing their lean-to by the racket of helicopters, the military setting up roadblocks and stop groups.

The platoon was given enough beer for a piss-up and then granted forty-eight-hour passes; Josh was promoted and posted as an instructor to Voortrekkerhoogte to get him out of the way; I was confined to barracks, hauled in front of the battalion CO, given a bollocking, handed an official reprimand, fined three months' pay and reduced to the ranks and shunted off to the quartermaster to spend the rest of service handing out shirts and sheets. I should have been court martialled for assaulting an officer and refusing to obey a lawful command, but they knew it would bring out the sordid details of the massacre and they couldn't have that.

Lawful command? I would have had something to say on that subject.

I can't say I was sorry at the abrupt decline in my military prospects. I had learned an essential truth at first hand. It was no longer a theory: the lives of so-called kaffirs did not count for anything, and the truth did not matter to the authorities, and never had. I shared the guilt for what had happened, my professionalism and pride in setting up the ambush had in no small measure contributed to the murders. I tried to console myself with the thought that I had not fired my rifle – I had had the safety catch on throughout. It was nonsense, of course; the moment I had turned up for duty at the Castle I had signed a blood pact with the authorities. I wasn't fooled; I knew what I was doing, and the Party was just an excuse. If I had really decided not to take part I could have done a runner, fled abroad like so many other draft dodgers. But I didn't do so; I had taken the line of least resistance and as a consequence I was part of what happened. Josh was not alone. He did not shoulder all the blame. I could not condemn him, either. I had prepared the ambush, sighted the weapons, briefed the section commanders, inspected the killing zone in person. At the very least I was an accessory to a war crime.

When it was all over and I was back in civvies, sitting next to Stanko in a borrowed car and reporting all this to him, he was thoughtful for a while. Then he turned to me and told me how hard it must have been to carry that around for all those months. He asked me if I wasn't tempted to publicize the incident back at the newspaper. I said they'd never run it. They'd be closed down. The story would never come out. It would be suppressed. Even if it was published abroad, it still wouldn't see the light of day in South Africa, and that was where it mattered.

I said I owed Stanko an apology, and the Party. I was supposed to be building my cover, not throwing my teddy in the corner like some pathetic liberal bourgeois. I had acted true to my class, not to my beliefs. It had been unprofessional. I had let the side down. If anything, I should have led the massacre and shown myself to be an iron man of the white Right, a defender of the *volk*, a true soldier, loyal and obedient to the hierarchy that placed 'us' over 'them'.

'No, Sebastien. Don't let this get to you. You have nothing to blame yourself for. The Party can use it. We will use it. Those people will be avenged. What you witnessed is a weapon and we will show you how to make full use of it. I make you a solemn promise.'

He stared out of the windscreen at the dark suburban street, both hands clutching the wheel. I swore I saw tears roll down his face. I envied him; I wished I could weep my pity and sorrow to rest.

I thought he meant it would be published in our banned newspapers and pamphlets, but I was wrong. Back then, in 1972, I had no inkling of what he meant, and, in time, Josh and I found it within ourselves to be reconciled, the one to the other, although in my case I had been equipped by Stanko with an ulterior motive that overrode my personal feelings.

That made it so much easier.

What I had no inkling of was how I too would end up with blood on my hands in just a few years, how I would turn killer out of duty and justify my cold-blooded murders in the name of a higher cause.

Just like Josh.

SIX

Breakfast consists of black coffee and we drink it in the same tin mugs we used for our cognac the previous night; to make the bitter liquid seem like a real breakfast we sit opposite each other, the wooden table between us, and we stare out through the salt-rimed panes of the front windows at the sea below. If I glance away over Josh's shoulder and through the open front door beyond, I can check the path up the cliff as far as the road. We do not want visitors; they will only complicate matters for us both.

We both know Josh can't hide indefinitely.

It is just a matter of time before the rest of the world finds out and Viljoen in particular.

The shack itself is all wood aside from the glass windows and tar-paper roofing, and no part of its interior is painted. It is everything a beach shack should be: there are bunks in pairs along the walls, benches instead of chairs and plenty of clutter, including lobster pots, rods, nets with cork floats and belly boards, empty kerosene cans, whisky bottles, black rubber face masks and snorkles, three sets of flippers, tins of fishing hooks and lead weights and a rack of ancient, yellowed magazines and paperback novels, several missing their covers.

Sand blows in from a thousand chinks, up between the floorboards, down from the roof. If the place is left empty for more than a couple of weeks, the sand piles up and makes it hard to open the doors.

I don't know what it is about this place, but it always reminds me of somewhere else, somewhere similar, somewhere familiar, a home the conscious part of my mind can't grasp. I don't know anywhere else like this, that is the trouble. Perhaps when people talk of inherited memory, of a remembering buried in our genes, this is what they mean. It isn't quite déjà vu, more a pang of loss, a yearning for an atmosphere, a presence of someone long gone, an emotion I can't quite define.

Josh tugs a cigarette out of a crumpled packet.

'Want one?'

I shake my head and look at him; with every passing day the sheen of his affluent, protected way of life is worn away, like a mask falling from his face. He looks a wreck, yet paradoxically healthier. His face has regained its colour, but the skin is rougher, the hair wilder and bleached by the sun, the faded blue eyes brighter, even if the skin around them seems more wrinkled than ever. The stubble is turning into a thick, red beard streaked with grey. This is no corporate player; he is part-prophet, part meths drinker on his way down to the very dregs; yet again he is part man, part boy. Here he washes in cold water if he washes at all, there is no skin cleanser or softener, no aftershave, no soft towels, no under-floor heating, no servants to serve the toast and tea, no one to trim his hair, no butler to put out a custom-made suit and Charvet shirt, no air conditioning, no television, no radio, no chauffeur to drive him to his board meetings and City Club luncheons.

He's already lost weight, and the swimming has toned his arms and shoulders.

'I remember you used to live on Lucky Strikes and black coffee, Seb. What's happened? You've become a health freak, or what?'

In a few more days, perhaps a week, he will be unrecognizable.

We both will.

He draws hard on the cigarette and leans back, head up, savouring the moment and blowing smoke rings at the spider webs above our heads. He looks at me through narrowed eyes.

'What now, Seb?'

'Why ask me?'

'You must have a plan.'

'I don't know what makes you think I should have.'

'So what's this, then? A last interview with a fugitive tycoon wanted for his own father's murder? An exclusive for that London comic you write for? Man, don't tell me you came all this way on a whim, out of friendship – old Bishops boys sticking together. For old times. For old soldiers. Please. Don't give me that crap. Not from a KGB hood like you.'

'Something like that, but for the record I was never KGB.'

'Suit yourself. It makes no difference. Call it whatever you want, but you were Moscow's man all these years.'

I am not going to confirm or deny it.

He leans towards me, both forearms flat on the table

top, the cigarette between the fingers of his right hand, and fixes me with his eyes, giving me the famous Schuter stare. I don't answer him. His temper doesn't frighten me. I tell myself it's an act, but instinctively I measure the distance between my left hand and a boathook propped up in the corner.

'So tell me, Seb, what's it to be – a fishing boat after dark? A rendezvous beyond the twelve-mile limit with a Panamanian freighter heading out to Maputo – or is it Melbourne?'

I shake my head.

'What do you want? Is it money? Is that it? Did she put you up to this?'

'She?'

'Frances. Or Zak?'

'Oh, Christ, Josh. Don't be a bloody fool. Is that what you think?'

He is paranoid. He thinks we've ganged up on him, in a conspiracy to rip him off, and that his dad somehow got in the way.

'You tell me, man.'

'There's nothing to tell. You don't seriously think Frances and I planned all this—'

He strikes the table with his fist.

'You know who killed my father. We both do. So does Frances. The only people who don't know are the cops.'

'I don't know what you mean.'

'The fuck you don't.'

The solitude is turning his mind.

'I think you'd better explain.'

'We all killed him,' he shouts, flinging the words at me, flecks of white froth gathering in the corners of his mouth. 'We might not have held the knife to his throat, but we did it. I did it. You did, too. And Zak. So did Frances. I don't say he didn't deserve to die, the bastard, but not like that. Not – not humiliated. What they did to him was terrible. I am guilty, just like they say, but so are you. We all had a hand in it. Don't you see?'

He points an accusing forefinger at my face. 'You want to know, Seb? You really want the truth? Do you? Then I'll tell you, and when I'm finished you can fill in the missing pieces, my *rooinek* friend, because you know a bloody sight more than you're willing to admit. I know you do and I'll prove it to you – and then you can fuck off out of here and crawl back into whatever miserable hole you came from. You were always a secretive bastard, but this is one secret too far.'

'You remember Whitey's Place, don't you, Seb? That's where I think you first met Zak. Maybe you don't remember. We're talking 1969 – maybe '70. It was a shebeen a few blocks from the Argus School in downtown Jo'burg. Nice place. In those days, blacks weren't allowed to drink "whites'" alcohol, but this place was really humming. The woman who ran it was called Mercy and she was paying off the cops, but it didn't last long. There were too many cops, and they got too greedy and Mercy had to disappear.

'There weren't many survivors from those days. Drugs, alcoholism or John Vorster Square accounted for most of the clientele sooner or later. Anyway, there we were, at the bar, surrounded by pissed black artists, musicians, journalists, and there he was, grinning at us rookie reporters – Zakaria Wauchope.'

I listen. I remember.

'He was quite the man about town. I remember what he was wearing when we both met up with him – he had on this wide-brimmed fedora, he was speaking his *tsotsi-taal* out of the corner of his mouth, and he was using a cigarette holder. He was the Godfather and Damon Runyon all in one; he had on a loud Hawaiian shirt, all palm trees and blue sea and yellow-haired girls. He was playboy and hoodlum, press photographer and artist, pimp and dealer in Colombian marching powder.'

How could I forget? To a white kid from the suburbs, it was all so exotic that any critical faculty was quite numbed by the shock of this other world.

'He carried a shiv and a marked deck. He was what anyone wanted him to be – gangster, card sharp, freedom fighter – you name it, he was it. I remember the look on your face, Seb, and he saw it too. You were impressed but trying to hide it behind that snooty, stuck-up expression you English like to hide behind when you're faced with something a little odd, something beyond your experience, something scary.

'And I could see why you were nervous. Until you went on that course you thought of blacks as "them" – anonymous beings quietly queuing up at a separate window in the post office, dark faces at the back of the bus, the kids playing in the dust at the side of the road.'

Who wouldn't have been scared?

It is just not something I'd want to admit, especially not to Josh. So I say nothing, and Josh continues.

'They weren't really people, now, were they? Just a fuzzy background. They were the quiescent masses who shined your shoes, laid the table, cooked your breakfast, made your bed, polished the silver and cut the lawn, then vanished at night back to whatever shithole they lived in out in the *gramadoelas*, Guguletu or Langa, Alexandra or Sophiatown. Right?

'And there you were, in the midst of them, and fuck me, they're human after all. They're all talking at once, shouting to be heard, they're smoking *dagga*, popping dexedrine and drinking like the world's about to end. You'd suspected as much, but this was for real.'

And what of Frances? God, the exhilaration, the arousal, the sudden self-consciousness, the fear of rejection as she moves past me, the scent she leaves in her wake, her head held high, her proud smile, that V-shaped back, the swimmer's shoulders, the long thighs.

Such longing.

Oh, Africa!

I am daydreaming, and Josh brings me back down to earth.

'What a surprise, eh? You could smell them, touch them – in that crowd we were wedged in pretty tight – and hear them, oh, boy, could we hear them, and they took no notice of a couple of whiteys. Shame on them – the cheeky kaffirs showed us no respect. They couldn't have cared less.

'This was social equality. The great taboo. *Gelykstelling*. Admit it, man, you were asking yourself whether you really liked it after all. Maybe it was just a little too real, a little too scary, even for a textbook Red like you.

'No, don't fucking interrupt. Don't tell me you were a snivelling little liberal with your values straight out of the Reformation and the Enlightenment. Keep it for those books you used to read. Keep it for those shirt-lifting

Anglican priests at Bishops. This was for real, pal. Be honest: you were nineteen and momma's little boy and you were shitting yourself.'

I stare back at him. I'm not going to let myself be intimidated by this ritual display of male competitiveness – the flexed arms, the shoulders pushed forward, head down, glaring at me from under the thatch of Viking hair.

'Still don't remember?'

It's a snarl.

Who do you think you are, Josh?

You don't have a monopoly of recollection, of feeling.

But I say nothing. I don't move as Josh leans forward.

'Now I'll tell you something, so pay attention. Zak had said he wanted to meet you. It was Zak who suggested we visit Soweto. It was Zak who arranged our programme – the football, the Green Door, the shebeen in Orlando. Oh, yes. It's true. And it was Zak who saved your ass when we were arrested – yes, mine, too. And maybe, watching Frances and me snogging on that sofa while that other chick was trying to get you to join her outside so she could give you a blow job, maybe you thought that was just a coincidence. Wrong. That was Zak's doing too. He fixed Frances up on a blind date with this rich white boy, and he had – what was her name? Jesus, I forget – arranged one for you. Constance. That's it. It was Zak's way of making us feel welcome, at home so to speak. There was more to it, and I suspected as much at the time, but I thought, what the hell. You only live once. Put it down to experience. Live a little. I didn't care what Zak's game was. I should have, but I didn't. I was having too much fun. My only concern was that I didn't have any protection and I was scared stiff of catching a dose. But then Frances was one hell of a woman. She was only seventeen, and she wasn't putting on an act. She wasn't some two-bit tart, either. She wasn't going to put out that night, or the next. It was weeks before we went to bed together, finally. Bet you didn't know that, did you?'

I clench my fists under the table.

Damn your patronizing mouth.

Damn you altogether.

'We fell for each other. No question, Seb, no question at all, man, it was love at first sight.

'Sure, I was being used. So was Frances. But that's life, isn't it?

'We all get used one way or another. The key is to know it.

'Am I boring you? Let's get out that brandy you brought. We'll drink it with what's left of the coffee. Sure you don't want a smoke?'

I shake my head.

'I'm quite happy to admit it, man; I wasn't thinking straight that night. I was thinking with my dick. Hey, we were kids, right? Old enough to fight, sure enough, to fuck too. Fucking and getting stoned was about all I did think about in those days. But kids all the same. It was my mistake and I take full responsibility. It was the start of my troubles, only we didn't know it back then – and I don't think I ever told you, did I, that I'd known Zak a lot longer than that, and that Zak had us in his sights right from the start?

'Not just me, Seb. You too. He wanted you.

'You were the fucking prize.'

Congratulations, Josh. You took your time, but you got there in the end.

I'm just surprised it took so long for you to understand.

Josh returns to the table with what's left of the cognac; there is about a third of the coppery liquid left. He holds the bottle by the neck and slops a generous measure into our mugs, setting the bottle down between us. He hesitates, as if he's forgotten something, putting a forefinger to his lips.

'Wait a moment.'

He vanishes behind the partition that separates the living area from what there is of a kitchen – a basin and a couple of cupboards. I hear banging and shuffling and a couple of four-letter expletives, and Josh returns with a dusty box-file. He drops it on the table.

'Something I want to show you.'

He sweeps the dust off with one hand, releases the spring that holds the cover in place, and pulls out a leather pouch and puts it to one side; I can tell from the way he holds it and from the thud it makes on the table that it's heavy, and I know at once what it is.

He shuffles through the envelopes and files and pulls out a sheaf of papers held together with a metal staple. He holds it up, stares at it a moment, then flips it over to me, drops the cover back in place and sits down heavily.

'Go ahead. Read.'

He lifts his mug and drinks, then turns to the pouch, unfolding it and sliding a small black pistol into one palm. He releases the magazine out of the butt, clears the breach, squinting into it to make sure it is clear, and puts it down.

'It's a 6.56 mm Mauser,' he says. 'German naval officer's sidearm, and it's got the eagle and swastika engraved on the inside of the butt to prove it – see? I nicked it from the old man some years ago. Still works a treat, though not accurate at more than about twenty metres. It was a gift from a U-boat commander who surrendered at the end of the war and whom my old man befriended. They had a lot in common. Aryans and all that.'

He continues to talk, but I'm trying to concentrate on the pages in front of me. The document is typewritten on a manual machine, and the ink has faded. The paper is cheap, a dull grey colour. It is also official; each section is stamped and someone has initialled each page. These are, yes, depositions. Witness statements. I catch the word Palmiet and another phrase – female survivor.

The date is 24 August 1973.

'You get it now, do you?'

There are seven signed and initialled statements, all witnessed by an attorney of Williams and Mathers Pty Ltd of Port Elizabeth. I know where Port Elizabeth is; it's a dull little dorp on the Eastern Cape coast. It is more than that, of course. Port Elizabeth was one of the first towns where a black workforce organized itself to fight against the theft of their land, and in the face of segregation laws.

Joshua says, 'It's one of three originals – that is, it was typed up three times, each signed and witnessed.'

'And the other two?'

'Ask Zak.'
I read aloud:

Irene Toomi, aged 47, widow.

They came in the night with dogs. They wore masks and hoods. They had askaris with them. They asked for my husband. They pushed me and our two children into one room and then they found my husband under the bed and they took him outside and I could hear him screaming. They beat him with a metal rod and a bicycle chain. They were shouting at him that he was a terrorist. They wanted names of other terrorists. I ran out and they caught me and beat me and pushed me inside the house again. He was on the ground and they stamped on him. They stood on his head. They came back again to the house and one of them, a white man with a gun, said we must leave at once. The place we were living was not our land. It was illegal. We had to leave with the others. Then they set fire to the house, and we left, running. They used petrol to burn down the hut and the two other huts. My husband was dead. They would not let me go to him. I tried. They chased us away with the dogs. I saw two other bodies. They were neighbours. Then we all left on foot. It was very dark and they told us to go south. I did not know where south was. We had the clothes we were wearing and my daughter had a blanket but nothing else.

I say, 'So there were survivors, after all.'
'Read it all.'
'This has been happening all over the country, Josh.'
'Read it.'
'I'd get rid of it if I were you.'
'What do you care? Read it.'

**Thomas Ketli, age estimated as late 30s,
labourer.**

We reached the river they call Palmiet and I
showed people where the white man's cattle
crossed to find pasture. We walked along the
bank until we came to a path the animals had
made down to the river. The water was cold and
came up to our waists. We held hands to cross
over because the water was strong. We stepped
on the stones that lay under the water. We did
not know how to swim. Some of us had some
clothes and pots and blankets and they wrapped
their things up in the blankets and tied them
to their shoulders or put them on their heads.
There were sixteen of us, including nine
children. Once we crossed we said to each other
we would rest on the bank as best we could
until it was light and we could see where to go.
So we put down our belongings and some of us
lit cigarettes and others looked for a place to
lie down to try to rest, though we were wet and
cold and had nothing to eat. We decided to give
the blankets to the children to share. We were
talking quietly and then we heard something

and a voice called out just in front of us. The voice told us to stand still or they would shoot. This was said again in Afrikaans. We were surprised. I stood still and raised my hands but right then the shooting started. Some of us fell down. Others tried to cross the river but were shot. I saw my neighbour's little girl. She was shot in the water. The river took her away. I hung on to the bank under the bushes, just my face out of the water so I could breathe. The shooting went on and then stopped and the soldiers used torches and when they found someone they shot them or stabbed them with their bayonets. I knew they were soldiers because I saw them very close to me and they wore uniforms of soldiers. I heard crying in the darkness and the soldiers were laughing, saying they had found a kaffir. There were more shots and then it went quiet. The soldiers buried the bodies and their few things. I think they wanted to hide the evidence. I stayed there as long as I could and then I came out of the water when the soldiers left. I saw no one else alive.

I thought I was the only survivor.

I read all seven statements, but the last, the shortest, is the most affecting.

Alice Ngika, aged 9.
When they shot us I lay down and shut my eyes. My uncle picked me up and told me I must

be brave and hold on to him. He put his arm
round me and ran to the river and jumped in and
told me to stay on his back. It was deep and the
water was very dark. It was night. The white
men were shooting. The shooting made a big
noise. The bullets hit the water. The bullets
made lights over the water. I held my uncle
round the neck. He kept close to the bank, under
the bushes. He swam like this [breaststroke]. He
told me it was all right. He said I must help
by kicking my legs in the water. I wanted to
know where my mother and father were. I wanted
to go back to find them. But I couldn't let go. I
was scared. We swam into the night, away from
the shooting. My uncle kept swimming for a long
time. I was cold and wanted to sleep. I miss my
mummy and daddy. The soldiers killed them.
The policemen burned our home, and they
chased us with dogs and the soldiers shot my
mummy and daddy. They didn't do anything
wrong. They killed them because they were
black. I am black. I think they will kill me,
too. I dream of the white soldiers with guns.

Josh stares down into his mug. The bottle next to him
is empty. He doesn't speak; he waits for me. But what
can I say to my old friend who was also my enemy? I am
no priest; I can't offer him absolution. What can I say that
each of us has not, separately, told ourselves? That he
didn't cover up his crime sufficiently? That these depositions were gathered by people looking for ammunition to
use against him and his kind? That I deflected him from

his purpose? That I was to blame not just for bringing dishonour to the unit, the paratroops, the ethos of the South African Defence Force, but for diverting him from the task of finding and silencing all the survivors? Is that what he blames himself for? For the incompleteness, the sloppiness, of his crime?

Memory is comforting, but not the memory of a child's murder. It is murdering the future. His and mine as well as the victim's.

His fault was not killing, but failing to have killed enough.

Is that how he was looking at it, even now? Or perhaps I should tell him there are different kinds of guilt, that he isn't to blame because he was only obeying orders. There is the political guilt of politicians and senior commanders who approve such activities, and Josh isn't one of them. There is the criminal guilt of those who carry out their orders, and, yes, perhaps those depositions are a prima facie case against Lieutenant Joshua Schuter, platoon commander. Then of course there is moral guilt for those who don't act to stop what they know is happening. Well, in that case, we are all guilty, all of us with white skins. How many years passed before we finally woke from our self-absorbed indifference and did something? Perhaps that is how I can tell it; that we are all in this together.

No one is innocent.

You see, part of me wants to offer some comfort; another to raise my hand and slap his ugly face. To spit on him. To wrestle that little Nazi popgun out of his meaty, freckled hand and press the muzzle against his ear and squeeze the trigger, ending the Schuter line for all time, blowing those bloody X and Y chromosomes of his all over the walls.

I do none of those things; I push the papers back over to him.

'How well did you know my father?'

'I met him a few times. When we were boys.'

'Up at the house in Bishopscourt?'

'Yes. Once at the farm, I think.'

'What did you think of him?'

I shrug. What am I to say? That I envied Josh for what had then seemed a normal family life, with a mother and father and a fashionable home; that I saw Cris Schuter as a hero figure. That the swordfish and those sporting trophies had impressed me even if I learned to deride them later. His laid-back manner, that day he cleaned his Purdeys and let me handle them – hell, as a kid I thought he could no wrong. What did I know about the Land Act, the Suppression of Communism Act, Section 10, the Group Areas Act and all the many legislative instruments of racist dispossession and repression?

Nothing.

I was a cuckoo of a child, wanting to nest in homes better than my own, more comfortable, lighter, prettier, larger, more affluent, where the grown-ups were smart and beautiful and kind, and seemed to love children and perhaps would love me, too, and I could forget my own name and who I was, who my own absentee parents were, forget my mother's shameful illness, our relative poverty, my reliance on grandparents for everything I needed.

No wonder espionage turned out to be my vocation.

'You know how my dad made his money?'

'I heard it was in the wine industry and then banking.'

Josh smiled. 'Seb, that's what he wanted you to think.'

'So?'

Josh starts to explain by saying that under apartheid the state had intervened heavily in the economy, to the detriment of growth – something I already know. He says that by refusing to let black and Coloured people get a decent education, industry was starved of the skills it needed, especially after the boom years ended in 1973. The country had virtually no machine tool production – something else I know – and manufacturing fell behind South Africa's competitors. The country's share of world trade shrank to nothing. State monopolies were created. The wine business, Josh says, was no different. It was dominated by the Ko-operatiwe Wijnbouwers Vereeniging – KWV. They established quotas. They limited the wine to chenin blanc – they called it *steen*. They relied on a shrinking domestic market for sales. It was a recipe for self-destruction.

'Do you remember any of this?'

'No,' I lie. 'I think I was overseas, but go on.'

'No one was buying our wine abroad – not just because the quality was poor, but because of the race issue and because of sanctions. So my father, who was on the KWV board, organized a sanctions-busting exercise, sending the wine abroad in bulk and relabelling it as produce from Chile and Portugal. That's how he made his fortune. He took a commission. He was bringing in hard currency, and he made big profits in a shrinking industry. So the authorities turned a blind eye when he started breaking

KWV rules by producing pinot noir and chardonnay, and by focusing on *terroir* – the issue of soil and location for planting different varieties; he was breaking all the rules – and he was making money.'

'I'm impressed.'

'Bullshit – you're not.'

'I am, Josh. He was smart as well as cynical. He built his fortune while wrapping himself in the flag. He had no illusions. He knew what he was.'

'He was a patriot – at least to his mates in the Broederbond.'

As Josh says, how else would he have succeeded? In those days everything was run by the secret society, from banking to rugby internationals. But there is more. Josh's father wasn't a national socialist like some of his comrades: he hadn't studied in Germany in the 1930s as so many in the leadership had. No, he wasn't a philosophical racist. But he earned the reputation of a firebrand because in his youth he'd joined the OB.

'The Ossewabrandwag.'

Josh says that, like a lot of young Afrikaners, his father joined because he supported the Nazis against the British, whom most Afrikaners saw as their main enemy in those days. He was seventeen. The OB had their own Fascist-style militia with uniforms and armbands, and they waged a guerrilla campaign against the Allied war effort. And like many others, Cris Schuter was locked up during World War Two. Josh said the differences between OB members and Afrikaners who supported the Allies could be compared to the rivalries between the Zionists of the Palmach and the extremist Irgun. The distinction was lost on Palestinians – as it was on the black majority.

I know about his war record, but I'm not going to interrupt.

'Interned – like Balthazar John Vorster, the man who was to become one of our most *verkrampte* prime ministers.'

'So where's this leading?'

'I'm saying my old man was a complex character. Like most people, he was both good and bad. He couldn't be pigeonholed as left or right, reformer or racial purist. For the ANC and their allies, of course, he was the enemy.'

'You're telling me his murder was political – is that it?'

'I'm trying to say that at one level he was a modernizer, at another level a traditionalist. You've heard of the "dop" system?'

Josh says wine growers in the Cape paid their workers partly in cheap wine – 'dop' as in 'tot'. They were drunk most of the time and many were alcoholics. Infant mortality, always high, was even higher in the vineyards because of the impact of alcohol on the fetus; it was called fetal alcohol syndrome. The farmers believed the 'dop' kept the workforce pliant if inefficient. It went straight back to the era of slaves. Cris Schuter was no different. Josh says he remembers the flagons of cheap white wine, and the drinking that went on in the workers' cottages.

He has my full attention now. 'You mixed with them?'

Josh gazes out of the window, remembering.

'I played with their children, sure. You see, Seb, that's how I knew Zak. His mother was one of our household servants. I remember her. She was young and pretty. Her name was Clara. She was nice to me. She sat me on her lap and told me stories. I was very fond of her. It was before I went to boarding school. It was around the time you and I met. When I was on the farm Zak and I played all sorts of games. We had catapults for hunting and we swam in the dam and went fishing. We spoke Xhosa to each other and we played war games, too, only they were re-enactments of the colonization of the Cape. I played a commando leader – usually Piet Retief or Cilliers, and Zak always played the Xhosa leaders who fought a long resistance war against the settlers – either Maqoma or Hintsa. Until my father told me I couldn't see Zak again. He didn't say why. Something about him not being suitable company. I didn't listen, of course. When my dad was away or busy, and that was most of the time, I would seek Zak out. Like you, he was a good friend, full of mischief and daring. He taught me to track game, to lay traps, and I let him shoot with my air gun.'

Something in my memory stirs.

Viljoen's question in the hot sunshine.

'I didn't know.'

Not true. I remember the brown boy.

'One day my father found me in our house with Zak, playing with my toy soldiers. My old man had given me a puppy when I was very young and now it was nearly three years old. I was very fond of it. I called it Voetsek, a name everyone disapproved of. The rule was that I was never to let the dog in the house, but this time he was there, too, playing with us. My dad lost his temper. He took his *haelgeweer* – his shotgun – and ordered me outside on to the stoep along with the dog. He carried it by the scruff of the neck. It was a King Charles spaniel – you know the breed, I think, quite long ears and thick fur – and he asked me if I knew the rule and I said I did. He asked me if I remembered what he'd said about Zak –

Zak was there, too, listening – and I said, yes, I remembered. What was it? I said I was forbidden to play with my friend any more. My father said he would teach me an important lesson – to follow orders. Then he put the gun to Voetsek's head and pulled the trigger. He fired both barrels. There wasn't anything left of the dog's head. At first I didn't believe what I was seeing—'

'Josh—'

He shakes his head.

'You know the farmhouse. It's beautiful. It's built in the traditional Cape Dutch style by Malay artisans. Out front are the jacaranda trees, carpeting the street in flowers. The floors are wood throughout, and the ceilings are very high. There are a couple of feet of clay above the ceiling for insulation and the long sash windows help keep the breeze moving through the place. When you open the huge front door you can see straight through the door out the back that leads to the garden and the great clouds of purple bougainvillea spilling over the walls. The house is warm in winter and cool in summer. At the rear, on the way to the servants' rooms, there's a brick bench, plastered and whitewashed, and you can see the indentations made by the rings that held the chains of the slaves. The rings had gone and so had the chains and the slaves, but I used to think I could still feel their presence.

'It should have been paradise on earth, Seb. It wasn't, though.

'I had some kind of fit. They took me to the doctor and he prescribed pills. Someone told me years later they were tranquillizers. In those days that's how they used to treat kids for depression, apparently. It was about a month or so after this incident when Zak and his mother disappeared. Clara didn't come to work as usual and I went to their cottage – it was just one room, really – but they'd gone, taken everything with them. No one in the servants' quarters would tell me anything, and certainly not the truth. They dared not. I looked everywhere. I searched the whole farm. I asked everybody. I saw suspicion and distrust in their faces. I didn't think then it was because I was a white boy and the son of the master, a man with their lives in his hands. I wouldn't have understood their hostility and fear, not then To me Cris was like nature – the natural order of things, like the wind, like fire.

'Clara and Zak – I grieved for them.

'It was like a secret, something bad. I thought they were dead, like my own mother, and like Voetsek. In my childish mind, I couldn't think of any other explanation. After that, I didn't go to the farm much. I lived in the new house my father built at Bishopscourt and you became my only friend. I learned to play English games, with English heroes, but I was always the Boer. I was General Botha, or Cronje, or Reitz on a commando raid.'

Josh picks up the bottle, puts it to his mouth, tips his head back and finishes the last few drops, then wipes his mouth with the back of his hand.

I have to give it to Viljoen; he has set the hares running, and his suspects are interrogating themselves and each other as he knew they would and I see now what he meant by the choices we make and live by.

'What you have to understand, Seb, is my sense of failure.

'See, I always loved my father; I looked up to him, I

wanted to be like him. I didn't judge him and I certainly didn't condemn him for what he did to me, my dog or to Zak and his mother, Clara. I thought I must deserve it. I wanted so much to be strong like him. I couldn't be, you see. Strength is what we Afrikaners are all about.

'Power. Power of the masculine kind. Power on the rugby field, in battle, in business, in the bedroom. Godlike power. But it wasn't in me. I didn't have it. I felt a failure. Stupid? Of course. The way he looked at me, I knew he thought so too. I felt guilty; I felt I had let him down by failing to come up to his standards. I didn't deserve his love. It wasn't that he was violent and cruel – it was that I wasn't cruel enough. I wasn't indifferent to suffering and that meant I wasn't manly. I blamed myself. There was something wrong with me – not with him, you see.

'It must be the brandy talking, because I've never spoken of this to anyone, not even Frances.

'Can you understand, Seb? Can you really?'

SEVEN

I leave behind my biltong and chocolate to augment Josh's peculiar diet of burned pancakes, sea urchins and abalone. My step is lighter; I carry a good deal less weight on the return hike.

The moment the train rounds the bend in the coast, past Glencairn and coming into Fish Hoek, my mobile starts to ring. I have several messages: would I contact the foreign desk? Would I be in a position to work up a thousand-word profile of C. Schuter for Tuesday's paper? And could they have a tight update on the murder inquiry? Was I able to visit the townships to gather first-hand colour in time for a Saturday Review piece? All very polite; that's the way editors ask their reporters to put their necks on the line for a few column inches of newsprint to fill the space between the ads for mobile phones and hardwood flooring.

At least I can console myself with the thought that I am needed. A journalist who takes a couple of days off and returns to find no one has noticed must know his star is in danger of total eclipse. And then of course there are two brief calls from Viljoen, and one from Mabaza, both asking me to call back urgently. It will all have to wait.

*

Flashback; a memory undated. Unusually, Frances and I were alone.

She took my hand in hers. A strong hand, its grasp firm, palm to palm. Her long fingers curled around mine. She held me tight. She was close; our faces not more than six inches apart. Those basilisk eyes peered at me, gauging me, excavating my dark places. I was so close I could pick out the little ridge of skin that ran around her full Cleopatra lips, the light burnishing those Nilotic cheekbones and long, straight nose, the prominent chin. I thought: she's flawless. I could smell her – I breathed in her peppery, sun-warmed skin. Chanel, too, if I wasn't mistaken. A gift from Josh.

My heart was on full automatic fire, trying to burst its way out of my chest.

'Hey, white man.'

I was speechless. Dumb.

'We are friends, aren't we, Sebastien?'

'Of course.'

We'd polished off a bottle of Chardonnay and I could feel it.

She shook her head, frowned.

'No, not like that. No. I mean, really.'

'Really.'

'Really? Say what you feel. Try not to be so English.'

So white.

I nodded, petrified like a deer caught in the middle of the road, immobilized in the headlights of an incoming car. Desire rose in my throat. I had the most awful ballsache. It was sheer frustration. She smiled as if she knew.

'I need a friend, white boy. A real friend.'

I said nothing.

'I'm a woman, Seb. Friendship is important to a woman. A woman can have a deep friendship with a man, but I'm not so sure that a man can do the same. Young men – all they think about it is sex. I know how you think you feel about me, Seb. You are in love with my womanhood. With my being black. With my being African. You are crazy about Africa, I think. It is – what you call it – a passion. An obsession. Yes? You have a crush on a continent, not me. You don't love me. It's not possible. You don't know me. You know you don't have to be jealous. No.'

She placed a finger on my lips. Don't talk.

Mention of the word jealousy brought the colour to my face.

'Now I am offering you the chance to learn who I truly am by being my friend. Yes. It's true. Don't look so disappointed. I want your friendship, Seb. I don't think you've really known a woman before. Not like this. Can you give it to me? Can you – can you be my trusted friend?'

She threw an arm around my neck and pulled me even closer, our foreheads touching. I wanted to grab her.

There was only one thing I could say, for God's sake.

I wanted to say no.

You know what you can do with your friendship.

But I didn't.

She'd got my dick in the wringer, all right.

Yes, I said. Yes, of course. Yes.

It came close to costing me my life.

The unmarked car is still there in the street; I turn tail and make for Greenmarket Square instead, clearing my back en route, and find the photographer's shop in Plein Street; the name is emblazoned in blue neon on a yellow background: Zak's Studio. It's smarter than I imagined, with an automatic door and air conditioning, recessed lighting, chrome and black leather, glossy foreign fashion magazines scattered about and a receptionist with long black hair, kohl and gold bracelets busy painting her nails a deep pink.

She raises her head, inspects me with a chilly glance and goes back to her nails, announcing that Mr Wauchope is out and not expected back today. I can leave a message or make an appointment. I keep going, smiling at her and moving on past the counter and a series of Zak's best pictures, tastefully enlarged to poster size, framed and hung on the brick walls. I take the stairs two at a time down to the basement. I rather think she smudges her nail varnish because she looks none too pleased, jumping up and almost knocking over her swivel chair. I hear her punching numbers on her silver phone and announcing my imminent arrival.

What would Comrade Dr Stanko make of Zak's emporium now?

There is a vast seascape on one wall, on the other a brass-framed mirror, topped by a crescent. A stinkwood desk dominates the far end, and there is more leather and chrome.

Zak is on his knees on a Turkish rug in his shirtsleeves, his waistcoat undone, his jacket left on the back of his executive chair.

At first I think he's ill; then I realize he's performing his noon prayers; he is just beginning the first cycle of prostration, or rak'ah. He gets to his feet, ignoring me entirely, and raises his hands to the level of his shoulders. His hands are open and his fingers almost touch his ears. It's a gesture of tolerance, of submission.

'Allah is great.'

He puts both hands on his chest, right hand over his left, the act of a penitent.

'You alone we worship, and to You alone we turn for help.'

Not Marx or Lenin. Not any more. Well, I never suspected Zak of being susceptible to any religious thought or feeling. He bends forward from the hips, back straight, leaning on his hands, which reach down and clasp his knees.

He is muttering, but I can't make out the words.

Then a gruff voice, right next to me, speaks for him, making me start.

'Glory be to my God and praise be to Him.'

Zak straightens up. I see him glance at the doorway.

'God listens to those who thank Him, O Lord, thanks be to you.'

The man standing just behind me is entirely bald, and he wears a white skullcap. He's a good foot taller than me, and very broad. His expression is deadpan. Then he moves past and joins Zak. He looks like a weight-lifter or wrestler. He wears a loose cream shirt down to the knees of his baggy pants – the shalwar kameez favoured by many Asian Muslims, from Karachi and Kabul to Gujarat and Dhaka.

'God listens to those who thank Him, O Lord, thanks be to You,' they say in unison, and both men get down on their knees. They bend forward, rumps in the air until forehead, nose and both hands are touching the prayer rug. No other human posture expresses such humility.

This is not the Zak I remember; this isn't the kid in faded shorts, the wide boy in the fedora, the guerrilla cadre or Zak of the flat cap and mirror shades behind the wheel of a city cab, decanting Frances on to the pavement, or tipping a homeless, glue-sniffing street kid to deliver the pathologist's autopsy report on Schuter.

'Glory to my Lord, the Most High; God is greater than all else.'

They kneel again.

'O my Master, forgive me.'

Down once more – forehead, nose and hands on the floor.

They sit back.

'Peace be with you and the mercy of Allah.'

Zak struggles to his feet and comes over to me, smiling broadly, his fingers doing up the buttons of his waistcoat.

'This is Omar, head of my close protection team.'

'*A'salaam Aleikum,*' I say.

'*Wa'leikum Salaam.*' Omar nods in acknowledgement, but he does not offer his hand, or smile. He stands behind his boss, watching me.

'Since when did you need protecting, Zak? You seemed to manage pretty well on your own, if I recall.'

He laughs without humour, leading me by the elbow over to one of the leather armchairs.

'Make yourself comfortable. Tea? Coffee?'

I sit.

'When did you convert to Islam?'

Zak puts on his jacket, then sits behind the desk, shoots his cuffs and places his hands together. 'I had a religious experience.' Why is it that I don't believe him? He repeats the question. 'Tea or coffee?'

'Coffee.'

'You've caught the sun. You look as if you've just come from the beach.'

'I have.'

He looks sleek and well-fed. He keeps pulling at a double chin as if it will help make it disappear.

'And how is our mutual friend?'

Something in Zak's face tells me I shouldn't mention Josh by name.

'As well as can be expected.'

'If you didn't look so healthy, Seb, I'd say you'd turned into a beach bum.'

'Thank you.' I smile. I refuse to take offence.

'Omar, it's okay, man. He's a friend. A *rooinek*. It's true, man. I've known this *Engelsman* for more than twenty years. He's a rascal like me. You can go. I won't be long.' Zak turns to me. Omar hesitates. 'He'd like to frisk you. He doesn't trust anyone, particularly infidels of European descent. And he's totally loyal. One hundred per cent.'

I say, 'That must be reassuring.'

Zak nods again at Omar, who leaves, giving me a last threatening look as he goes through the glass door on his way to the stairs. Zak presses a button on his desk and speaks over the intercom.

He is more at ease, I feel, without Omar's presence.

'Fatima, two coffees, please.' He puts one small, brown hand over the mouthpiece. 'Sugar?' I nod. 'Both with sugar. And bring some of those almond biscuits. My friend here is starving. *Dankie*, Fatima.'

'Know who she is, Seb?'

I shake my head.

'That's my wife, man. Her family's Muslim. That's what I meant by a religious experience.' He grins, revealing two gold crowns. 'She's expecting our first, a boy.'

So he's converted out of love, or to ally himself with a Muslim family, or both. I'm relieved; there's something rather unnerving about faith in a divinity, at least to me, and particularly on the part of a hard-case leftist, news photographer, former *skollie* and Resistance hero.

I pull myself up out of my seat and go over and shake his hand.

It's soft and plump, a pen-pusher's paw.

'Congratulations. I didn't know.'

'Thanks, man.'

'Since when did you need bodyguards, Zak?'

'It's business, Seb. It's going very well, and the better it gets, the more some people seem to resent it.' He opens his hands and raises his eyebrows, still smiling with his mouth while his eyes remain wary.

'It's a precaution, that's all.'

He reaches for a silver box on his desk, takes out a cigarette and lights it with a massive desk lighter.

'Smoke?'

I shake my head. 'I never associated fashion photography or running a cab company with high risk.'

Zak shuts his eyes, puts both hands in the air like someone surrendering.

'Okay. Look. It's like this. The cab company runs itself. So does the studio. I have six cabs and I have four full-time drivers and two full-time photographers. But that's not what I mean, okay?'

Zak gets up, goes to the door and closes it. Josh was

right – Zak has put on a lot of weight. His suit looks like a lightweight mohair and silk affair; he wears what appears to be a Rolex. His shoes look Italian and he has on a black poloneck under the jacket. Always a snappy dresser, Zak exudes a certain kind of wealth, the conspicuous kind beloved of footballers and nightclub owners.

I'm sure the Wauchope dustbins would reveal a large number of cash receipts.

'So what do you mean exactly, Zak?'

'Did you know – ' he settles himself behind his desk again – 'did you know that at any one time only six per cent of our wonderful South African police force spends any time investigating crimes like murder, robbery, burglary, muggings and the rest of it?'

I say that presumably the other ninety-four per cent have been pursuing the likes of Zak and myself as part of their Total Onslaught against international communism, Jewish bankers and terrorists.

Zak doesn't think it funny.

'Right now, Seb, this country is knee-deep in cheap heroin and cocaine. The Russian mafia have got into bed with our local gangs and it's a sweet deal for both sides. The drugs are paid for with cars stolen to order and then shipped out to places like Sydney and Melbourne. The cops haven't a fucking clue. They're stupid. So there's a huge need for security, both residential and commercial, and I saw it as an opportunity for a little private enterprise—'

'You run a protection racket, in effect—'

'Jesus, Seb, do me a favour. Cut me some slack. I'm a businessman, all right? I'm married, and there's a kid on the way. I've settled down. Forget all that other stuff. It's over. I see a niche that needs filling and I provide a service. So I make money. What's wrong with that? I've got the contacts—'

'And the skills,' I interject.

The smile fades and is replaced with a pained look.

'What is your problem, Seb? I did my bit. So did you. Now it's time to look after number one and get a life. Security is the country's only growth industry. It's perfectly legit. In fact, I could do with some help. There's more than enough work for all of us. Quite honestly, I can't expand fast enough. I need an English-speaking sales manager, preferably white, someone reliable to deal with these city types, someone they'll respect, someone who can talk their talk, knows about wine and books – not some kaffir off the farm like me. If you've ever thought of giving up the newspaper—'

I cut in. 'What's this got to do with your having bodyguards?'

Zak stubs out his cigarette with more vigour than is strictly necessary.

'Some people don't like the fact that I'm in a position to protect prominent citizens and their interests – I'm taking bread out of their mouths. So they tell me. That's how they see it. They don't like the fact I have armed fast-response teams – and believe me, they are fast and they don't mess around. They're good boys, and they're all well trained. Ex-Comrades, many of them. They get the best pay in the business, and I issue them with Heckler & Koch sub-machine guns, Glock pistols and Kevlar body armour. Quality. We're a class act, Seb, believe me. So I've had a few warnings – enough to take them seriously.'

'And Frances? Where does she fit into all this?'

The words aren't out of my mouth when the office door slides open and Mrs Wauchope appears, carrying a tray with two coffees and a plate of biscuits. Zak introduces us. Whether she's heard my question about Frances I can't tell, but when she gives me my coffee and offers me a biscuit and a paper napkin she doesn't seem at all pleased to see me again.

'Give him the plate, Fatima, darling. I don't think our friend from the press has had a square meal in weeks.'

I'd known what Zak did in the Struggle, but only in the most general terms. On only one occasion did we team up for a specific task, and it was not something either of us was keen to revisit. I wasn't supposed to know much. He was MK, and at some stage had commanded an SDU, a self-defence unit, the MK's basic tactical fighting unit, responsible for attacking the enemy, for defending the home turf – usually a township or sector thereof – for seeking out informers and destroying them. It required balls, self-discipline and a certain ruthlessness, an ability to handle young toughs itching for a scrap; leadership, in other words, and the resolve to enforce rules of one's own making. To do it well, and to survive, required a sixth sense, an acute awareness of danger. The secret police became very skilled in penetrating SDUs, at soliciting the *impimpi*, at using coercion to start the business of betrayal which, in less well-organized units, worked rather like dominoes: Dirk cracks and gives up Jack, Jack betrays Pieter, who gives up Andries, who fingers Bert and so on, until the whole sorry bunch have been turned, their weapons caches seized, their dead letter boxes and couriers compromised; and they are used to work against other

Comrades, the infection spreading its poison of fear and distrust until, of course, Jack, Pieter, Andries and Bert outlive their usefulness and can be picked up at leisure, and, after the usual assault and battery, sent to the Pretoria hangman who used to string up seven in a row, side by side, every week.

Aside from Zak's initial overture, his introduction to the good doctor and that single operation, we'd kept well away from each other. He was military. I was intelligence. The two never did mix. Except the once. Bangs and skulduggery play havoc with a spy's task. The agent needs tranquillity, he needs an opponent at rest, at his ease, his guard down. He needs empty streets, not police patrols, helicopters, flares, roadblocks and cordon-and-searches.

We Communists could be faulted for a great deal, and we have emerged from the twentieth century not as we saw ourselves, as liberators, but written into history as oppressors, executioners and false prophets. Nevertheless, we always had one incontestable strength: our security. We were hard to break. Zak might have deduced that I worked for intelligence, and that my initial targets included the Schuter family, but no more than that. Our lines of command were entirely separate and there was nothing to link us save for those two meetings; the first in Soweto and the second at Dr Stanko's safe house – unless our entirely circumstantial cover roles in the media were taken into account, and why should they have been? Even so, we quickly went our own way, and I lost track of him.

There was just that time in the Swartberge.

What had Josh said? Something to the effect that he had been aware that night in Orlando that his first meeting with Frances was no coincidence, that we were both in some way set up by our host, Zakaria Wauchope.

'That evening in Orlando, Zak. The first time Joshua met Frances, and I had my little misadventure with Constance. You remember?'

'Sure I do. It's a long time ago, but I remember. Constance wasn't so much a misadventure as a lost opportunity.'

He waits. He plays with his cuffs. It is safe to speak of such things now the new Mrs Wauchope has left us, but he doesn't look comfortable.

'Did you fix us up with those two girls?'

Zak grins. 'Hey, is that what's bothering you? What's Josh been saying to you?'

'I just wondered.'

'I might have asked them to come and meet a couple of white boys.'

'That's all?'

'Sure. What else?'

'Was Frances going out with you back then?'

'I wouldn't put it quite that way.'

He purses his lips, curling his mouth down at the corners, puts his palms together and raises them to his face. He's hiding something.

'How would you put it, Zak?'

'We were seeing each other. I was helping her with her career. Introducing her to people in advertising and so on.'

'So you were her boyfriend and her patron.'

'Hell, what is this – an interrogation? We went together,

maybe a couple of times. And yeah, I was her first. So what? What are you trying to tell me, Seb, that I was jealous of Joshua Schuter when he and Frances got together? No way, man.'

He shakes his head, his expression solemn.

'You don't get it, do you? I wasn't going out with anyone, as you put it. I'm not the possessive kind. In those days I was young and I had money in my pocket and people looked up to me. Word got around that I was ANC. You know how it works. I could pretty much choose any girl I wanted to, and once I had a decent set of wheels it was a different one most weekends. So what? I wasn't into wedding bells and all that shit – not then. I had no claim on Frances.'

'So it didn't bother you.'

'You crazy? Why should it?'

'But she must have learned a good deal of what you were doing.'

He shrugs. 'She helped out. She was a courier. For a while.'

'You told her stuff?'

'Nothing important.'

'Pillow talk.'

'If you like.'

'You weren't worried she'd pass it on to Josh?'

'A security risk? She was too low level to be a problem.'

'But she told him you were MK and I was SACP.'

'Is that what she says?'

'It's what Josh says.'

Zak raises his eyebrows and grimaces.

As if to say, what do I care?

'So what can I do for you, Seb?'

'Can you tell me where I can find her?'

'Frances? You know where she lives. In Observatory.'

'She's moved out, Zak. I checked.'

'I tell you what. You tell me where your friend Josh is, and I'll help you find Frances. How's that? We got a deal?'

'I promised Josh I'd find Frances and take her to him.'

'You spied on the Schuters, but you don't want to tell your old comrade-in-arms where that rich white fucker is? You're a little confused, Seb, aren't you?'

'Somebody's after him – and I don't mean the cops. They're the least of his worries.'

Zak places a hand on his own chest.

'Man, my heart bleeds for the Boer.'

'You can do better than this, Zak. Josh told me you warned him to get out of town and lie low a couple of days before his father was killed. Maybe you didn't know Cris Schuter was going to be murdered. Or maybe you did. You knew something, for sure. Then you popped up with a stolen report on the killing which you presumably intended me to pass on to Josh. So tell me. Where do I find her? It was you who dropped her off outside Minetti's only last week for a meeting with Josh that never happened.'

Zak sighs, shakes his head wearily.

'Didn't anyone tell you, Seb? Joe Slovo declared an end to the armed struggle. Wasn't he your boss man? MK's Chief of Staff? A Communist like yourself? Yes? I thought you commies were disciplined, obeyed orders. Yes? Something wrong with your hearing? Or is it your sight? It's over, you hear? It's finished, Seb. It's time to get on with life.'

'I don't go round wearing mirror-glasses and pretending to be a cab driver and sidling up to the rich and famous at art galleries and giving them advice about their personal safety.'

Zak raises his voice. 'Hey, she called the firm and asked for a cab and I took the job.'

'And what was that all about with the kid and the autopsy report at the railway station?'

'What did you want me to do, Seb? Walk right up to you in broad daylight with the cops watching and hand over a stolen document?'

'The cops weren't there.'

'You were being watched, Seb.'

'They weren't cops.'

'Whoever.'

'So why take the trouble of giving me a copy?'

Zak doesn't respond. He takes a pen out of his inside jacket pocket, tears off a strip of paper from a notepad on the desk and scribbles something. He's got quite a paunch and it's between him and the desk. The lean-jawed young guerrilla with the shaved skull and designer stubble in black T-shirt and jeans with the fighter's alertness has given way to comfortable middle age.

And yet . . .

I am down to my last card. 'I think you're fighting your own very private war, Zak. Question is: who for? Old Comrades like us are supposed to wait for the Truth and Reconciliation Commission to sort it out, not take matters into our own hands. And I'm including you and me that morning in the Swartberge. You remember that, don't you, Zak?'

He knows only too well what I mean.

He rises to it as I hoped he would.

'And you think, do you – ' he smacks the top of the desk with a palm – 'that the other side is going to sit nice and quiet – ' he smacks it again – ' and wait for this commission, do you?' Smack. 'Then we can all be pals again.' Smack. 'One big, happy, multiracial family.' Smack. 'Is that how you think it's going to be, Seb?'

The open right hand curls into a fist.

'You tell me, Zak. Didn't I just hear you say the war's over?'

But Zak doesn't answer. I've struck a nerve. He just holds up the yellow slip with a telephone number and waits for me to get up and walk over to the desk and take it from him.

I've exhumed a past he wants buried for good.

Just as Viljoen intended.

He won't make eye contact. He looks away, past me, at the wall.

I go back to my chair but I don't sit down. I pick up the last biscuit and put it in my mouth. I watch him while I chew and swallow. I empty my coffee cup, still watching him.

The interview is over.

It isn't rational; I know the sensible thing to do is to answer those messages, go home, clear up the mess and start work. Instead I go straight to a payphone – one of the few still working – and call the number Zak has given me; there is no answer and no machine to leave a message on.

I still don't go home; I believe the term psychologists use is displacement activity. I call it instinct, and on occasion it has saved my life, or I like to think so. My

211

instinct tells me to waste a couple of hours, and I do so by taking a walk such as a tourist might make through the city centre.

It isn't just irrational, it isn't even a conscious decision, but I check every dead letter box I've used in two years. I look for emergency signals. I certainly don't expect to find anything, and I don't know what I'd do if I did, so I don't honestly know why I bother. It sounds stupid. All I can say is that it's part of our natures; some people shop when there's nothing they need, others drink more than they should even if it makes them ill, or they pig out on a chocolate bar despite feeling guilty. Old spies hunt for traces they know aren't there.

We all do things that don't make any sense.

I do it by the book, mirroring all the way, doubling back, leading my imaginary shadows a merry dance. I begin in Plein Street, strolling past Parliament, turning left on to Wale and into Bree, a right this time down to the Strand and a right and a left into Long Street. This is backpacker and busker territory; I rest my feet with a toasted sandwich and beer at the Long Street Café and watch the crowds of young people coming and going from the bed and breakfast places.

I make another call; still no answer.

This time I drift from St George's Mall to Greenmarket Square and the Old Town House and its collection of Flemish art and antiques; not my taste, certainly, but with a sense of purpose I head through the cool interior for the central brick courtyard and the giant pots of lavender. Pretending to read a street map like a careful tourist, I sidle up to the clay pot in the north-west corner and put my back to it, sliding a hand down among the plants, feeling with my fingers in the earth for anything hard, metallic, perhaps a little rusted.

Nothing.

Up through the Gardens next; I sit on the first bench on the left-hand side of the gravel walk, watching the squirrels and passers-by, mostly office workers heading for the concrete eyesore of a rail and bus station. I put my left arm up, resting it along the back of the bench, feeling with my fingers for three drawing pins – but they aren't there.

Three, close together, would mean a demand for a meeting.

I get up and stroll towards the Mount Nelson Hotel where the wealthy gather among the hollyhocks for cucumber sandwiches and tea each afternoon. Just where the path divides into four I turn left, towards the National Gallery; on the corner is an immense oak which was probably planted by van Riebeeck's men; after all, this was the original garden that provided the Dutch settlers with their greens. I look up at its wide girth vanishing into a profusion of leaves.

Nothing there, either.

The trail has gone cold.

Is it really all over?

No sooner was I elevated to the Central Committee with oversight of all intelligence-gathering than the war came to an end. It was a huge relief, for the higher the Party post the greater the risk of betrayal and assassination. I was as surprised as anyone by the sudden turn of events: the Afrikaners were a truly remarkable people; they surrendered while still undefeated on the battlefield, handing over a state apparatus damaged but still intact, still powerful, still dangerous.

Is there anything comparable in history? As an example of intelligent self-interest on the part of an entire nation, of realpolitik, it has no equal.

None I can think of.

No one gives up power voluntarily.

It broke all the rules of class warfare. Marx would not have approved.

The Berlin Wall came down, the Soviet Union imploded and we were unbanned. So much for the march of history, the victory of the proletariat.

I tell myself I'd better get used to the capitalist peace.

It is time to go home.

I've cleared up enough of the mess to be able to work. I have replied – in the affirmative – to the rag's several messages, and am summoning up the courage to speak to Viljoen and Mabaza, when Frances calls. As I put the phone to my ear I peek through the blind.

I think she's using an outside phone, certainly not her own. She doesn't give her name, but I know it is her. She doesn't say much.

The car is still there.

'We need to talk.'

'Yes, of course.' What I need is eight hours' sleep in my own bed.

'Along with George.'

'George?'

'George's place, okay? At seven.'

She rings off. Frances has not given me much time. It is already six-forty. What on earth does she mean?

I pull on jeans and a short-sleeved shirt, grab my keys, drink some water and try to think. I leave a light on in the hall, push my feet into a pair of black loafers and lock the front door behind me. Only when I'm outside, on the step and staring at the car, do I realize where she means us to meet.

I'm late; evensong had already started, so I sit at the back. Frances is sitting on the opposite side, well forward. It's the usual multiracial congregation, no more than thirty or forty people, the majority women of a certain age. They call St George's Cathedral, at the top of Adderley Street, right next to the entrance to the Gardens on Wale Street, the People's Cathedral because its doors stayed open to members of every community throughout the apartheid years. Five years ago, Desmond Tutu, the first black Anglican archbishop of South Africa, led 30,000 people to the Grand Parade, signalling the beginning of the end of the white regime.

Frances goes through the motions, getting down on her knees to pray, rising to sing, opening and closing her mouth and holding her hymnbook in front of her; is she playing a role, trying to merge with the devout? It occurs to me I have no idea whether Frances is religious. As for me, I don't bother to pretend. I stay seated.

We are the last to leave, waiting until everyone has passed out of the doors except for a young cleric who's extinguishing the candles; he smiles at us as I wait for Frances by the font. Perhaps he thinks we are lovers of the new rainbow nation. I'm happy to oblige him: I take Frances's hand and we hurry to the door; Africa's sunsets are brief, and the city is bathed in the final golden glow of a dying day.

'Where to?'

'You're in danger, Seb. All three of us are.'

'What are you on about?'

'We have to talk – but not here.'

'Fine – you want to eat? There's a new place on de Waterkant—'

She shakes her head. Frances is scared, looking around her constantly, as if afraid the lengthening shadows might hide an assassin. Nobody pays us the slightest attention; the last of the commuters hurrying home wear that mask of indifference that a lifetime of routine brings. I feel invisible, and my mind goes back to the student protests on the cathedral steps thirty years before. It was about the same time in the evening that, as a local reporter, I was roughed up by a trio of neo-Nazis, forerunners of the grotesque AWB or Afrikaner Weerstandsbeweging.

Now it's so quiet it is hard to believe anything could be amiss.

'Come on.'

She waves her arm at a passing taxi. He slows and we run down the cathedral steps and jump in the back, Frances getting in first and sliding across the seat to make room.

I've forgotten how tall she is.

'Tafelberg,' she tells the driver. Her anxiety is infectious; for a moment I think it might be Zak behind the wheel, but one glance at the eyes looking back at me in the rear-view mirror is enough. It would have been too great a coincidence, after all.

From Firdale we enter Kloof Nek Road, with Signal Hill on our right and the mountain on our left. The road takes us up above the city, and, before it dips down to Camps Bay on the far side, we turn left into Tafelberg. The road twists sharply into a hairpin bend and then I recognize the lights of the lower cable-car station just ahead.

This time Frances grips my hand and squeezes it.
Just like old times, eh, Frances?
We're going up to the top of Table Mountain.

The round car rises vertically, then tilts and swings forward into space, nothing but night between us and the
city below, the pale line of the surf breaking on the shore,
the grids of streets, the fireflies of cars crawling home-
wards along the coast road, then the dark torn open by
the lights illuminating the amphitheatre of rock. The cables
stretch out ahead, curving away and down and vanishing
into the cliff face; only at the last moment do we seem to
avoid a head-on collision with the mountain by rising
steeply, feeling the tug of it under our feet. The floor
revolves on its own axis, so one moment we hang out
over the city, the next the rock face sweeps past, so close
we feel we can reach out and touch the roots and ledges
as we are drawn up.

We are the only passengers; it is the last trip. We'll have
forty minutes on the crest before we have to descend at
nine p.m. when the cable-car system shuts down for the
night. As we step out on to the mountaintop, Frances
shivers. I don't think either of us thought about the abrupt
change in temperature three thousand feet makes, especially
once the sun has set. In her pink, short-sleeved cotton
dress, she must feel the difference.

'Do you want to sit inside?'

No, Frances doesn't.

There is a large rest house with a bar and café – a poor
attempt to render an alpine hut out of concrete.

We find a flat rock and sit side by side. To our left lie
the Twelve Apostles, clear now of the mantle of cloud that

usually shrouds the peaks by day; directly in front of us the huge vista of southern ocean goes on and on to the vast, limitless horizon; closer, to our right and between our feet, lies the city itself.

Frances hugs herself.

'I love it up here. It's the only place I feel completely solitary. To think it was here all that time and we couldn't come up here. Even the mountains were *slegs blankes*.'

I wait.

The air is cold and clean on our faces. The stars are of a brilliance I've never known. We can see for hundreds of feet in all directions; there is no need for a torch. Just in front of us the plateau of mountaintop that gives it its name falls away abruptly; now I have some sense of what it must be like to be an eagle or seagull, though I suppose it is something birds take for granted, without thought, a physical, instinctive freedom.

'Seb—'

She slides her arm through mine and moves closer for warmth.

We lace our fingers together, and I think of all the years I've wished for such a moment. Now it doesn't seem to matter.

Frances laughs.

'What is it?'

'Look.'

She means her feet. She wears pointy pink shoes that have straps, little buckles and three-inch heels – fine for a cocktail party but hardly appropriate for wandering around Table Mountain. He expression changes and she turns to look at me. She isn't laughing any more.

'Seb, this is a difficult thing for me. I want to talk to you.

I don't know if I can trust you, but I have to talk to you. I do know that if I can't trust you there's no one in this world I can trust. We used to be good friends, you and I. We had a pact. Remember? I know there's a hell of a lot I don't know, and even more that I don't understand, but maybe if I tell you my story, you will see I'm telling you the truth and trust me enough to take me to Josh, because I know you've seen him. You have, haven't you, Seb?'

Her voice is deep, husky.

'I promised Josh I would,' I say, quite flustered. I still don't know whether to be annoyed or pleased, so I end up, as usual, confused. 'I mean, I promised him I'd take you to him.'

She gives my arm another squeeze.

'Seb, I'm sorry. You always had feelings for me. You were always kind, always the English gentleman. I didn't always appreciate it. I should have. Looking back on it, I know now how difficult it must have been for you back then. I'm truly sorry. I just know we don't have much time left and I do love him so very much – despite everything.'

She leans forward and I feel her cheek against mine.

Her lips brush my ear.

Desire creeps out of its pit and crawls away again, ashamed.

Did she say despite everything? Everything? Everything is so much. Too much. I wonder if Frances has any idea just how much it includes.

Like murder, for instance.

219

EIGHT

'When we met, the three of us, for the first time – you remember, Seb, don't you? It was in Soweto, and it was no accident.' She notices the expression on my face because she says, 'Yes. Of course you do. The other girl, Constance . . .'

It's a long time ago, but still a little embarrassing, and I don't like being reminded of it, least of all by Frances.

'Poor thing, Seb, she drank too much.'

Frances watches me carefully.

'God,' she says, 'it's so long ago it's as if I was someone else entirely. My former self. Your former self. Memories like ghosts, Seb, they haunt us and keep popping up when least expected. You probably guessed, I don't know, but I was there because Zak wanted me to be. That's the truth of it.'

I sense her awkwardness, the tension in the way she holds herself. I sit quietly, face in neutral, waiting. She says she didn't just happen to be there. She didn't simply turn up. Oh, no. She hadn't been in the habit of visiting shebeens at night, not even in Orlando. She wasn't that kind of woman. Zak had wanted her to go out with him that evening, and Frances had agreed.

'I was with Zak back then, Seb.'

'You mean,' I say, 'you were sleeping together.'

I try to sound matter-of-fact, disinterested.

Frances says she was living with him. Am I disappointed? I shake my head. Of course not, she says. It's too long ago to be shocked, and we are too old for surprises. We've both seen too much. Not under the same roof, mind, but all the same, Frances says, she was what some people would call a mistress. How would I put it?

I stay silent.

A kept woman, Frances says, adding that she isn't ashamed of it.

Maybe, she adds, breaking eye contact, she should have been.

'Seb, I owed him so much. I don't say I loved him, then or later, but I looked up to him. I respected him . . .'

She goes on to say that she saw Zak as her protector, the father figure she never had. A lot of women wished they could say as much about their husbands, so it wasn't all bad. In traditional African society, well, I know how it is, and that's where she came from. It was what she was. You don't get a choice. It was a matter of bride price.

They were better than married. They were friends. Frances could talk to Zak. He was a good listener, and he gave her sound advice. He never took a hand to her. Zak was one of those men who was good at giving someone practical advice, but not very good at taking it himself.

I interrupt to say Zak was always a terrible risk-taker, but Frances isn't listening.

She says she had her own place, which he paid for, and he would visit whenever he felt like it. But he always called first. He respected her privacy. He wasn't unattractive in those days, and he was generous with money, when he had it, that is, and they'd go out and have fun. He made her laugh, he made her feel special. Men didn't seem to realize the way to a woman's heart and into her bed was laughter. Zak knew. He was a charmer. Life with him was never dull. How many married people could say that of their partners? He had lots of friends, some of them gangsters. Frances didn't care. He helped her career. That was the important thing. He introduced her to people who could help her, and because of who he was, what he was, they agreed to help. Frances thought that in some cases they'd been afraid not to, but she didn't know that then – not at first. Or perhaps she just didn't want to know.

This is still painful for me, more than she'll ever know. But I have to hear it – all of it. I have to know. I've listened to Josh, and have squeezed a good deal out of Zak.

Now it's her turn.

Frances says Zak was the first man she had sex with. He didn't force himself on her. It wasn't rape. She wanted him. He was gentle. She was fifteen the first time. Old enough – many girls lost their virginity a lot earlier; Frances was lucky, or so she says. It is taken from them in most cases, not given freely.

'He cared for you,' I say, and she nods enthusiastically.

'It mattered to Zak how I felt. He had enough experience to know what a woman feels, what she should feel. If I'd said no at any stage he would have stopped. He wanted me to want him. You're thinking: she's been taken advantage of. No. Not at all. I knew what I was doing. My eyes were open. I made the choice. There's no blame. I became one of those loose women they talk about back where I come from. The women my mother talked about; she had this image of painted, seductive creatures with white people's ways who take the men's wages, who flaunt themselves, get their hooks into some decent, simple working man so he can never send money home to his family, never go home himself. Don't think I didn't know all that. I lay awake thinking about it, but I made up my mind.'

'It's okay,' I say. I take both her hands in mine.

She doesn't seem aware of me at all. 'That's what happened to my dad, you see. That's why I ran away from home in the Transkei. I went to the city to find him and bring Pa home. I had no idea of Johannesburg, how big it was, how impossible the task I'd set myself was. I was the eldest of three girls. My mother couldn't feed us all. We had no man in our home. There were no sons. We were left on the margins. We had no – how do you say – weight in the community. Do you say weight? Influence, then. My father left when I was nine or ten and to begin with he'd send wages home. Not regularly, but it kept us going. Then it stopped completely. Nothing came. No word.'

Her mother had been a proud woman and she'd tried to instil some of that in her children. She used to tell Frances stories of the old days. She'd said her daughter's great-grandfather used to be quite wealthy; he'd been a farmer, what I'd call a share-cropper. As a black man he wasn't allowed to own his forefathers' land, his by right, by custom, by blood, so he'd rented from a white farmer, and he'd done well. Then, even renting land and working it was outlawed by the Boer government. If you were black.

They'd become serfs, and finally the family's only wage-earner disappeared.

Her father.

They were a people who'd gone downhill, though it wasn't their fault. Their land used to be rich and green and covered with cattle. Now it was dust, cut by big *dongas* – gullies. There was no grass. All this brought shame as well as poverty. Frances vowed to go after him and confront him and force him to come home or at least send them money again. She wanted to shame him.

I think: it was probably shame that forced him to leave in the first place, but I don't say so.

She left when she was fourteen. She ran away, and left a note.

As the eldest, Frances tried to be the son her parents had never had.

'To this day my mother places her bed on bricks because she fears the *tokolosh* might be hiding underneath. We worship our ancestors. The spirits are always telling us what to do. They are with us. They are our shadows, they follow us, guard us, protect us and advise us. The spirit world is real to us – good spirits and evil – as real as anything you can see and touch. That is the world into which I and my sisters were born. It's our culture. You call it magic. You white people laugh at us and our beliefs because you don't try to understand.'

Not me, Frances. I'll never laugh at you.

Of course she couldn't find her father. She worked as a maid in a house in Parktown, then Houghton, looking after two white children: a nanny. She sent back a few rand every month, but it wasn't nearly enough. She was very unhappy. Lonely. Then Zak found her. He told her she was beautiful, that she had presence, that she could make a career for herself as a model. She could build up her own business, become financially independent.

He was persistent. He wouldn't take no for an answer.

I could well believe it.

Frances believed him, too. She'd wanted to believe him.

He kept his word – he introduced her to people in the clothing and cosmetics business. She started work as a photographic model and began to send home some real money.

He ran the business side for Frances. He negotiated for her.

He encouraged her to sit her Matric and study by correspondence.

Zak bought her flowers, perfume.

He helped her choose clothes and shoes.

Oh God, Frances. I don't want to hear any more.

She says no one is all good or bad.

Yeah, sure.

'By the time I met you and Josh I was seventeen. I was still taking Zak's money and going out with him, but less often, and I was earning enough to pay my own way, even then. I was studying, too. I felt I owed him loyalty and gratitude. He made me feel safe, though I knew what he was, and I knew what I had become. Because of that I could never go home. Perhaps in his own way, that's what had happened to my father.'

She says she and Zak were still good friends. They respected each other. They made their own rules. Zak had never said to her: here are two white boys and I want you to give yourself to one of them because he's the spoilt son of a rich Boer.

Of course not, I agree, nodding my head.

'He'd never do that. He knew I'd refuse.'

We believe whatever we want to, Frances.

She says that when she met Josh something happened to them both. Josh knew it and so did she. It was thrilling. What they were feeling – and later what they did – was illegal. Frances thinks the illicit nature of their relationship only added to the attraction they felt. They were so very different. There'd been a sense of wanting to explore a forbidden land, forbidden bodies, forbidden souls. To Josh she was uncharted territory. Years later, she says, he told her he'd been worried back then that he wouldn't rise to her expectations, that he wouldn't perform to her satisfaction, because, he'd said, he knew black men had much bigger dicks than white guys and maybe if she'd seen his tackle she'd have laughed.

Thank you for that subtle insight.

Frances says Josh measured up pretty well, in fact, but then she'd only ever known one other dick, and that one belonged to Zak.

Enough already.

To Frances, his red hair, his blue eyes, his soft white skin belonged to a strange being, and the ambitions and expectations he had to a world away from her own.

She was curious, too.

Frances made Josh wait. She decided she wasn't going to sleep with him for a long time. There were white men, she knew, who thought they could have any black chick they wanted because they were poor and didn't know better except to say 'Yes, baas' and spread their legs for every white prick who looked at them.

Not Frances.

'I knew Zak wasn't faithful. Not that I expected him to be. He went with other women. I knew that. He didn't tell me, or introduce them to me. He tried to be kind, to make me feel special, but Zak just wasn't the monogamous type. I don't know any black men who are, to be honest with you. I've heard of some, men like Mandela, but they are very special people. It takes a very special man to love just one woman, Seb. For us women, loving is all too easy, and that's the burden we bear. We are trapped by our biology.'

She looks at me, trying to weigh my reaction.

'Zak didn't ask me if I was sleeping with Josh.'

So what did he want?

What Zak had asked Frances to do was to befriend Josh, gain his confidence. He hadn't suggested how she do this, and Frances is of the view that he didn't want to know how she did it. Zak wanted information about the Schuter family, especially the father. Where they lived, how many people lived in each place, how secure it was, how many servants they had and who they were, their names and so on.

'Zak told me I would be serving the Cause.'

Now we are getting somewhere.

Frances agreed.

'Why am I telling you my story, Seb?'

'Go on, Frances. I'm interested.'

'I don't think there's one reason. There are several. I felt for a long time you disapproved of me, Seb. I felt – I don't know – it was just a feeling, that you thought I was doing a bad thing by being with Josh. I felt you despised me. No? Perhaps I was feeling guilty because you and Zak were so involved in the Resistance and there I was, a model, making money and having an affair with a rich white friend of yours – on the enemy side – and you were taking all these risks.'

It was envy, but never mind that now.

'I also want you to understand, Seb.'

'Of course, and I want to understand.'

'That's okay, isn't it? I'm not boring you?'

I'm loving every moment. Carry on, please.

In time Zak told Frances many things about Josh's father. She says she realized that while she could give him small details – the type and registration number of the car the old man used, where his gun cabinet was, the unlisted telephone numbers of his homes and private office lines, that kind of thing – he knew so much more about what Schuter, the father, was doing, his secret life. Zak was getting all this from somewhere, secretly. From the Comrades.

Zak must have realized at some point that Josh and Frances were together. He didn't say anything. Zak and Frances had become more business partners than lovers and weren't so intimate. They'd grown apart. Or maybe, Frances says, she'd just grown up. Zak was deep into politics, and he was involved with the Youth. The ANC. It became his life. Zak was powerful, but always in danger from the Security Branch. He was on the run much of the time. He had to sleep in different places. It was a dangerous game, and it went on through the seventies, when the secret killings started, and the eighties, when the Boer repression was at its height.

'He'd ask me to try to get Josh to invite me to the farm,' France says. 'He wanted details of Josh's movements, his activities, and his father's. Zak wanted to know the layout of all the Schuter properties. Could I get into the South African Broadcasting Corporation headquarters in Johannesburg? The old man was some kind of special adviser there. But I couldn't help. I tried, but I couldn't get inside.'

The modelling business was going well and Frances did travel, so she used to meet Josh at his family's home in Cape Town – yes, that was right, Bishopscourt. She only went once to the farm, and she did visit the house in Stellenbosch, but again only for a few hours, and in secret.

Then it all fell apart.

'One day Zak said to me I would have to choose. This came after an argument. He was upset that I had not spent more time in Franschhoek, or got more of the information he wanted from the Schuter winery there. He'd wanted details of the combination locks and copies of keys. He said I was in a dangerous situation, playing both sides. It would not be understood, and who would believe me if I were to say my association with Josh was really a cover for spying on behalf of the Resistance? He said I could be hunted down and hacked to pieces by the Comrades if it was known I was sleeping in the bed of a Boer like Joshua Schuter. I'd be accused of being a collaborator, and, worse, a white man's whore.

'I replied that I had chosen. Wasn't I collecting good information? Hadn't he asked me to do so? Didn't I work as a courier, meeting an agent in a café, taking them on the bus or train to the next agent? Or choosing a safe house on the pretext of being a purchaser? Looking for places with two entrances and exits, on two streets, preferably a corner, and on the edge of town. You know this, I think, Seb. Zak said you were smarter than you seemed, and knew more than you let on. He likes you, you know. But he's a little afraid of people who are quiet. No offence. Anyway, I tried to convince him of my loyalty, of my dedication.'

As Frances had spoken the words, she said, she'd known it was a lie.

She had chosen, but not the way she'd told Zak. Not the way he'd wanted her to choose. She couldn't help herself no matter how hard she tried. She says she thought then that he'd guessed, but he didn't say anything.

'You think he's a crook and a killer. Many people think that. Of course Zak changed, Seb. We all changed. The Struggle changed his personality. The fun went out of him. He was colder, more calculating. Zak said I must prove myself, again and again. He had a test for me. He had orders, he said. From his people. It was my chance to show my devotion – and my courage.

'You weren't around, Seb. I think you were in England. I couldn't refuse – even though it would finish what I had with Josh.

'It would destroy him.'

We break off while Frances finds her cigarettes and lights up.

'We have to go back a bit,' Frances says. 'This was when Josh went into the army. You did military service too; at least I remember that's what he said. Something bad happened, though he didn't tell me. It was afterwards when Zak found out through his Comrades. He said it was information that originated with a white Comrade in Joshua's army unit. He didn't know the details. He used to say very little to me about his political work, but because I was part of what he was planning, he had to let me in on a bit of the background. I think it was around 1971 or 1972, I don't recall exactly, but Zak had this information of a massacre by soldiers under Josh's command. This was intelligence he had received from outside the country. The incident occurred in the Cape, so Zak compiled a dossier of evidence. He sent people to the area to find survivors and get depositions which were witnessed and then he had the dossier copied and the originals kept with lawyers who were sympathetic to the Struggle.'

Frances had read it. She says all she remembers is that some squatters were chased out of their homes in a raid by the Security Branch and forced to flee – they crossed a river and were shot down by soldiers. The soldiers were commanded by a National Service lieutenant, a paratrooper. Josh. There were several witness statements, and Zak found a soldier who swore an affidavit that Josh was his commanding officer who had initiated the slaughter.

Her job was to get a copy to Josh and another to his father.

'You see, these rich white people are surrounded by servants and assistants and people who try to keep the unpleasant things from them.

'How do you say it? Protective.'

Zak told Frances he wanted her to plant the dossiers where both Josh and his father would find them. She would report back on the initial reaction; Zak's people would then decide how best to exploit the situation – by blackmailing one or both of the Schuters, or by leaking the material abroad and discrediting the father by implicating him in a cover-up of his son's crime.

That would have been my task.

The goal was to neutralize Cris Schuter's political effectiveness.

Spot on, Frances. That was it exactly.

Zak told her the old man was too well guarded to try an assassination.

But it didn't happen.

Cris Schuter found out that Josh was having an affair with a black woman.

'Me,' she says, and sucks at the cigarette before flinging it into the night.

It was a routine security check carried out by the cops because of Cris Schuter's prominent role; he was a leading Broederbond member and he was an adviser to the SABC, the main propaganda tool of the white government. He also had another very secret job Frances didn't know anything about and which only came to light much later. So from time to time security checks would be made on the old man's different homes, his associates and family members.

She turns away and stares off into the darkness.

'The first thing Josh knew that anything was wrong was when he noticed he was being watched and his phone was being tapped. He was followed everywhere. His flat in Cape Town was watched twenty-four hours a day, and wherever he stayed, the same thing happened. His mail was opened. His homes were searched.

'I couldn't go near him.

'Josh thought they didn't know about me and he was anxious to protect me as much as possible. Because I was black and a woman I effectively had no rights at all. They could bundle me in a car and take me out of town and do whatever they wanted and no one would care. No one with the power to do anything about it, anyway.'

So the plan to plant the documents misfired. It was postponed.

Their separation gave Frances time to think. She said she was still very busy with her own business, but she knew she had to make a decision about Josh and Zak.

Frances lowers her head, resting her forehead on her forearms. She bends forward like someone praying.

We're almost there. This is what I've been waiting for.

When she speaks again, it is with a muffled voice.

'I chose Josh over the Struggle, Sebastien. I chose a white man over my commitment to the liberation of my country and my people – and yes, I'm ashamed of it. I was ashamed of myself then and I'm ashamed now. I keep telling myself what I did was the human thing to do. I could not give him up. I just couldn't do it. I loved him. I knew I could not just turn my back and forget him. I wanted Josh more than anything else, no matter what. At any price.

'God forgive me.'

For what seems to be ages she doesn't speak or move.

I put out a hand and touch her arm. I'm all sympathy.

Frances raises her tear-stained face and looks at me.

'I was a love-sick fool. I still am, I suppose.'

About three months after it started, she says, the sur-veillance stopped as suddenly as it had begun. Cris

Schuter called his son to the farm and told him that if he did not end his affair with the kaffir girl, he would be disowned. He would inherit nothing. He was a *kaffirboeti*, a kaffir lover, a *kommunis*, a debauched creature who did not deserve to carry the family name, disloyal to the *volk*, the country and to his own kith and kin.

'The old man had a police file on us.'

Recordings, photographs.

'They shouted at one another. Cris raised his fist, and they started wrestling with each other. Rather than hurt his father, Josh stormed out of the meeting, calling his father a racist and a fascist. That's how he described it to me.'

I say, 'I'm truly sorry, Frances.'

She plays with her cigarette lighter, turning it over and over.

'I sometimes wonder, Seb – and I know it's terribly unfair to someone who was so good to me all those years – whether Zak didn't tip them off about me and Josh. I had to wonder because, let's face it, my affair with Josh was almost as effective as a massacre in driving father and son apart and discrediting the family. It wasn't just fucking across the colour line and breaking the Immorality Act. It was more than that – and that's what they could never forgive: a white man and a black woman having feelings for each other. Lust is one thing, love something else entirely.'

No, Frances, it wasn't Zak. You're close, but it wasn't him.

It was me. I'm the bastard. Your Judas.

All it took was a phone call and a paragraph on the

gossip pages of one of Britain's meretricious tabloids, and the story was out.

I let the moment pass. I say nothing.

Frances says Josh reached a crossroads.

He had to make a decision, too.

Frances says she told Josh everything.

She told him about her relationship with Zak, how they'd met, what Zak did, his role as an activist, his interest in the Schuter family, and how he'd used her to spy on Josh and his father, and how willing she'd been not just to serve the Resistance, but to have a good reason for seeing Josh again and again. She told Josh she'd fallen for him almost from the first moment. She warned him that Zak knew about an incident involving Josh in the army – an incident in which a number of civilians had been shot down, murdered, by soldiers under Josh's command.

She told him the kinds of small things Zak was interested in: the layout of the house, where the safe was, the combination to the alarm system, the location of the guns and ammunition on the farm. How he wanted to discredit Cris, how Frances was to have planted material on the massacre in their homes in such as a way they'd both find the evidence that had been compiled.

'I told him all of it, Seb. All of it. Everything.'

She gave Josh Zak's code name: Maqoma.

'I could see the shock on his face. He did a very good job trying to hide what he felt, even to himself, but it was there, I could read it in his expression. He was badly shaken.

'I told Josh that you were an important Communist, Seb.'

I shiver, but it isn't the mountain air.

Josh was right all along.

She'd blown my cover, and Zak's, just the way he said. All that had stood between us and the hangman all those years was Joshua's conscience, God help us. His friendship. This was why she's hauled me off to talk to me on Table Mountain – to unburden herself, to make her confession. It wasn't cowardice. It was self-preservation. To save her relationship. She'd been prepared to sacrifice everything and everyone in a desperate effort to save it.

And Josh has kept silent all this time.

What was it? Friendship? Friendship with two men who were doing their best to demolish his family fortune and reputation, who sought to topple the state? Yet he'd kept it all to himself. In a funny sort of way, we owed our freedom – and possibly our lives – to a wealthy Afrikaner who'd valued friendship more than we had.

Why?

She is still talking, hands writhing in her lap.

Frances says Josh was a liberal, but I knew, didn't I, what a white liberal was. He was liberal until his own interests were threatened, and she thought that at that moment of revelation Josh felt very threatened. They were at her place. It was an autumn night – beautiful the way the Gauteng nights at that time of year could be, but chilly. They sat at the kitchen table. They ate linguine with lemon oil and Parmesan and they drank wine. It was one of his favourite meals, but Frances says she didn't think he tasted anything and neither did she.

They grew reckless. In her case, it was the relief at having spoken the truth. They made big plans. Josh became expansive, loud. The wine helped. It seemed to cheer them up and they opened a second bottle.

'We would leave the country separately, meet up, marry and Josh would get any job he could find. He didn't mind. He'd work as a dish-washer if he had to. It would be a new beginning. As long as we were together, it wouldn't matter. Who needed money? Who needed the Schuter empire? Who needed South Africa?'

They'd escape to London. They'd join the thousands of other expatriate South Africans already there. They could make a new life for themselves even if they were poor. Frances could try modelling – the African look, they decided, was just coming into vogue – and Josh could use his limited newspaper experience to write the definitive words on South Africa's agony. He could use the business connections he'd already made in London.

Maybe Josh would go into business on his own account.

After the Sauvignon, everything seemed possible that night.

'There was no limit to our dreams, Seb, but the more Josh talked, the more scared I could tell he was. I'd never seen him frightened – it shocked me a little, but I said nothing. I went along with it all, adding some dreams of my own, anxious to keep the mood happy, positive. Which it wasn't.

'We tumbled into bed, cold, a little drunk and scared – scared of what? The future? Each other? Our love-making was, well, it was clumsy and awkward and neither of us really got into it, but we pretended it was wonderful, and

237

then we lay there in the dark, Josh smoking one of those cheroots of his. Then he said he had to leave.

'I went to the door and I kissed him.

'He put his arms around me.

'It was the last time I saw him for more than ten years.'

It was exactly a month later that the Soweto student revolt erupted.

16 June 1976.

The era of Steve Biko's black consciousness movement, remember?

'How much time have we got, Seb? My God, I had no idea.'

I tell her we have ten minutes. I'd like to haul her to her feet, but I don't do anything of the kind. I've got what I want. I can hold on a little longer, surely, make a pretence at being patient.

She thinks I'm sympathetic, her one true friend.

Don't go and spoil it.

Frances says she fled to Durban. She sought to escape the township violence and her memories of Josh. He never called or wrote. She couldn't bear it. She had to get out. She knew no one in Durban, and no one knew her. She had a three-month contract with a ready-to-wear fashion house, and she knew she was getting to the upper limit of her modelling career. The girls were getting younger, prettier – 'The writing, as you say in English, was on the wall.' She decided to bury herself in her work, to make as much money as she could before she found she wasn't getting the jobs she wanted. She was still supporting her mother and paying university fees for one of her sisters. She used work to try to forget Josh, to forget her friends in Soweto, to forget everything. She had no idea what had happened to Zak. The Youth had taken over; they ran the townships and fought their daily battles with the cops in their armoured vehicles – those *cesspirs*. She didn't want to get caught between the two, as an activist or as a white man's woman.

'I heard you on the radio once, Seb. You were being interviewed, so I knew you were back. Your voice was so much deeper. You sounded so much older, so serious. I didn't know who it was you were working for, and had no way of getting in touch. I shut out the politics. I tried not to read the newspapers.'

In all that time she never spoke to Zak.

'Sometimes I'd see Josh in a magazine. It would be a sporting event, or the launch of a new restaurant. That was how I found he had married this English-speaking girl. Helen.

'It was September 1977; I remember it because it was the month that Steve Biko died of head injuries during police interrogation. They kept him naked, in chains, then threw him head first into a wall, repeatedly, and flung him into the back of a van, still naked and manacled, and drove him a thousand miles or whatever it was to hospital. He never made it.

'I turned the page and there was Josh with his bride, in full colour. She had such blue eyes. All in white, of course. Vast wedding cake. God, it was awful. I threw up right there in the hairdresser's.

'Man, I'm such a fool sometimes.

'The caption-writer described Josh as one of South Africa's new generation of business leaders and patron of the arts.

'Wedding of the year, they said.

'Fuck, I sobbed my heart out.

'It's funny now, Seb.'

She covers her face with her hands.

'It wasn't funny then.'

Mist rises, swirling around us.

'My God, Seb, it's scary.'

We can see the lights of the cable station, but those of the city have vanished, swallowed by the cloud.

'You don't mind if I take your arm, white man?'

Mind? When had I ever minded?

Frances says she can't see where she is putting her feet. She says she feels she might fall off the edge of the mountain. She is cold – she can feel drops of water on her arms and legs.

We're not more than a dozen feet from the edge.

I think, just for a moment, that I can finish it.

Right here. Now.

I can lead her to the edge and with one shove put an end to my jealousy, our betrayals, hers and mine, her big mouth. No one will see.

They won't hear her cry.

I picture her in freefall, spinning in the darkness.

Then I remember my nightmare.

I brush the murderous thought aside. Sometimes I disgust even myself.

'Viljoen thinks we all did it, Seb – I mean the murder of Josh's dad.'

'Together?'

She leans heavily on my arm.

'Surely you're not surprised. He thinks it's a conspiracy. He can't quite figure out how we all fit into the plot, and that's why he hasn't arrested anyone quite yet, but I'm sure he will.'

Frances says he told her that each had ample motive to kill old Schuter. Josh had. His rows with his dad, their political differences, Josh's childhood – Viljoen has it all worked out, or so he told Frances that night in his office. Frances has a motive, of course – for his wrecking her relationship with Josh. And because she is a black woman, was the mistress of an ANC activist, thwarted lover of the son. Viljoen thought that by keeping her in his office for hours – oh, no, not that, he'd behaved very correctly, he wasn't stupid like some of those bastards – he could work on her emotions, wear the *meid* down into confessing.

'You have a motive, Seb, because of what you are, or what you were.'

We'd all wanted to destroy the Schuters, hadn't we?

'And then there's Zak. Poor Zak. They want so much to nail him. With Zak, you see, it could have been any one of several motives, or maybe all of them at once. Revenge for what happened. Greed – Zak was always interested in where Josh and his father stashed their cash at home. Or simply because of what Cris represented. A long-held wish to smash the Schuter empire, just because it existed.'

Like me.

'Josh was your friend, Seb, but don't tell me it wouldn't have made you happy to see them brought down a peg or two.'

A palpable hit. Frances snuggles closer.

'Of course, Zak himself isn't an easy target now. They

say he might get ministerial office after the elections, so Viljoen has to step carefully where Zakaria Wauchope is concerned.

'Mabaza – you met him, I think – wanted to have us all rounded up and held on remand. Viljoen is more political. He thinks that by letting us out on a long leash he can watch what we do, see if we make mistakes. He doesn't have enough evidence, you see, and he doesn't want the whole thing to become a media frenzy again because then there's no chance anyone will know for sure what really happened, and, because Cris Schuter was what he was, Viljoen is being careful not to make things worse just before the elections.'

Frances has a point. Everyone is terrified of a general bloodletting that would throw everything off track.

'Viljoen predicted you'd go to Josh, Seb, but he thought he'd be right behind you, watching your every move. He didn't reckon on your getting away undetected. But he knew you were holding out on him over Josh's whereabouts. And that, so he says, is enough to charge you with being an accessory to the murder. He's pretty mad at you, and for all I know he could be waiting for us at the lower station to haul your cute white ass off to jail.'

She expects me to say something.

'You're taking me to Josh now, Seb?'

'Tomorrow,' I say, then instantly regret it.

We pick our way across the rocks, watched by a group of teenage backpackers peering out of the cable car, waiting for the last journey down.

'I have my own theory,' Frances says. She still clutches my arm. 'I'm keeping it to myself. But then, let's face it, Seb, I'm just a nigger woman. That's two strokes against me. My views never did count. Maybe they never will. We may be liberated as blacks, but as women? We'll need another three hundred years and a second revolution for that to change.'

DAY FOUR

NINE

I call Potgieter the next morning, and ask him to fill the
Peugeot's tank, check the water, oil and tyres and tell him
I'll need him all day; we won't be back until well after
dark. He arrives an hour later, at eight-thirty a.m., pleased
to be needed. I grab my laptop – they've not found that,
at least – pull the front door shut behind me and get in
next to Potgieter.

I have an idea.

'Have you got your hat?'

He frowns, baffled.

'That old hat of yours. The straw job with the band
around it, the panama. You wore it last summer. Where
is it?'

'Agh, man, that hat . . .' Gesturing with his head, he
says, 'In the boot.'

I can tell he doesn't like what's coming.

'Get it, please. Put it on.'

When he gets back behind the wheel, looking puzzled
and not a little self-conscious with his battered panama
in place, I tell him to drive – anywhere, I say, it really
doesn't matter – while I code up my replies in the
affirmative to the foreign desk's queries. The car outside
my place has changed colour; that is to say, it's a similar

model, but a different paint-job and registration. It has its usual complement of two anonymous watchers, and, yes, two rear-view mirrors and no bumper stickers, and as Potgieter rolls downhill, it falls in behind us, taking little trouble to keep at a discreet distance.

They don't care if we know we're being followed, so much so that even Potgieter notices within a minute or two; perhaps Viljoen or Mabaza want it that way.

At Constantia Nek we pull over on to the verge under the pines, and with my satphone I find the Indian Ocean satellite signal without difficulty, log on and send off the messages, our followers waiting patiently fifty yards away. I download some SAPA and Associated Press files, using the key words Schuter, murder and police. Then we move on.

Potgieter tries to take off the hat – he doesn't like his image as a Cuban sugar-cane worker – but I won't let him. By the time we reach Plumstead I've called Malherbe, who kindly fills me in on what I've missed, which is very little. He's as curious as ever, with more questions than I have. Have I seen Joshua Schuter? Am I planning to run an interview? Yes and yes, I say. Is he still in the country? Yes. What are his plans? Uncertain, I say. Aren't I concerned that by failing to inform the authorities of his whereabouts I could make myself liable to prosecution? No comment. By now I have enough to cobble together a two-hundred-word update on the murder investigation and without a single original source of my own (I ask myself will anyone really care or notice in this age of microwave journalism), but it's obvious from our chat that the issue has slipped off the front pages on to the inside. The elections are close and are squeezing out everything that isn't directly related.

When I catch sight of the sweep of Muizenberg beach and the lines of multicoloured wooden bathing huts, we are joined by a second pair of watchers riding in a metallic blue five-series BMW. They settle in just ahead of us. It's becoming quite a party: Security Branch ahead, CID behind. That's what I assume they are. We're the filling in the sandwich.

I finish the story over a generous plate of kingklip, chips and salad in the café that stands at the entrance to Fish Hoek beach; a cheap and cheerful place where I bought ice cream as a child, standing at the window in my sandy shorts, coins clutched in my fist. If I'm about to go to prison, the condemned man should have a decent meal. Potgieter and I follow up our main course with coffee and banana sundaes. Our watchers park and enter the café, and self-consciously sit two by two at separate tables.

We studiously ignore one another. The Security Branch and CID men stare down at their plastic menus and thumb their neat moustaches and pretend to be happy to be there, no doubt wondering if kingklip – a meaty fish hauled out of the sea that very day – can somehow be massaged on to an expenses sheet.

We take our time.

After I call for the bill I lean across the table and ask Potgieter, 'D'you think you can lose them?'

I have a rendezvous with the delectable Frances and no intention of arriving mob-handed.

'I think so, boss.'

I'm not so sure. Potgieter doesn't sound confident. Sweat is visible just below his hairline and it isn't a particularly warm day; the southeaster is blowing hard across False Bay, whipping up white horses and raising sheets of sand off the dunes. The stuff patters against the glass windows like a silica rainstorm.

'Ready?'

He mops his mouth, watching me leave a generous tip.

'This is how it's going to be,' I say. 'You'll lead the way, walking slowly. I'll follow. You open the door and go first, and then we'll saunter over to the car, taking our time. No rush, no panic. Everything's cool. We're relaxed. Enjoying ourselves. Tell yourself you're on holiday. Okay?'

A nod. His adam's apple goes up and down as he swallows. Potgieter is frightened. He doesn't believe a word, but he's trying hard.

'Good,' I say. 'That's the spirit.'

We have parked on the road that runs along the seafront. We face north, towards Kalk Bay. To our right there is the sea, the beach, the dunes, the railway line, a fence, the road and us. To our left there's a line of boarding houses, hotels and flats, and beyond that strip the main road running through the centre of the tidy, booze-free conservative dorp that is Fish Hoek.

The BMW is parked ahead, but faces towards us. If they want to follow they'll have to turn. The Ford is behind us. The four men with crew cuts are emerging from the café just as we reach the Peugeot.

I go around to the front passenger door, turning my face away from the stinging sand coming across the railtracks. I wait for Potgieter to unlock the doors and we both climb in.

'Give me the hat,' I say.

He reaches over to the back seat and hands it to me.

'The keys.'

I hold out my hand.

'Switch places – quickly.'

I have the hat on and am behind the wheel, watching the mirror. The first two – the men I assume are CID – have reached the Ford, the other pair are perhaps ten yards away when I pull out and slam the accelerator to the floor, scorching rubber and narrowly missing the BMW.

I glimpse the two Security Branch men running for their car.

The Ford starts to move, or am I imagining it?

What I am looking for is perhaps a hundred and fifty yards ahead.

It's still there – a Shell petrol station with a forecourt that provides access to the main road.

'Hold on.'

I swing the wheel hard, we seem to topple to one side as we go into a slide, then I flick the wheel into the skid and we shoot across the forecourt, two employees diving out of the way, a pressure hose dancing away like a snake. Potgieter holds the dash with both hands as I rotate the wheel again, burning more rubber, and we bounce on to the main road, picking up speed in the wrong lane, and I watch the needle dart up the gauge.

Just as Potgieter thinks the worst is over, I stamp on the accelerator and pull hard on the hand brake. We spin 180 degrees and face the way we've come.

'Christ, chief—'

I think Potgieter is more appalled at the damage I'm doing to the tyres than anything else.

'Get out.'

There's nothing in front of us. Not yet.

I don't think he's taken in what I've said.

'Go on.' I lean across him and open the door. 'Travel agent's – see it? Five minutes, then get a cab or a train. I'll call you.'

I leave him on the pavement, bemused and not a little afraid. I'm moving again, turning across the traffic, broadside on, and there's the BMW coming into view, just ahead of the Ford for whatever reason, and now I'm across the central island, heading back into the town, building up speed. I pass the BMW and Ford but I don't wave; I don't look at them. I'm staring at the amber lights.

I slap the horn.

And just as I thought, they don't follow.

They have seen us stop, a door open and close, someone leave the Peugeot. They've seen a man in a hat, my driver, all alone. *Die snaakse Engelsman* has vanished. Are they going to follow the man they think is Potgieter, or try to find the missing Palfrey, their murder suspect, out there somewhere and on foot?

I go through the red lights, and the last thing I see is the ashen faces and open mouths of other motorists and, behind them, four men pounding along the pavement, two one way, two in the opposite direction. I hope they don't find the unfortunate and bewildered Potgieter, no doubt hiding behind a glossy holiday brochure and regretting all that chocolate and vanilla ice cream he's consumed.

*

I mutter an apology to the absent Potgieter and get rid of his hat by flinging it out of the window once I'm moving up from Fish Hoek through Nordhoek; the wind carries it off like a kite. This is a valley that was virgin fynbos forty years ago; now it's covered with a virus of detached bungalows with pools and built-in barbecues out the back, SUVs and postage-stamp-sized lawns out front. The honeycomb pattern of identikit homes eating up the landscape includes a number of retirement villages and shopping malls. I know I have to get rid of not just the panama but the car, too, and as soon as I can.

There are three options: I can dump it and steal another, I can fake an accident by rolling it over a cliff, leaving myself stranded, or I can hide it among others and pick up a hire car. The last makes the most sense, but it means I will have to wait until I cross over to the Atlantic seaboard and the fishing harbour of Hout Bay, newly discovered watering hole of that globalized brotherhood of the idle: minor foreign royals on the run from tabloids or creditors – or both – and, inevitably, a sprinkling of anorexic models, verbally challenged footballers and surgically modified Hollywood wannabes.

The route there is described in tourist guidebooks as one of the country's most striking scenic drives. Chapman's Peak Drive is certainly scenic and could strike in unexpected ways. Imagine, if you will, a mountain rising directly out of the sea. This spiny ridge has twelve peaks known as the Twelve Apostles. These are cloaked in fluffy white cloud. Halfway up the steep side of the mountain is a two-lane road, twisting in and out, hugging the boulder-strewn slope; the verge is unprotected except for a few white stones spaced out at wide intervals. Otherwise, it is a clear and a precipitous drop of six hundred feet to the Atlantic rollers. The winds are capricious, often gusting to gale force, and rockfalls commonplace. Many people who stop their cars to get out and admire the view slip on the gravel verge, the wind sweeping them to their deaths.

South Africans still drive on the left, part of their imperial British legacy. It means I'm on the outside of the road, my left-hand wheels inches from the cliff edge and the afternoon sun in my eyes. I slow right down. I know what the wind can do on a sharp bend. The sea is immense: its gunmetal-blue expanse spreads across the horizon to the west; to my right rises the mass of mountain, topped by cloud.

I'm concentrating so hard I don't see the blue BMW until it's right there in the mirror, its grille snarling at me; it isn't five metres behind. It makes no attempt to slow down, and I don't have time or room for evasive action when it strikes the Peugeot hard from behind.

The driver tries to overtake; I speed up and shift into the centre of the road, but oncoming traffic forces me to move back into the left-hand lane again. This time he almost draws level and I feel the weight of the 5-series as the driver edges against the Peugeot, trying to push me on to the verge and over the side.

He tries twice, striking the Peugeot's offside rear. I fight to keep control. I know I'll be fine as long as I don't panic. That's what he's counting on – that I'll make a mistake, or lose my nerve.

All it needs is a moment's loss of concentration.

So this is it; there isn't going to be an arrest, or even an attempt at one. They want me dead, out of the way. I hold on, and, glancing to my right as my pursuers draw level for a third strike, see one of my adversaries in the front passenger seat: he's a blond *borselkop* thug. Except for the tan, he could be an English football hooligan.

He grins at me; he seems to relish the chase. He's wearing sunglasses and is turned towards me, holding out his right arm, gripping his wrist with his left hand. I look across a second time and realize he's pointing a pistol at me; he uses a double-handed grip, bracing his left shoulder against the backrest of his bucket seat. The driver swings the BMW into the Peugeot a third time, but I see it coming and swing back at him and have the satisfaction of watching them struggle to stay on the road and out of the ditch on the far side. I'm getting the hang of it now, and even beginning to enjoy it. It all seems to be happening in slow motion as the adrenalin kicks in, speeding up my reflexes.

I tell myself this must be an old score they want to settle. They know what I was, what I have been.

We are locked together, hogging the road between us. A white truck heads our way, and the driver flicks his lights at us. It won't do him any good. This time the passenger in the BMW isn't smiling; he must have pulled the trigger at this point because I register two loud cracks close to my head, then the double boom of the gun going off.

Nothing else, though.

My first sensation is of being held very tightly. I can't tell what it is that has me in such a vice, but I realize after a moment or two that I'm wrapped in it. Only my head protrudes. My ribs ache and my left leg throbs. It's the pressure of the wrapping that makes them painful, and I decide I've either cracked a couple of ribs, or bruised them. My head hurts, too, above my left eye, and the eye itself isn't functioning properly. I can open and close it, but there's something clogging it and I don't have a hand free to explore what's wrong. As my mind returns to full awareness, I grasp the fact of it being blood – my blood, fresh-tasting and warm – from a cut somewhere on my forehead where the pain is, a stinging, because I can see it now, dripping a dull red on to the floor in front of my nose – a concrete floor, harshly lit. No windows I can see.

The blood forms a little shiny pool of scarlet.

Somewhere . . . industrial.

Not a hospital, certainly.

A factory.

I've been rolled up tight in a carpet. Its hard folds are just below my chin. I can make out the tufts, the rough backing.

I smell diesel.

No, not a factory. An indoor car park?

I'm naked.

That's a shock. I feel the panic run through me – the sudden rush of sweat as the adrenalin kicks in. My body wants to react. It wants to get away, it wants to crouch in that primeval, instinctive way of all primates, to run or to fight, or to curl up and protect its vulnerability.

I can't move at all.

Hearing movement very close, I shut my eyes.

Someone holds a match to my nostrils and blows it out. I must have moved my head away and opened my one good eye, too, because the movement stops and I can hear breathing, very close.

'The *rooinek*'s with us again.'

The voice is right next to my face.

The speaker's hand – a burly hand, with fat fingers and a gold ring so tight on the pinkie it vanishes into the flesh – withdraws.

It hurts every time I breathe, but I have to breathe because I feel that if I don't, the carpet's going to crush me like a boa constrictor so I won't get air back into my lungs. I have no choice.

There's a noise, a guttural sound, a panting that seems to go faster and faster. I realize I'm making it, sucking in air and expelling it.

'Mr Palfrey, sir . . .'

Feet moving away, a chair scraping the concrete. A blurred shape, of a man sitting, leaning forward, looking at me, his elbows on his knees. His feet seem very big.

'Pleased to make your acquaintance, Mr Palfrey.'

A snigger behind me.

Two men. Industrial lighting. Concrete floor. Cool air. No door or window, but then my field of vision is acutely limited.

'We're going to ask you two questions, Mr Palfrey. Just two. We like to keep things simple. You will tell us the answers to those two questions. You see, Mr Palfrey, we're experts. We don't waste time. We know you want to get dressed and go home. So we keep it simple. And I want to tell you something, Mr Palfrey, we always get the answers. Always. And something else. You will give us those answers within thirty minutes. We've asked questions of hundreds of people like you. Hundreds. Black, white, male, female, big and small. Strong and weak. Communists like you. Activists. Comrades. And you know what? All these kaffirs give us the true answers, Mr Palfrey, and all within thirty minutes.

'There are no lies, and no exceptions.'

Feet moving again. Coming around me, very close, stopping, then moving on.

Veldskoene.

Shoes of soft leather up to the ankle with thin, rubber soles.

'This is my friend, Mr Palfrey. Look, we're professionals, my friend and I. It's a job to us, nothing more. Whether you live or die doesn't matter to us. It's not personal in any way. We're just going to ask you the two questions. Okay? As soon as we have the answers, you can go. You can put on your clothes and you can walk out of here. We'll even give you the fifty cents for the bus back to town.'

Another chortle.

The sound of a match struck, the smell of a cigarette.

The figure on the chair rises. I can see him a little more clearly as he steps forward. A burly man in a light sports coat and khaki trousers, well pressed. Rubber-soled shoes, the brown shoecaps burnished.

A cop.

I tell myself this is just the warm-up, the preparation.

I can't see as far as his face.

'We know everything about you.' The second voice is smoother and and up an octave on the first. 'We've got the file right here, Mr Palfrey.' Papers are shuffled. 'Let me see – you're Mr Sebastien Edward Latymer Palfrey, born Cambridge, England, 1950? Is that correct? I take it from your silence that's affirmation, Mr Palfrey. You were recruited into the South African Communist Party by a Dr Stanko, since deceased, and worked for three months as a probationer before your membership was accepted. Is that an accurate record, Mr Palfrey?'

Stanko dead. Is it true?

Toecaps: 'Mr Palfrey signals his assent by his silence.'

'Okay. Fine. Let's move on. Mr Palfrey travels abroad and receives training in Angola and Tanzania, and also behind the Iron Curtain. We have a note here that he attended a special intelligence school near Grozny. That's in the Soviet Union, somewhere in the Caucasus, I believe. Only for the best students, it says. I'm impressed, man. Is that correct, Mr Palfrey? You must have been very good at your job as a spy for the Russians, eh? Did they give you a medal?

'Let's not waste time. The wife and kiddies are waiting. Okay. You then worked in an intelligence capacity, reporting as head agent to your Case Officer who happened to be the Cape Town resident of the GRU – that's Soviet military intelligence. It's an interesting career, you've had, Mr Palfrey, really. Oh yes, we mustn't leave this out. Mr Palfrey's cover was as a correspondent for a British newspaper. We've seen all sorts, I must say, but you're one of the most interesting we've had.

'How you doing? Still with us, Mr Palfrey, yes?'

Veldskoen moves back.

His voice, to my left: 'I think we've put to rest any idea of mistaken identity. Wouldn't you agree, Mr Palfrey, that we've got the right man?'

Toecaps grunts with the effort as he squats down.

'Now, pal, our two questions. Just two. You can remember two questions, Mr Palfrey, can't you? I know you're not feeling very comfortable, but that's the idea. Or maybe we'll just start with the one. That will be easier, won't it, hey? We don't want to confuse Mr Palfrey, now, do we?'

That snigger again, a snort from Veldskoen.

Toecaps: 'Where is Joshua Schuter, Mr Palfrey? His current whereabouts, if you will, that's what we're after. Simple, isn't it?'

The second, higher voice: 'The clock is running.'

The pair of polished shoes are on either side of my head.

'Where is he?'

I keep silent.

'One minute,' Veldskoen announces.

I tell myself that this isn't an official building of any kind. There are no desks, no noise, no shouts or doors banging. I just have to beat the thirty minutes. The other good news is that they have taken care not to reveal their names. That means, surely, that they have no intention, at least at this stage, of killing me once this is over.

I will keep silent.

I owe Josh that, don't I?

The man sits on me, straddling the carpet. He sits down heavily.

I think I black out momentarily from the pain.

'Where is he? Where is your old school friend, Joshua Schuter?'

I waggle my head.

'Oh dear. You want to make it hard on yourself. Give us the bag, man, would you?'

Something is passed between the two men.

'This is just a bag, Mr Palfrey. It costs about thirty cents. It's made of plastic, so it's airproof. It's also wet. Now what I'm going to do, you see, is put it over your head. Certain things will happen. You will try to breathe, but you won't be able to. I will leave the bag there and you will suffocate. First, you will lose consciousness. No, it's no good shaking your head. You can't stop it happening. The only way you can stop it happening is to answer the first question. You see, the way it works is that you don't have a choice. The decision is not yours. The sooner you understand that, the better it is for all of us. It becomes so much easier when you understand that there really is no alternative. You can hardly be blamed for the inevitable. There's no point in pain, in putting up a fight and then feeling guilty when you fail. It isn't your fault that you've failed, you see, because you could never win. The decision has already been made. You can't be blamed. So be sensible, man, and answer the question. Save yourself a lot of pointless grief, man. Now I will count up to three.'

I open my mouth and all I get is a mouthful of wet plastic.

The plastic is sucked into my nostrils. I want to use my hands to claw it away, but my arms are pinned to my sides. My eyes are open too, and the bag sticks to them. It's completely dark. I shake my head from side to side so that the carpet cuts into my neck.

It doesn't help. With every move, the bag seems to tighten and the sensation of drowning, of being throttled, increases. I try to bite through the plastic to make a hole in the bag, but it's too thick, and I can't get a grip on it with my teeth.

I forget my ribs. I forget my pain. I fight the carpet, but it has no effect. I can't budge, not an inch, not a fraction of an inch. It's like a straitjacket, only worse. I'm bathed in sweat. I know I have moments before I lose consciousness. My lungs burn like napalm.

I'm an animal fighting for life. Except I can't fight.

They have total power over me. I can't run. I can't do anything.

How long can I stay alive without air?

Lights burst inside my head, brilliant patterns of gold and silver and blue. This is what it is like to be a fish out of water. This is what panic means.

Powerlessness.

This is death by suffocation.

This is terror.

This is what it is to die a violent death.

'Three minutes,' intones Veldskoen.

'Welcome back, Mr Palfrey. 'You will remember I asked you a simple question. You don't need to be a rocket scientist. It's easy. I just want to know where we can find your friend, Joshua Schuter.'

'Please.'

'That's a nice word, "please". I teach my children to say "please". It's good manners. We should all learn good manners. I'm glad you were taught to say "please", Mr Palfrey. You were well brought up. Please what?'

The bag is right in front of my face.

'Please – stop.'

'But I can't stop, Mr Palfrey, until you answer my question – please.' His tone oozes sympathy.

The bag goes on.

'You can stop it, Mr Palfrey, by answering the question.'

He walks away.

I struggle. I choke.

This time the night descends like an old friend.

I don't know how often the bag goes over my head.

I lose count.

They light several matches and burn them under my nose. Once, the big man gets off me and slaps my face with his open hand and throws water over me. My cheeks sting from the blows.

'Twenty-three minutes,' says Veldskoen.

'Seven minutes to the record, Mr Palfrey. As long as your heart holds out. Not everybody's does. Think you can break the record, Mr Palfrey? You think you can make it? I don't think so, to be quite honest with you. It's not bad, but at your age I think you should be more careful, man.'

Snigger.

'My friend thinks you're funny, Mr Palfrey.'

The bag is dangled in front of my face.

'I don't think you're funny, Mr Palfrey. You're pre-dictable.'

I shut my eyes rather than see it.

No. No.

'Someone more intelligent would know this is a no-win situation, Mr Palfrey. Only stupid people try to resist, and I know you're not that stupid.'

Take it away.

'Where is Joshua Schuter?'

Yes. He's right; it's not your choice.

Give in. Give up.

I try to speak, but it comes out as a hoarse whisper.

'What did you say?'

I try again.

'Smitswinkelsbay,' I say.

The bag vanishes from my field of vision.

I cry then, out of a sense of failure, out of a sense of relief. I blubber like a child, snuffling with snot running down my face. It is self-pity coupled with the physical pleasure of betrayal. My own body has rewarded my cowardice with a surge of endorphins.

I suck in huge draughts of air.

A whispered conversation in Afrikaans follows between Veldskoen and Toecaps; it is very brief and I catch only the odd word. My impression is that Toecaps is telling Veldskoen where and what Smitswinkelsbay is.

Toecaps returns, his rubber soles squeaking on the concrete.

I flinch at the sound.

'You have another chance to break the record, Mr Palfrey. You'd like that, wouldn't you? I know you would. You commies like to suffer. Ready for the next question now?'

Veldskoen: 'Clock reset.'

My heart hammers in my chest.

'Question two: where are the Cris Schuter memoirs, Mr Palfrey?'

I am ice cold and shaking. My mouth is completely dry.

Not again.

'I'd like to give you time to rest and get yourself ready, but you see, Mr Palfrey, we have work to do, and this isn't a holiday resort for retired Communist spies. So if you don't object, I will press on.'

I do object. I think I moan out loud. I beg to be left alone.

Not again.

My bladder empties itself.

Veldskoen: 'Clock running.'

'I don't know anything about any memoirs. Really. If I did, I'd tell you. Honestly, I would.'

Toecaps: 'Oh dear. He's a tryer, is Mr Palfrey. You have to give him that. He does try. Or maybe he's a masochist and he enjoys it. Do you enjoy it, Mr Palfrey? Oh, he's gone and pissed himself. Don't worry, Mr Palfrey, they all do that near the end. The sphincter muscle will go next, but it does make an awful mess, and you will have to clean it up when we're finished. You won't mind. You'll want to help. You'll be grateful.

'Pass me the bag again, man, will you?'

TEN

I don't know how much longer it goes on, and I don't see the stun grenades roll along the floor from under the garage door and come to a halt near Veldskoen.

I don't hear the breaking glass or see them break in.

I don't see the flash or hear the bang of the first grenade.

Or the three that follow.

I do know there's a lot of smoke at some point.

I don't witness Veldskoen draw his standard-issue 9 mm Vektor pistol, and I don't see him thrown against the wall by James Mabaza's first two rounds, both .357 hollow-point, two tons of pressure and enough to stop an angry African buffalo in its tracks.

Someone pulls the bag from my head, but I'm not aware of that, either, because I've passed out again. It's become a habit, this floating in and out of consciousness. Somebody gives me mouth-to-mouth resuscitation, but even that I can't recall. They tell me about it later.

All I remember is the sight of Toecaps spreadeagled, face down on the floor, lying in his own blood, and Viljoen, wearing a gas mask, kneeling on him while I'm being freed from the brown carpet by a couple of medics in orange overalls, the fresh air and sunshine, the red blanket hiding my nakedness, the stretcher being lifted into the rear of the ambulance, the oxygen mask going over my face and I'm screaming at them to get it off, fighting them, using my fists, grabbing at their faces, getting a thumb in the corner of one of the medics' eyes, trying to pop it out the way I was taught at the camp near Grozny, then the needle punched in hard.

They strap me down.

'Fuck you—'

A curtain falls inside my head.

It will be many months before I can bear to have anything, even a bedsheet, near any part of my face.

Frances tells me later she waited thirty minutes and then ordered.

We hadn't planned on eating, but she was hungry. Dunes is a sprawling restaurant behind the dunes at Hout Bay; wisely, she stuck to fish and chips (the food isn't all that great, but it's hard to go wrong with fresh fish), and by the time the food arrived I was already an hour late. We hadn't called one another for fear of the phones being monitored; having been Zak's partner for so long, Frances has a well-developed sense of self-preservation. She settled down happily to eat, and was contemplating coffee – she said it was around noon at this point – when she heard police sirens and saw two patrol cars speed past. They were followed by an ambulance and then a fire engine.

She had a feeling it was somehow connected to me in some way; she drank her cappuccino slowly and tried not worry. Then she saw the Peugeot towed past, this time going the other way, heading towards Camps Bay.

The front seemed to have crumpled, but the bodywork was otherwise intact.

The ambulance returned along Chapman's Peak Drive, light flashing, using its siren to overtake the tow-truck.

Frances was on her feet, leaving a tip, pocketing her purse when she saw three patrol cars enter the car park and Mabaza get out of the first; he saw her and raised a hand.

He called her name and walked over to her.

She went out and stood next to her hatchback, key in hand.

She thought at that point: Sebastien's dead.

'But I wasn't. I was hardly scratched.'

'If that's what you call a scratch.'

She means my left ankle and a swelling above my left eye where I've been cut. The ankle is twisted and swollen. It doesn't even hurt now, just as long as I keep still. The cut has given me a headache, though, and a couple of ribs were bruised when I was pulled out of the Peugeot. The ribs are painful whenever I breathe in or out, and breathing is not something I am going to give up doing if I can possibly help it.

That was before the carpet and the wet bag.

'I was lucky.'

'That's what you call luck? I'd hate to be around when you get unlucky.'

'They say I can leave today. They want to run a few more tests, but they say I'll be fine.'

How will I ever be able to look Josh in the face after I betrayed him? Will anyone ask me what happened? In a sense, my breaking down, giving them what they wanted, has been overtaken by events, rendered irrelevant by Mabaza's quick trigger finger. With luck – that word again – it is just one episode everyone – except me, of course – will forget; I'll just have to learn to live with it.

'You'll be able to come to the funeral?'

'I wouldn't miss it for all the world.'

'I'll take you.'

'You don't have to.'

'It's no trouble.'

She means Cris Schuter's. The police have released his remains and they – the family, such as it is – are going to bury him in the Schuter graveyard on the Franschhoek farm. Everyone who's anybody in the great register of white supremacists is going to be there.

'I hate hospitals,' Frances says, sitting down on a chair next to the bed and smoothing her skirt over her knees.

'So do I.'

'Visitors are supposed to bring grapes or something, and I didn't bring you anything. I'm sorry.'

'Not grapes,' I say. 'Something will do.'

'Like what?'

'How about a kiss?' I take her hand.

'You're awful,' she says, pulling away. 'Josh and I are getting married, didn't I tell you?'

'It escaped my mind. I'd hoped you'd forgotten, too.'

'Foolish white man.'

'One can but try.'

Then she leans forward and kisses me on the forehead.

'You're quite cute sometimes,' Frances says. 'Especially when you're as helpless as this.'

There is movement behind the door and I think I see part of a uniform. I'm allergic to the sight of a policeman by now.

'What's going on?' I have a nasty feeling I'm about to be arrested.

Frances looks at the door and back at me. 'Relax. It's okay. You've got your own police guard. Two of them out there – with shotguns.'

'To keep me in, or others out?'

'The latter, honey, don't worry.'

'What's going on?'

I don't think I can run, but I'll have a go if I have to. I start measuring the distance between the bed and the window.

'I think I'll leave that to your new friends, Mabaza and Viljoen. It's rather complicated, and they can tell it better than I can.'

'I'm sure it's complicated,' I say.

'Potgieter says the damage to your car isn't too bad. It will be at the garage for the next week or two, though, and he says it'll cost around five thousand rand.'

'Bloody hell. The rag will be overjoyed.'

'I'll collect you at three. We'll stop at your place and you can change and we'll have a bite on the way. Would you like that?'

She stands up.

'I would – very much. But what about Josh?'

'He'll be very busy with the last-minute arrangements. He's already there, at the farm. Like you, he's got police protection and he's already complaining about it. You know what he's like.'

Yes, I do.

'You mean he's out and about? I thought—'

'I did say it's complicated, Seb.'

Baffled, I fall back against the pillows.

Viljoen must have whatever it was he was after.

Frances says, 'Where were we going? I mean, when you asked to meet me at Hout Bay, you didn't say what you had in mind.'

'I promised to take you to Josh, didn't I?'

'Oh. He found me.'

Flowers – lots of them, mostly white lilies and heavily scented – have always spelled death, at least to me. I don't know why. It must be some childhood incident, long forgotten. The sweetish stink hits me as I hobble into the cool gloom of Franschhoek's Dutch Reformed church, my ankle bandaged and my chest wrapped tight in crêpe.

I try not to breathe deeply because everything hurts.

The funeral of Cris Schuter marks the end of an era: the passage of the old order and the arrival of new uncertainties. When I lurch up the aisle on my shiny aluminium crutches to pay my respects, he looks a lot more alive than when I last saw him. The undertakers have combed his hair, brought colour to his cheeks, closed his mouth and shut his eyes. His throat is tastefully covered in a Regency-style collar of white silk. He lies on his back in the open coffin as if taking a postprandial nap, and the old South Africa and the emergent pay their respects before the solemn men in black screw the lid down and he is carried out and lowered into the rich earth alongside his parents, a black marble headstone marking the spot and engraved with words from the old national anthem, *Die Stem*. I can't imagine who's chosen them, or that Josh would have approved.

Or was the irony intended?

ons vir jou, Suid-Afrika.

There are three distinct groups of mourners; no, four. The first are the old men of the *ancien régime*, the Spartans of the departing order, a veritable roll-call of *verkramptes*, expressionless, grim, balding, straight-backed. I recognize a former minister of law and order, a former police chief, an ex-army commander presently under investigation for alleged extra-judicial killings, several SABC executives and National Party leaders, and, to my surprise, the Great Crocodile himself, none other than that stubborn old Boer P. W. Botha, who slow-marches stiffly down the aisle of the kerk, stands for a moment at the head of the coffin, clutching his fedora at his side, head bowed, and moves away. He doesn't say anything or look at anyone; he doesn't stay for the actual burial or the wake that follows; instead I see him helped into the back of a black Mercedes by his white bodyguard and driven away, no doubt back to his home in the aptly named Wilderness.

Then there are the patricians, come to pay homage to one of their own: the good burghers of Franschhoek, contemporaries of Cris Schuter with gnarled hands and weathered faces in ill-fitting suits and wearing black armbands; wealthy, most of them, but not the kind given to display of any kind, several accompanied by their wives, women hidden in veils and ankle-length black dresses and gloves. To me, they are a living reminder that this fertile, well-watered valley is, together with neighbouring Stellenbosch, the very heartland of Afrikanerdom. The faces of the men show it all: independence, pride, faith in a wrathful God and conformity to a rigid social and racial hierarchy which their Lord has seen fit to place under their unbending and exclusive stewardship.

I recognize some of these gentry: there are Cloetes, Cronjes, de Villiers, two Malan brothers and a handful of van der Byls, to name but a few – several are fathers of boys Josh and I knew at Bishops.

The third group is the strangest of all: the Schuter farmhands and household servants. They enter as if nothing has changed. They shuffle in, heads down, meek and submissive in the house of the white God, not knowing what to do with their hands, shuffling from foot to foot, awkward and embarrassed. Have they been compelled to pay their last respects? Is it a matter of keeping a pay packet of twenty dollars a month, of losing their foothold in the Schuter estates if they fail to put in an appearance? Or do they feel a genuine loyalty, a sorrow at the old bastard's passing?

The Dutch Reformed Church has felt little obligation – until the arrival of missionaries – to baptize or confirm the servants and slaves of its white congregation, in contrast to the Roman Catholics of the Portuguese and Spanish empires, and that goes a long way towards explaining the rigid hierarchy of the Afrikaner. So what are these descendants of Ham thinking, how do they feel as they troop up in their Sunday best to the coffin and out again into the sunlight?

Only one of these looks up at the white faces in the

pews on either side. She must be sixty at least; she moves with dignity, her venerable grey head covered in a black *doek* that matches her wide skirt. She's in no hurry, undaunted by the place or the worshippers. She seems curious, as if searching for people she knows.

Our eyes meet. She gives no outward sign, but I feel a jolt of sudden recognition. It's in the intelligent eyes.

Zak's eyes: hazel with a glint of copper fire in the iris.

It is only when I swing my way under the oaks, the rubber feet of my crutches sinking into the dust, the ground underfoot scattered with acorns, when I breathe in the rich, tannin smell of the trees, Frances and I swallowed by a green twilight so dim it's like being underwater, that I recall coming here as a child and playing with both Josh and Zak.

The memories reel through my mind like an old movie, long forgotten.

It can't have been more than half a dozen times, all told, but yes, I remember all this. I remember climbing the oaks and sitting in the swaying branches, I remember Josh, and I vaguely remember the little Coloured lad roughly our own age – a rival for Josh's friendship.

He never mentioned it, not once.

I have to wonder why.

I say, 'I didn't see you at the service.'

'I was right at the back with Zak,' Frances says. 'We decided to keep a discreet distance. We didn't want to embarrass Josh. These are his people, not ours. He must be the grief-stricken son and heir, not the *kaffirboeti* with terrorists as friends.'

We – Frances, Zak and myself – form the fourth and

smallest group of mourners; and a more unlikely, disparate and out-of-place bunch of people would have been hard to find in this ultra-conservative place.

Frances leads the way.

She goes quickly across the wooden bridge with its white superstructure and rough wooden boards that shake underfoot. She waits there for me to catch up. The stream below rages with dark brown water and foam in the winter months; in summer its boulders lie exposed like beached whales, the stagnant pools stinking in the heat. Nearly half a century ago Josh and I used to hunt rats, leaping from rock to rock, and, on cornering one of the beasts, we'd bombard it with rocks as it scrabbled uselessly with its claws on the smooth, sun-warmed stone to escape, until we crushed it and it died – a cruel, agonizing and fearful death that could take as long as half an hour until we'd smashed the creature to a bloody pulp.

Lapidation is a vicious way to go, even for a rodent.

The sight of the blood, the frantic final fight for a life already doomed and the animal's broken, split body, its guts everywhere, excited us. I know it did me, and I imagine it was the same for Josh. It made the heart race, took away the breath, made me feel giddy with the slaughter.

Boys, and some girls, like to kill. We begin with curiosity, and end with the enjoyment of absolute power that makes us murderers. Add a sexual frisson and we have the simple, universal recipe for exquisite sadism.

Trouble is, some of us never move on to true manhood. We graduate from birds and rats to deer and other people and stop there, forever child-killers, from Rwanda to the

Katyn forest and Srebrenica, the execution cell in the Lubyanka to the roll-calls at Auschwitz, the chimneys of Sobibór, the mass graves of Treblinka and the use of children under the age of six for target practice by teenage soldiers in Gaza and Jenin. In the name of peace. In the name of security. In the name of justice. In the name of civilization. In the name of history. In the name of freedom.

That night on the banks of the Palmiet River.

And that time in the Swartberge – the Black Mountains.

We are far away from the winelands now, from the Great House with its superb Cape Dutch gables; we emerge from the oak copse and the river to face a line of tiny cottages with small gardens, washing lines in front of each, bright bedlinen and scraps of clothing hoisted like signal flags at a regatta, a deep blue sky and the hazy outline of the mountains behind. The workers' homes are terraced and consist of a room each, the outside walls a yellow wash, much weather-stained, the thatch in some cases replaced by rusty corrugated iron sheeting.

Pretty, a colourist's joy, but a rural slum all the same, well hidden from the white man's house.

I swing over towards the nearest, feeling like Long John Silver with my left foot bound up. Frances opens the gate for me and a mongrel, its tail flailing, flies at us, yaps at my metal legs.

Zak's mother sits outside, hands in her lap, waiting.

We drink mint tea and wait for Zak and Josh; they appear after a few minutes, walking side by side, Zak in a grey suit with black armband, no tie of course, Josh in black suit, black tie and white shirt, using his hand to try to flatten his unruly mop of red hair. He looks his normal self again, shaved and civilized, though as we take our places in a half-circle around the old woman he looks subdued. That's only natural, all things considered.

Zak hugs his mother, then she turns to Josh and stares up at him. She takes hold of his arms and looks into his face.

'Are you going to sell the farm, Joshua?'

'No, Clara, I'm not going to sell.'

Then we all sit down, using chairs and stools brought out for the purpose. Frances, I note, sits on the ground at Josh's feet. The men remove their jackets, Zak slipping his gold and diamond links into a pocket and rolling up the double-cuffs of his striped shirt.

It's what they all want to know, all the vineyard workers and servants, but only the old woman with the bright, mischievous eyes has had the courage to ask the new owner directly.

Clara makes a fuss of me, ordering Zak to find me a comfortable chair. He doesn't argue; I have the feeling this is the one person in the world Zak will always obey and without quibble.

'What happened to you, Sebastien? We expected to see you yesterday.'

'I had a little accident, Clara.'

Self-consciously I touch the crust of dried blood above my eye.

'Ja, I can see that.'

They all want to know. Frances explains how she was waiting for me, how she heard the sirens and saw the ambulance and feared the worst. I tell them about my escort, how I assumed I was being followed by a combination of

CID and Security Branch, my frantic efforts to lose them in Fish Hoek, the attack by the occupants of the BMW, using the car like a battering ram to try to drive me off the road and over the cliff. Josh purses his lips, Zak laughs and Clara looks appalled. In trouble with the police – that's just about as bad as it gets.

I take up the story from the point at which they opened fire.

The cracks I heard were the rounds going past my head, the bullets ending up in the car roof in one case and, in the other, lodged in the window pillar. But the shooting served its purpose – I lost concentration and in that fraction of a second I missed seeing the boulder lying in the road. It wasn't that big, perhaps two feet across. If it had been bigger I would have seen it.

The Peugeot slammed into it and I found my rear end slewing around to my right. As I fought to get back some degree of control, it struck the BMW – not what my assailants had in mind at all – and they were taken by surprise. One moment they were enjoying the spectacle of their quarry in trouble, the next they had a wheel over the cliff.

They regained control in time to watch me hit the ditch.

I vaguely remember being pulled out, hands gripping my arms.

Stupidly, I thought I was being rescued.

They must have put me in the boot of the BMW, but I knew nothing of it until I found myself swathed in carpet, blood dripping off my nose and running into my mouth.

The main sensation then was pain in my chest and leg.

The garage, the police said, was at a detached house in Camps Bay.

Josh says the man I knew as Toecaps is in intensive care and under close guard. His condition is described as critical but stable.

Veldskoen is dead. He was killed at the outset of the rescue.

Zak says, 'Who the hell were they?'

Clara hasn't gathered us together to talk about my accident, or about politics. She has something else to say to us, and a girl she introduces as her niece brings more tea – it's the pungent rooibos this time – along with plates of shortcake and ginger biscuits. After the tea is poured, the cups and plates handed around, we begin. Or rather, Clara begins.

'The Old Man has gone,' Clara says, 'and Joshua, I am genuinely sorry for your loss.' She turns to look at Josh, who drops his eyes, not knowing how to respond. 'To some people he was a national hero. To others – ' here she looks at her son, Zak, who lowers his head and examines his feet – 'he was the enemy, someone to be fought and destroyed. To Thérèse, his first wife, he was simply a loving husband.'

She looks around at us. Frances has cupped her chin in the palm of one hand and gazes at the cottages. Joshua doodles in the dust with the toe of one of his black loafers.

'To me, Cris was many things. He was my employer. He was the *baas*. His word was law. Yes, he was a white supremacist. He could be a cruel man. Of course. But he was more than that. No one is all good or all bad.'

She pauses. The use of Schuter's first name, the familiarity of it, should have told me what was coming.

Clara says, 'I used to say to Zak when he was a child that his father had gone away. When he was a little older I would say he had gone to the city to find work and send us money. The trouble with a lie is that it has to be constantly updated if it is to be believed. Zak wanted to know what he was like, this absent father. Didn't I have pictures, couldn't I show him, and why didn't he write? The questions came thick and fast. After all, other boys had fathers. Joshua had a father, the great Cris Schuter, so why didn't he? Was there something wrong with us that he never returned? Didn't he love us? Zak started to blame himself for the lack of a father in our home. His boyhood friends had fathers, so there must be something wrong – something he'd done – that prevented him from having a dad just like everyone else.'

I know just how he felt.

Mostly anger.

Clara drinks from her cup and sets it back on the tray.

Am I imagining it, or do I see tears roll down her brown cheeks?

'Mama . . .' Zak looks worried.

'Don't interrupt, my son. I have never told you the truth. I never told anyone. I gave my word I would not tell. I kept my word. Now is the time for the truth to come out. I owe it to all of you. You have all been friends of my son. You, Joshua, you, Frances – and you, too, Sebastien. You are Zak's family. He never had one of his own, not really.'

Zak gets to his feet.

'Sit down, Zakaria. You will have your turn. Now sit.'

He sits.

Does Frances understand? She bends forward, head in both hands, staring down. I can't see her expression.

'When Joshua was born and his mother died in labour, Cris was beside himself with grief. He would see no one. He did no work. He stayed indoors. He wouldn't shave or bathe, or change his clothing. He wouldn't eat. He lost the will to live. He wouldn't let anyone come near him, not even his own family. Not even his newborn son. He stayed in his room, the shutters drawn. He drank himself insensible, sitting there in the dark.

'I was the wet nurse. I tried to take the baby to him. He wouldn't open the door. So I sat outside and talked to Joshua. I hoped that by doing that, by letting Cris hear his son through the panelled door of the bedroom, he would relent. I used to put the cot there, and sit rocking Josh back and forth, sometimes all night.

'Nothing happened for five days and nights. Then he opened the door and told me to bring the child to him. He turned his face away from me, and he wouldn't let me draw back the curtains or open the windows – but I took out his washing, and later brought him some breakfast. I think it was the first food he'd eaten since Josh's mother had passed away.

'Little by little he began to improve. He would carry the baby around himself, talking to Josh. It seemed to calm him, and cheer him up a little. In the weeks that followed we talked. We became friends. I was the only servant he would allow in the house. I realized then that he was terribly lonely. I would try to lift his spirits by telling him news of the outside world, of the farm, and he started to show an interest in me and the other servants. I also told him he was feeling sorry for himself, that we grieve for ourselves as much as for the person who has left us. He didn't like it, but he thought about what I'd said and I like to think it helped.

'The cook returned, and the gardener, Abraham, and Cris began to venture outside. He would take his horse and ride while I held his son.'

She stops. She takes a deep breath.

'It was two months after Josh was born that we first slept together.'

Clara pauses, watching us for any reaction.

All I can hear are the oaks creaking in the afternoon breeze that has sprung up, and in one of the cottages a child wails. Josh, Zak and Frances all seem preoccupied with their own thoughts. Did they suspect? Did Frances know intuitively? She's said nothing of it, though.

'Ma—'

'No, Zak. Let me finish. Please.

'He didn't force himself on me. I know that's what you're thinking. But it wasn't like that at all. Cris was a handsome man, and he was kind. Yes, he had a terrible temper. We all knew that. I felt sorry for him. I pitied him. His strength had left him, and I wanted to comfort him. When Thérèse died he lost the will to live. We had spoken together for so many days and nights, you see, and I had found the man himself, behind the name and the reputation. I went to him willingly, and every night thereafter until my condition prevented me. For it was that first night that I concieved my only child. It was a week after my sixteenth birthday.'

Clara looks across at Zak.

'Cris supported me financially, but he told me that if I

breathed a word of this at all to anyone during his lifetime, I would get nothing, not a cent – not for me, and, more important, not for Zak. So I kept quiet. And when we were sent away, I made no complaint. I did not protest. I said nothing to anyone. It was not in my interest, or Zak's.

'Until today.

'My son, I ask for your forgiveness – your father, Cris Schuter, was buried today. I am so very, very sorry it had to be this way. I pray that in time you in turn will learn to stop hating and that you can find it in yourself to forgive us – both of us.'

Zak is back on his feet, hands at his sides. He's turned away from us, uncertain what to do, which way to turn. I think I know how he must feel, but of course I don't, not really. I imagine him being pulled in several directions. Part of him must want to run and hide. The small boy in him would want to flee, and the grown man, the guerrilla, to strike down a man already dead and buried that very day.

His father.

He turns back, takes two strides past me to Clara.

Zak drops to his knees in front of his mother.

I can't see his face.

They say nothing for a long time.

Mother and son simply hold each other, rocking gently.

When the rest of us reach the bridge and I look back, they are still there.

ELEVEN

Viljoen and Mabaza want to talk to us; according to Josh they've something they want to say, but he won't be drawn on what it is.

They can speak to us individually, or together, and Josh resolves the issue by inviting everyone to a meal at La Couronne, a formal eatery in one of Franschhoek's smartest hotels. It's magnanimous of him. On the face of it, a celebratory occasion seems in bad taste; nevertheless we gather at eight-thirty at the round table under a vaulted ceiling in a private room, an alcove off the main restaurant: Clara and Frances, Zak and Josh and myself. Viljoen and Mabaza arrive last, completing the guest list. I end up seated between them, directly opposite Clara.

I dread the prospect of my interrogation and its sordid details emerging into the open; I hope – hope is not strong enough, but I can't say 'pray' – that everyone else will be too preoccupied with their own issues and one another to take much interest in me and my squalid defeat at the hands of Toecaps and Veldskoen.

The old-fashioned way of doing these things would be not to make any mention of the business in hand until the coffee, but Josh, always impatient, is having none of it; as we study our menus he clambers to his feet, tapping the white tablecloth with a spoon to get our attention. We fall silent. I think I know what's coming, so I keep my eyes down, staring at the candlelight dancing on the silver cutlery.

'Thank you for coming tonight. I know some people will regard this as an inappropriate day for such an announcement, but I am going to break with convention and announce it anyway: Frances and I are engaged, and we will marry once the elections are out of the way – ' he beams down at the policemen – 'provided, of course, Commandant Viljoen and Lieutenant Mabaza will allow us our liberty.' He pauses, then raises his voice. 'We have set May the seventeenth as the date for the wedding, and we hope you will all be able to come – in fact we both insist you do.'

If the departed ever do turn in their graves, Cris Schuter's is spinning at this moment and I for one will not be sorry for his sorry soul's torment.

We all clap. Zak whistles. I punch the air with a clenched fist. No, my jealousy has truly run its path. I'm happy for them. We all are. Josh blushes, his face turning the colour of his hair, and Frances smiles up at him, an expression of sheer, unadulterated happiness spreading across her face.

Josh isn't finished.

'Today I lost a father.' He waits a beat. 'But I gained a brother.' He nods at Zak. 'Some of you will know I've built a career as a businessman. But I'm no farmer. I know nothing about wine. It was my father's interest, never mine. So I have come to a decision. As of now, the Schuter place belongs to Zak. We've talked about it. Zak will take a fifty-one per cent interest in the business – his wish is that the estate workers will share the remaining forty-nine per cent; henceforth Schuter Wineries will be a cooperative venture, with Zak as chief executive, and I personally hope Zak and Clara will make the homestead their permanent residence. It is theirs, and it is right and just that it should be theirs. I spoke to the lawyers this afternoon and have asked them to set it up.'

More applause, and Frances hugs the lachrymose Clara.

It is Zak's turn to rise, a glass of the Uittyk estate's finest sauvignon blanc in a right hand that I can't help but notice is trembling. 'Here's to my two oldest friends – my very best friends. I wish Frances and my brother Joshua every happiness. And my mother and I warmly accept his gracious offer ... to the new Mr and Mrs Schuter!'

We drink. Zak drains his glass. So much for his new faith, but then Fatima is not there to witness the heresy.

The waiter takes our orders. Our glasses are charged.

A sense of anticipation – even apprehension – overtakes us as Viljoen and Mabaza lean across behind me and discuss who will make the delivery. Viljoen insists it will be Mabaza. The lieutenant shrugs. Okay, he says, so be it, but they can share the burden, can't they?

'Ladies and gentlemen, we both have an apology to make to you – a double apology, in fact. First of all, let me assure you there's no question of our denying these two people their liberty. That goes for all of you, even our friends of the ANC and the SACP, so you can all relax and enjoy your meal tonight, and our first apology is for the worry we've caused you.'

Zak winks at me; Josh smiles at Frances, who still has hold of Clara's hand and now squeezes it.

'It was all my idea,' Mabaza says, 'but I could not have implemented it without the Commandant's help, and especially not without his trust. Yes, it's true, with the exception of Mrs Wauchope – Clara – everyone had a reason to hate Cris Schuter and wish him dead. In theory. In so far as that's true, you were, very briefly, suspects. Each of you had to be eliminated from our inquiries. We apologize for the deceit – for failing to tell you that you were in the clear – but we needed you, Mr Schuter, and especially you, Mr Palfrey, to be our tethered goats, at least for a while.'

Viljoen puts a hand on Mabaza's sleeve and addresses me.

'You remember, Mr Palfrey, when I showed you the crime scene? Yes? I mentioned memoirs Cris was working on – you remember? I told you they were being dusted for prints, I think.'

'Yes,' I say. 'I do remember. I put it in my story.'

'As I hoped you would.'

We are interrupted by the arrival of our starter courses.

'Cris Schuter was writing his memoirs, ladies and gentlemen. He was putting the final touches to the second draft at the time he died. They were not a self-justification by any means, or an excuse. I've read the document – twice. It's a remarkable work; remarkable for its frankness, for its detail.'

Mabaza glances over at Viljoen, on my left. The commandant puts down his soup spoon and takes over.

'Schuter was a frequent visitor to Auckland Park.

Perhaps you know the SABC headquarters and its *brein-toring* – its brain-tower – where the blacklists and other propaganda tools of the system were devised. The old man, with his wide experience abroad, his government service and his financial acumen, was a valued asset. As such he got to know members of the National Security Council, the Sanhedrin, as these secret leaders of the Security Branch and Military Intelligence were called – yes, it's true: they were named after the rabbinical judges who sent Christ to his death on the cross.'

Mabaza takes up the tale.

'It wasn't long before he became a member of the Western Cape's Joint Management Committee, or JMC. These regional bodies reported to the Security Council. They were part of the apparatus for waging total war against the enemies of apartheid. You know this already, I think.

'The JMCs have been involved in every aspect of security, from hearts and minds campaigns to the pursuit and assassination of people the Security Council identified for what they called "permanent removal" from society.'

There's a chill around the table and no one is eating.

Mabaza goes on to say Schuter has described all this in his book. He left out nothing. Trouble was, it became common knowledge that he was writing his memoirs, and that he was naming names. He had confided in one of his friends in the JMC, sounding him out, and word had leaked.

'The JMC relied on secret units made up of Security Branch and Military Intelligence personnel to carry out the killings. People from my own organization,' Mabaza

says. 'Naturally, when they heard the gossip that someone like Schuter was writing about what they were doing
– frankly and without pulling punches – they wanted to
put a stop to it.'

Once more, our glasses are refilled. This time Josh asks
that the bottles be left on the table and we will help
ourselves. Then the main courses arrive. I've chosen
Springbok pie and I switch to a delicious merlot, but by
this time I sense that few, if any, of us have much appetite
left.

'The murder,' Viljoen says, once our dishes are taken
away, 'was almost accidental. It was made to look like a
botched job by a couple of clumsy thieves. What we think
happened is that two officers – Detective Sergeant
Granger of the Security Branch, based at Stellenbosch,
and Staff Sergeant Metz of Military Intelligence – climbed
in the kitchen window of the Schuter city residence with
the intention of stealing and then destroying the memoir,
all one hundred and twenty thousand words of it.'

Granger is the burly Toecaps and Metz the wearer of
soft *veldskoene*.

'They knew,' Mabaza adds, 'that he worked in a study
area off the bedroom, and that he would copy his work
on to floppy discs as a security measure. So the target
was the manuscript, whatever he had on his hard drive,
and the discs. What they didn't know was that he had
copies made every week, and that they went by courier
to his solicitor, and his publishers.'

Zak says, 'So it was pointless.'

Mabaza nods cheerfully. 'Oh, yes, it was. Murder often
is.'

Viljoen explains that they made it to the bedroom. They had the typescript, had found the diskettes, and Metz, who knew something about computers, was sitting at the desk, hacking into Schuter's hard drive with the intention of deleting everything he could find.

'That's when the old man found them,' Mabaza says.

'They fought there, in the bedroom,' Viljoen adds. 'We found traces of Granger's blood on the carpet and the duvet. The old boy had managed to give him a bloody nose.'

'But they got him under control,' Mabaza says, 'and dragged him through to the living room. He was probably semi-conscious at this point.'

'The bare footprints you saw were Schuter's,' Viljoen says, addressing me. 'He probably made an attempt to escape when he came round, but they overpowered him a second time. We think they then discussed what they were going to do with him, and Metz, who was leader of a unit that had killed a number of ANC suspects, was most anxious to silence him. Granger went along with it, but they had to make it look like some crazed killer. So they staged it.'

Frances raises a hand. 'Please, spare us the details.'

Clara covers her face with her hands.

'I told you about the carpet, Mr Palfrey, sir, didn't I? I don't mean the one they used to interrogate you . . .'

'You did tell me, Commandant.'

'We got one of Granger's feet, right there. He stayed too long. Overconfidence, you see. It was a regular issue police shoe, with a rubber ribbed sole. Distinctive. Forensics did the rest. That put him at the scene and at the right time.'

'We'd nothing on Metz,' Mabaza says.

'Which is where you came in,' he continued. 'Along with our second apology. We concocted a story that Josh had the only copy of the manuscript, that he had given it to his friend, the English journalist. We faked a CID report that went through to Security Branch. It was leaked to the *Sunday Times*, of course. That was enough for them both to go after Mr Palfrey. We put people outside your place, ostensibly to watch your moves, and we put out a warrant for Joshua's arrest, but what we really wanted was any sign of Metz and Granger coming out into the open.'

Mabaza nods. 'We doctored the autopsy report, too, and let that slip through our fingers into certain black nationalist circles. We tried to put the fear of God into Miss Nqutu – yes, I'm very sorry for that – over Mr Palfrey's refusal to tell us where we could find Josh Schuter. We tried to think of everything, and make it convincing. We fed material indirectly to Zak, who'd already had word from his own sources of a threat to Josh and his father. In fact, he had approached Josh in person to warn him before the murder took place.

'You see, that's why I needed Commandant Viljoen's help. I couldn't trust anyone in Security Branch. This was a secret group within the secret police, and they had sympathizers everywhere. So I had to reach out to some-one I knew I could trust, and use his manpower in CID.'

Zak asks, 'Where are they now?'

Viljoen answers. 'Metz died when he pulled a gun and James dropped him with two rounds in the chest. Granger is still in intensive care. He's the one who took a couple of shots at you, Sebastien. He had quite a reputa-tion as an interrogator—'

'Please,' I say. 'I had first-hand experience of his thirty-minute rule. No more. Not now.'

'Unfortunately, our people couldn't catch up with the BMW. They were there to protect you, but the inadequacy of our police vehicle up against a BMW never occurred to us. It should have, Mr Palfrey, but I'm afraid it didn't. Our mistake. We owe you an apology.'

'What was it that they were so worried would emerge in public?'

Mabaza looks hard at me when he answers.

'They had been responsible for hunting down an ANC activist code-named Maqoma. They had orders to identify, locate and remove him. Permanently. They picked up three of his people, but they didn't talk. They killed them. They shot them and burned the remains on the outskirts of Graaf Reinet. As far as I know they never knew this Maqoma's real identity. Schuter had sanctioned the Maqoma operation, and he knew about the killings, and he wrote about it.'

I have a final question. 'Do you know now who Maqoma is? I remember you asked me who he was. I told you I didn't know.'

Viljoen and Mabaza look at each other.

'No,' Viljoen says, I thought a little too emphatically. 'We've no idea.'

I dare not look anywhere near Zak.

We are thinking the same thing, he and I. We are thinking about the Black Mountains.

I can still remember the road at night, the ribbon endlessly unravelling in the headlights, the double flash of the catseyes as they appeared and a moment later vanished below us, the weird shadows thrown by under-growth and trees, the telephone cable like a lifeline slung between lopsided poles, the hills' dark embrace, the road rising, twisting into endless hairpins, the air colder by the minute as we climbed.

Very occasionally we'd pass through the outskirts of a village, just a light or two showing from a lone petrol pump, the outline of a church steeple and we, not paus-ing, not slowing for a moment, my foot pressed to the floor, egging the little car on and up, getting through, getting past, leaving civilization behind for the great mass of the Swartberge ahead and above.

Up there, I told myself, we'd be safe.

Another hour. And another.

'Turn here.'

Nothing to mark the turn-off. Just tyre tracks.

Another half-mile and there was a farm gate, a simple metal frame and wire. I stopped while my guide got out and opened it and I drove through and waited for him to close it again. There was nothing here but a sandy track, low scrub on either side, the stars so bright and the night sky so dark I felt I could reach up and touch the incan-descence. It was midnight, the air as cold as iron, a sea of frost glittering at our feet.

It was a plateau, entirely without any landmark, not even a tree.

This place would be baking in summer, freezing in win-ter. There'd be snow sometimes, and on the few occasions it did rain, it would cause a torrent, sweeping off the topsoil, flash-flooding the gullies. The rocks would be infested with snakes, and what earth there was would be too thin even for the hardiest sheep.

On arrival a cadre with a rifle checked my papers wordlessly and showed us to one of the rondavels, a simple affair of plaster with an earthen floor and thatched with river reed.

There were two camp beds. I collapsed fully dressed on to the nearest, kicked off my shoes and pulled my sleeping bag up around my chin. My last action was to check that my pistol had a round in the chamber and that it was on safe. I fell asleep to the sound of bullfrogs in the creek and the hacking cough of jackals and wild hunting dogs, my right hand on the heavy Tokarev at my side.

It was September 1984. The same month, in other words, that the township uprising began and the government declared a state of emergency. That was bad enough, but there were more pressing issues closer to home. My orders were straightforward. I was to rendezvous with the agent known as Maqoma and identify the two suspects he held, and, once I had identified them, witness their punishment.

Simple. Nothing to it.

There had been too many extra-judicial killings in which the innocent had been hacked to pieces or burned alive simply on the say-so of a neighbour, a *sangoma*, a rival – whatever. The Youth was overenthusiastic at times. Meaning, the boys were murderous, and didn't take care who they killed. Once a man kills, he finds it easier, and then he starts to enjoy the power killing gives him. Our excesses were giving the Struggle a bad name. This time was different; this was going to be an exemplary punishment, and it was going to be seen to be done properly.

There was another reason. Maqoma had lost an entire

network. One after another its members had been ambushed and killed – on country roads, in town, on their doorsteps: all in all, seven operatives in six months. Someone was talking. Someone on the inside. They weren't bothered about taking people alive. They had the intelligence they wanted. They were confident in what they were doing. And we had to admit it: their intelligence was spot on. Three arms caches in the Stellenbosch area had been compromised. Three couriers had been caught, tortured and killed. The Western Cape sector was a mess, and Maqoma, long a hunter of men, was now the hunted.

The man behind it all was a Security Branch officer named Granger. Based in Stellenbosch, he was too well protected to get to. Maqoma had lost two of his best people trying to do just that.

He had a reputation for effective interrogation – and for cruelty.

That's why they wanted an external arbiter brought in, someone not directly involved in military operations. Someone the Party trusted, someone in the intelligence business, someone with Moscow's imprimatur.

Me.

I was shaken roughly.

'That's enough, for God's sake. I'm awake—'

It was first light already. I'd had about three hours' rest, and I was still groggy as I crawled out of my sleeping bag and swung my legs off the bed, feeling the sand cold underfoot.

'Here – take it.' Whoever had shaken me awake now pushed a tin mug of hot tea into my hands.

'Smoke?'

'Thanks.'

A hand appeared with a light.

'We're ready, Comrade.'

I burned my tongue with the first gulp of tea. Someone had laced it with something much stronger, and I was immensely grateful.

Perhaps whoever it was knew something about executions I didn't.

It was that flinty, early light that hurts the eyes, so I had to squint up at whoever it was, still standing over me, waiting impatiently. It took a moment or two for it to sink in. I was going to say something to the effect that I had often wondered if Maqoma was my old friend and playmate, but Zak gently put a warm hand – the hand that had held the mug of tea – over my mouth and shook his head.

No, his look said. Don't speak. We don't know each other.

We don't know who we can trust any more.

'The prisoners are outside, Comrade.'

The breakthrough had come four days earlier when a faux barrage had been mounted on a bridge over the Touws River by three of Maqoma's men – Zak's fighters – wearing stolen police uniforms. Three more cadres lay hidden in the scree at the side of the road with an RPG just in case things went awry.

It was just after sunset when a rather smart little Fiat hatchback with two occupants drew up at the barrier.

One of the 'policemen' recognized the man behind the wheel at once.

His companion was a young black woman.

*

Their wallets and identity papers lay on a flat rock.

I had brought photographs and photocopies of their details with me, and I started to compare them.

The woman's purse was an expensive crocodile skin affair. It contained several hundred rand rolled up and held in place with an elastic band and a number of snapshots, showing herself and her companion and the man known as Granger, the same man I would get to know later as Toecaps. The threesome looked very happy. They were drinking, sitting on a rug on the grass in the sun, and the woman was laughing. She was only partly dressed, with her companion's arm around her, one hand suggestively cupping a breast, while Granger appeared to be cooking something on a barbecue behind them.

Her name was Miriam Sipole, and she carried a police warrant card. She held the rank of detective constable in the Security Branch, and her companion was a white detective sergeant, Prins Grobbelaar, right-hand man to Granger himself.

I compared the photographs with those in my file.

It was Granger, of that I had no doubt whatsoever, and this Grobbelaar was indisputably his number two.

I nodded at Zak. 'It's them.'

The prisoners stood next to each other in the sandy clearing, Zak's men around them in a semicircle. They were both in good shape. Neither had been knocked about at all, but I could tell they hadn't slept much, and I thought I knew why. This was their last day in this world and they knew it, but like most people in such a situation, hope sustained them even now, to the very end.

Zak started with the man, Grobbelaar, calling him forward and asking for his full name, his home address.

He was a big fellow, powerfully built, I thought, until I looked more closely. His body was too long for the rest of him, his legs were short and somewhat knock-kneed. There was something wrong with his mouth despite the disguise of a straggly moustache. It was soft, almost womanish. He kept smiling in a foolish way. I put it down to nerves, and a desire to insinuate himself into our favour, to placate us the way a dog wags its tail and licks its master's hand for fear of a thrashing. Grobbelaar's hands were plump and soft, a paper-pusher's hands.

The prisoner answered clearly, preferring Afrikaans. He didn't hesitate at first. He denied nothing. He must have known there was no point. He seemed almost eager to talk. Maybe it was the waiting. Maybe he thought frankness would win him a brownie point. But I knew Zak better.

Zak held Grobbelaar's big police-issue pistol down at his side, and, to begin with, Grobbelaar couldn't keep his eyes off it.

The questioning centred on loss of the arms dumps, the betrayals, the killings of Zak's cadres. Grobbelaar began to slow down, to hesitate, to stammer as it got down to precise details of who did what to whom.

But he always answered.

Then it was the woman's turn.

She was a piece of work. I put her age at around twenty-eight. She was expensively dressed, from the well-cut suit to her long pink fingernails and her red shoes. But she wore too much make-up. It was pasted on, presumably to make her look whiter, or less black, and

her fingers were thick, like slabs of meat, and the mani-
cure did nothing to improve them.

As Zak started to ask her questions (he spoke to her in
Xhosa), she edged slowly closer to him, keeping her gaze
on his face all the time, looking intently at him as if
searching for a sign that his manhood could somehow be
drawn out of him and used to her advantage, no doubt
as had been the case with some of Maqoma's dead agents.
She was certainly desirable, and she knew it, and had
used it for Granger's benefit, and her own.

Again, she didn't know Zak as I did.

Zak spoke to one of his men.

'Get the shovels.'

We watched as they were made to dig their own graves
in the sand. It wasn't hard work, because the sand went
down several feet. The woman slipped a couple of times
and her shoes had fallen apart by the time she was down
to her knees. The graves were several yards apart, as if
they didn't want to be associated with one another as
they had in life. They had been lovers, of that I was
certain, but they didn't so much as glance at each other
as they worked.

The woman kept her composure. She was dry-eyed.
She kept looking about her, especially at Zak. I would
have said that at this point she had written off her
Security Branch lover. He couldn't help her. Grobbelaar
was a dead man, and she seemed to accept it. He's going
to die, she was thinking, but not me.

I am going to get out of this.

I've made it so far, using my wits. I'll get out of this,
too.

They won't kill a woman like me.

A sickly stench of her perfume and his deodorant filled the clearing.

Grobbelaar finished first. He tidied up his own grave, polishing off the sides and edges, making it as neat as the sandy soil allowed. What was he doing? Buying time? Finally he clambered out and flung the shovel aside. He looked around him, as if seeing where he was for the first time.

He asked for a cigarette, but no one moved.

At this point a change came over him.

It was a very cold morning. The sand underfoot was icy, and wet from dew, but Grobbelaar was sweating. His clothes were soaked. It was partly the hard labour of shifting wet sand, but it was also fear.

He looked at me. I was the only white face – perhaps that was it. Perhaps he thought he would find sympathy. Or even a word of help. Perhaps he had thought one member of the Master Race would help another. Now he knew better. A shudder went through him. It was involuntary, starting in his knees and working its way up until he quivered all over as if in the grip of malaria.

Then he ran.

He must have known he didn't stand a chance, but I don't think he could bear to just stand there and take what was coming to him.

Grobbelaar hadn't taken more than three or four wobbly strides on his thin legs when one of Zak's men brought his Kalashnikov up to his shoulder and fired an aimed burst of three rounds. The first struck Grobbelaar in the small of the back, the other two between the shoulder blades.

Grobbelaar's shambling run ended when he seemed to trip, arms flung forward, then crashed down on his face.

The firing seemed terribly loud in the clearing.

Zak turned to me.

'Would you?'

He sounded so polite, as if offering me the wine list.

After all, I was judge and jury. I might as well provide the *coup de grâce*. I was the Party. I was Authority. I took my pistol from my waistband, pushed the safety off and walked over to where Grobbelaar had gone down, sliding slightly forward on his front. He wasn't moving. His right hand was under him, his left arm stretched out wide to one side. I thought he was dead, but it was better to make sure.

His shoes had come off. I noticed a hole in the heel of one of his socks.

He looked like the victim of a road accident.

Was this the victory we'd dreamed of?

There wasn't any hesitation. I didn't even think about it.

I took aim at the base of Grobbelaar's skull and squeezed.

Sipole pleaded for her life. She said she knew what Zak wanted. He wanted Granger, didn't he? Of course he did. She would take him and his men to Granger herself.

Or better still, she would lure Granger to a rendezvous where they could kill him. They could do it now. They could take the Fiat. He would suspect nothing. He was expecting them. She could get them money, and she knew where the police kept the arms they had recovered from the MK dumps. She would work for him, Maqoma. She wanted to work for the Struggle, but until now she'd never had the chance.

She made it sound so reasonable.

Oh yes, she would prove herself in the Resistance by handing over Granger and all those who worked for him.

She dropped to her knees and clutched at Zak's legs. She looked up at him, eyes wide, then, bending forward, pressed herself against his shins.

There was promise in her eyes and lots of cleavage.

'*Asseblief, meneer.*'

Please, sir.

She reached up to him, but Zak moved his arms, the right hand still holding the pistol, out of reach.

'*Asseblief*. Please.'

Zak held both his arms stiffly behind him, like a bather about to dive into a pool. He turned his head and looked at me. It wasn't a question. He gave a slight nod.

The sand was soft, so when I stepped forward, I did so quietly, putting my weight on my toes.

Sipole wept, still looking up at Zak, pressing her upper body against his legs and thighs. Zak's mouth twisted in disgust.

Now is the time for all good men to come to the aid of the Party.

I had my duty. My orders.

I raised the Tokarev, pointing the muzzle just behind Sipole's ear.

The shock of the explosion travelled all the way up my wrist and arm to the shoulder.

That moment, the precise instant of squeezing the trigger, repeated itself again and again in my nightmare. I was afraid of sleep. Eating became a treacherous and embarrassing process. I'd be in the middle of a meal with friends, and for no apparent reason I would leap up and run from the table, napkin over my mouth, only to be violently ill. And there were the daylight hallucinations in the form of Swartberge smells – a woman's scent, a man's sweating terror, the stench of cordite on my clothing and hands.

The Grangers of this world had more in common with the likes of Zak and myself than I'd ever care to admit.

I hobble out of the restaurant after the others into a moonlit rose garden, leaving Josh behind to settle the bill. It has been decided that Zak, the new owner of the Schuter homestead, will invite everyone back for a cognac, and that Clara, Frances, Josh and I will, at Zak's insistence, stay the night.

Josh is to be a guest in what has been his father's home.

Viljoen and Mabaza say they have to get back to Cape Town.

Mabaza pulls an object out of his jacket pocket.

At first I can't make it out. 'What's this?'

Viljoen and Mabaza exchange grins.

'We found it in your place,' Viljoen says. 'Under the floor.'

'Maybe it belonged to a previous tenant,' Mabaza adds.

I take hold of it. It feels and looks familiar. It smells familiar, too.

'Maybe you could pass on a friendly warning,' Mabaza suggests. 'He could find himself doing time if he's found with that in his possession.'

I get the point.

'I don't think he needs it any more,' I say. 'But I'll tell him all the same.'

'You do that,' Viljoen says. 'Smoking that stuff is bad for him, anyway.'

So we all say the right things, shake their hands and watch the policemen leave, then turn back to one another.

I kiss Clara on both cheeks, and she hugs me.

Zak offers me his hand and won't let go.

Josh pounds me on the back, then flings his arm around my neck.

We don't speak.

I think Frances is smiling, but I'm not really sure in the dark.

I squeeze her arm and she slips it around my waist, and whispers in my ear that her mother and sisters are on their way to the Cape, their first real holiday ever.

Out there, in the hotel garden, the heady smell of roses and jasmine all around, we cling to one another. We embrace. We huddle in a circle, heads together, our breath turning to cotton wool in the African night.

I drop my crutches. We know everything now. We have killed. We have murdered for an idea, for a notion, because of orders, a sense of duty. We have betrayed, too, and out of fear we have hated. We are old friends, old lovers and old enemies, also. Would the world have been any different had we not done these things? Would it have been any better, or worse? Better, surely, in that some people might still be alive but for us. Yet what kind of life would have awaited them, or any of us? We can't judge. We're grown men and women, but we are still those same children, a little lost, seeking answers, those clumsy and knowing children, both innocent and cruel, loving and desperately in need of love.

None can forget.

But can we forgive, and can we ask forgiveness, not of each other, not even of our victims, but of ourselves? For having survived. For having stayed alive. For having got through all of this more or less intact. If the future is going to mean anything at all, if the past is not going to rear up and crush us once again, if we are to be a part of what is ahead, if we are to be free of the guilt and pain we all feel, if we are to lay our ghosts to rest, if our survival is to mean anything, if we are to face our fears, if our friendship and humanity are going to be renewed . . . then we have no choice at all.

GLOSSARY

Askari	literally, soldier, but in this context a black collaborator and mercenary employed by white extremists to do their dirty work for them
asseblief	please
bliksem	term of abuse: scumbag
Boer	farmer, but often used as a pejorative term for an Afrikaner
dagga	South African marijuana
daggazolletjie	marijuana cigarette or 'joint'
doek	scarf, head covering
Dominee	Dutch Reformed Church priest
dorp	Afrikaans for town, often used in a pejorative sense, i.e. a dull little place
gramadoelas	the back of beyond, out in the sticks
haelgeweer	shotgun
impimpi	informer
Jou ma se moer	nasty Afrikaans obscenity, typical of

the lower ranks of the South African security forces and referring to the target's mother and her genitals

Kaapse Kleurling   Cape Coloured: a term used during the apartheid era to refer to people classified as belonging to the mixed race community (of which the components might be, severally, Khoikhoi, San, Malay, Xhosa, Dutch, German, French and British). In actual fact very few of the earliest Afrikaners were without a mixed heritage – partly because of the shortage of European females, at least until the arrival of Huguenot families in 1688

LMG   standard military acronym for light machine gun

pieds noir   French term for white colonists in French-ruled Algeria, often of Italian and Spanish origin, and major players in Algeria's long and bloody war of liberation

predikant   preacher

rooinek   literally redneck. Widely used as pejorative term for British and English-speaking people generally

sjambok   long rhino-hide whip

skollie   thug

soutpiel	salt dick: term of abuse for English-speakers who can't make up their minds whether they are British or South African, hence their dicks are constantly being dipped in the briny sea as they swing back and forth between Europe and Africa
tokolosh	malevolent spirit, demon of the underworld
tsotsi	gangster
tsotsitaal	gangster talk, a local patois not unlike Creole
verkrampte	repressive, inflexible right wing of the National Party
verligte	enlightened, usually a reference to the reformists on the left wing of the apartheid era's ruling white National Party. These were people in favour of some cosmetic change
voetsek	colloquial and abusive term: get lost
volk	Afrikaner nation, people
ware	Afrikaans adjective meaning true or genuine
zol	grass, pot, marijuana

Visit **www.panmacmillan.com** to read more about all our books and to buy them. You will also find features, author interviews and news of any author events, and you can sign up for e-newsletters so that you're always first to hear about our new releases.